"Y...

his voice curiously serious.

"I surprised *you?*" Brooke demanded. "I do not believe I was the perpetrator of surprises, Peter Cooper."

His chuckle was rueful and dark. "Oh yes, you were. You grew up."

"Don't be silly. I've had breasts since I was twelve. You were still around then."

"But you didn't have *those* breasts," he accused.

"Whose breasts *did* I have, then?"

Again he shook his head. "Having breasts doesn't make you an adult. It doesn't mean you've learned those...those things that make a man..." But he didn't finish.

Brooke was sure she didn't want him to. "I never learned those things," she protested. "If I had, I'd have fewer pals and more suitors."

"If you never learned those things," Pete retorted, his attention ostensibly on driving, both hands tightly around the wheel, "why did I spend last night dreaming about you? Very vivid dreams, I might add."

Dear Reader,

April is here and spring is in the air! But if you aren't one of those lucky people who gets to spend April in Paris, you can still take that trip to romance—with Silhouette Desire!

You can fly off to San Francisco—one of *my* favorite cities!—and meet Frank Chambers, April's *Man of the Month,* in *Dream Mender* by Sherryl Woods. Or you can get into a car and trek across America with Brooke Ferguson and Pete Cooper in *Isn't It Romantic?* by Kathleen Korbel. (No, I'm not going to tell you what Pete and Brooke are doing. You have to read the book!) And if you're feeling particularly adventurous, you can battle fish, mud and flood with Dom Seeger and Alicia Bernard in Karen Leabo's delightful *Unearthly Delights.*

Of course, we all know that you don't *have* to travel to find love. Sometimes happiness is in your own backyard. In Jackie Merritt's *Boss Lady,* very desperate and very pregnant TJ Reese meets hometown hunk Marc Torelli. Tricia Everett finds that the man of her dreams is . . . her husband, in Noelle Berry McCue's *Moonlight Promise.* And Caroline Nobel returns to the man who's always lit her fire in *Hometown Man* by Jo Ann Algermissen.

So, it might not be April in Paris for you—*this* year. But don't worry, it's still love—at home or away— with Silhouette Desire.

Until next month,

Lucia Macro
Senior Editor

KATHLEEN KORBEL
ISN'T IT ROMANTIC?

SILHOUETTE Desire
Published by Silhouette Books New York
America's Publisher of Contemporary Romance

If you purchased this book without a cover you should be aware that this book is stolen property. It was reported as "unsold and destroyed" to the publisher, and neither the author nor the publisher has received any payment for this "stripped book."

SILHOUETTE BOOKS
300 East 42nd St., New York, N.Y. 10017

ISN'T IT ROMANTIC?

Copyright © 1992 by Eileen Dreyer

All rights reserved. Except for use in any review, the reproduction or utilization of this work in whole or in part in any form by any electronic, mechanical or other means, now known or hereafter invented, including xerography, photocopying and recording, or in any information storage or retrieval system, is forbidden without the permission of the publisher, Silhouette Books, 300 E. 42nd St., New York, N.Y. 10017

ISBN: 0-373-05703-2

First Silhouette Books printing April 1992

All the characters in this book have no existence outside the imagination of the author and have no relation whatsoever to anyone bearing the same name or names. They are not even distantly inspired by any individual known or unknown to the author, and all incidents are pure invention.

® and ™: Trademarks used with authorization. Trademarks indicated with ® are registered in the United States Patent and Trademark Office, the Canada Trade Mark Office and in other countries.

Printed in the U.S.A.

Books by Kathleen Korbel

Silhouette Desire

Playing the Game #286
A Prince of a Guy #389
The Princess and the Pea #455
Hotshot #582
A Fine Madness #668
Isn't It Romantic? #703

Silhouette Books

Silhouette Summer Sizzlers 1989
"The Road to Mandalay"

Silhouette Intimate Moments

A Stranger's Smile #163
Worth Any Risk #191
Edge of the World #222
Perchance to Dream #276
The Ice Cream Man #309
Lightning Strikes #351
A Rose for Maggie #396
Jake's Way #413

KATHLEEN KORBEL

lives in St. Louis with her husband and two children. She devotes her time to enjoying her family, writing, avoiding anyone who tries to explain the intricacies of the computer and searching for the fabled house-cleaning fairies. She's had her best luck with her writing—from which she's garnered a *Romantic Times* award for Best New Category Author of 1987, and the 1990 Romance Writers of America RITA awards for Best Romantic Suspense and Best Long Category Romance—and with her family, without whom she couldn't have managed any of the rest. She hasn't given up on those fairies, though.

One

UPI New York—IBN News anchor Pete Cooper further enhanced the reputation of the newest network's news department by capturing a Peabody Award Monday night for the series he wrote and co-produced on the plight of mentally ill homeless in the big cities entitled *Nowhere to Go*. A well-respected veteran of ABC and NBC with awards for coverage of everything from war to the decay of family life, Cooper has been the lead anchor on the IBN national news for the four years it has existed. He is widely considered to be one of the driving forces behind the new network's growing credibility in the broadcast news field. When asked to comment, Cooper said that he has benefited greatly from the latitude network chief Evan Parischell has given him, and looks forward to seeing IBN take its place alongside the other major networks.

Entertainment World, May—News Tidbits: To-die-for newsman Pete Cooper has once again made the top-ten list of most eligible bachelors. Divorced and presently unattached at thirty-four, the oh-so-cool Cooper, who

8 ISN'T IT ROMANTIC?

stole our hearts with his unforgettable war reports (who can forget his élan during those missile attacks, decked out in leather jacket and scar), has an apartment in Atlanta where he now works, but also has a little flat in New York's Soho so he can keep up with the bright lights he left behind for IBN. He gracefully declined a questionnaire on likes and dislikes, but has been often spotted at symphony, ballet, opera and any tony fundraiser that's lucky enough to get him. From the sounds of the nightly newscast—that's become a must for women everywhere—it seems that all that slow, Southern living hasn't dimmed the edge on Pete's abilities—in any arena.

Western Union May 15 PETER COOPER, 1676 MAGNOLIA CRESCENT, ATLANTA, GEORGIA. COOPER. STOP. WHAT'S IT WORTH TO YOU TO KEEP THE SORDID TRUTH FROM GETTING OUT AND RUINING THAT SMOOTH REPUTATION? STOP. YOU'D BETTER BE THERE AT ONE, OR THE PICTURES HIT THE STREET. STOP. STUMP.

The Miller Family Funeral Home was open for business. A white colonial two-story building nestled between Chicken Delight and Bob's Carparts in the heart of downtown Rupert Springs, Arkansas, the home boasted two limousines, state-of-the-art refrigeration and stained-glass windows in the Chapel of Reverence. Two of its rooms could be opened to contain a larger-than-average crowd, and its morticians, Ray and Billy Lee Miller, stood poised at the head of the stairs in their dark suits, dark glasses and folded hands, nodding greetings to the mourners who were assembling to remember Miss Mamie Stevenson Fillihue.

Inside, Mrs. Marjorie Barlow was already playing a selection of reverential favorites on the organ, and the flowers that had arrived bracketed the pulpit. A fair crowd of townsfolk mingled in the heavily scented room to commiserate with Miss Mamie's two surviving sisters in their hour of need. Everything was ready.

Brooke Ferguson stood alongside the largest of bouquets with the minister, the Reverend Mr. Purcell, who was commenting on the lovely turnout. Pulling a little at the bright blue

ISN'T IT ROMANTIC? 9

cotton shirtdress she wore for the humid afternoon service, all
Brooke could think of was how very much she hated gladioli.
There was never a funeral bouquet without gladioli, and the
damn things stuck out of every arrangement in the room. Except, of course, the one with the pansies and lily of the valley
in the corner. The one given by Brooke and a certain missing
nephew who would go nameless—and headless if he didn't
show up soon.

"Oh, Brooke, dear, isn't this all too lovely?" Mamie's older
sister Letitia gushed, raising a perfume-drenched hankie to her
well-powdered nose. Brooke bit back the truth and smiled to
the fluttery little woman.

"Mamie was a lovely woman."

Everyone was beginning to find his or her place among the
folded chairs. Giving her skirt one more yank against the humid heat that had managed to sap even the Miller's legendary
air-conditioning, Brooke overcame the urge to yank out every
gladiolus she saw, and settled onto an end seat in the second
row.

She'd given up looking over her shoulder. It was already after one, and there was no sign of him. She was going to have to
get through this one alone, it seemed. It didn't leave her any
happier at all. Mr. and Mrs. Wilbur Renfield nodded their hel-
los as they took up their places on the other side of the chair
that held Brooke's purse and umbrella. She just smiled back
and left her belongings where they were.

She wasn't in the mood for this—not the weather, not the
service, not the disappointment. She was exhausted after the
past two weeks, and furious that she hadn't won even a single
argument in the past three days. Brooke would have much
rather been in her jean cutoffs, up to her elbows in dirt plant-
ing her annuals. Instead she was decked out in her brightest,
most attention-getting dress and hat like a peacock who'd
wandered into a field of well-mannered crows. Oh well, she
thought in resignation, at least it's for a good cause. God
knows, nobody else in this room would think to celebrate the
right way.

The Reverend Mr. Purcell marched slowly to his pulpit and
turned to face the crowd of mourners. "Open your books to
hymn number four hundred and fifty-three, if you please."

Clothing rustled and chairs clattered a little as the crowd
climbed to its feet for the opening hymn. Brooke followed

10 ISN'T IT ROMANTIC?

along, heaving a sigh of capitulation as the congregation swung into "Onward Christian Soldiers."

"Oh, for heaven's sakes," she muttered beneath her breath. Alongside her, Mr. and Mrs. Renfield made a show of offering to share their book as they joined in the town's second-favorite hymn. Brooke smiled and shook her head. They didn't seem pleased. Brooke went back to thinking about futility and a conspicuously absent nephew she was going to get on the next plane to personally strangle.

She was so busy muttering to herself that she didn't hear the surprised rustle in the room around her, the slight faltering of voices. Trying her best to ignore the music Miss Letitia had picked for the service, Brooke clenched her hands together to keep them still and wondered if she could get up to give her own eulogy to the little lady they were remembering today.

Not one thing. They hadn't allowed one of Mamie's requests to be honored at her own damn funeral. It seemed that the dead in Rupert Springs didn't have the same rights their fluttery, iron-willed surviving sisters did. Miss Letitia and Miss Emily, both often married and yet still clinging to that fond affectation of Southern womanhood, stood together in the front row, tiny sparrows in their old straw hats and organdy dresses, white gloves and prayer books. Dabbing overwrought and suspiciously dry eyes, they oversaw the funeral they'd personally planned for the sister they'd never quite agreed with. At least, Brooke could almost hear them thinking out loud, Mamie's done something correctly. It had almost been over Brooke's dead body.

"Excuse me, can you take that damn hat off?" a new voice suddenly whispered in her ear. "Person can't see over somebody your size, much less one with a Frisbee on her head."

All of Brooke's anxiety escaped her in a whoosh as she whipped around on her attacker. "Well, if it isn't the star of stage, screen and Saudi Arabia," she hissed right back, fighting hard to keep the delighted grin from her face as the congregation swung around in an attempt to read the second verse and watch the newcomer at the same time. "Where the hell have you been?"

Coop shot Brooke a brash, completely unrepentant grin. "It's one. I'm here. And I have the bribe."

ISN'T IT ROMANTIC? 11

Not even seeming to notice the people around him, he handed up a gold-wrapped box that Brooke knew was going to contain Godiva chocolates.

"One my cute little tush," she retorted, snatching the box from his hand. "When have you ever been on time for anything?"

"You forget," he answered. "I'm a respected newsman now. Six-thirty, every night. No matter what. In your living room."

Brooke snorted, upsetting the delicate tonal balance of the Renfields. "Not in *my* living room. I have better things to watch." She gave brief attention to the weight of the box and nodded. "You just made it, bucko. That shot of you and Bessie almost hit every wire service in the country."

Coop scowled at her. "I do not consider cow-tipping a sordid truth. And besides, it's not like I did it with a stranger. She was Mamie's cow."

"*Your* cow, now. Stand up here, you jerk, and pay your proper respects."

He looked so good. So much the same, and yet so different. Brooke had lied. She did watch him every night on the news, cheering for his successes and worrying through his crises. She hadn't eaten the entire forty-eight hours he'd been caught in Baghdad by a surprise war, had barely had the concentration to work while he'd dodged scud attacks in Saudi Arabia. And when he'd been hurt, she'd come very close to getting on a plane herself.

"Did I miss 'Streets of Laredo'?" he whispered in her ear.

Brooke was one of the few women Pete didn't have to bend to. At six-two, he was built like a runner, long, sleek lines and unconscious grace. Brooke, of course, remembered the years when that frame had been lanky, the legs too long, the arms too short, the famous Cooper profile still honing. She remembered the vast sea of insecurities that had finally launched his career in broadcasting.

No one would ever think it now. No one in Rupert Springs remembered anymore that Pete Cooper hadn't always been self-possessed and striking, that women didn't always fall dead away at his feet over that just-handsome scar on his chin and the devilish intelligence in those moss green eyes.

"Please be seated," the reverend intoned just as Pete gained the chair Brooke had saved for him.

12 ISN'T IT ROMANTIC?

"Yeah," Brooke informed her older brother's best friend. "You missed 'Streets of Laredo,' all right. You missed everything."

"Mamie Marie Ellen Stevenson Fillihue," the reverend intoned in his best preaching voice, "was a good woman."

Brooke couldn't hold back the groan. "I knew it," she said mournfully with a shake of her head. "I just knew it. He'd give this same damn eulogy if it were about Lizzie Borden."

"Where's Elmer?" Pete asked in her ear.

"Fixing fenders," Brooke informed him. "Just like he is every other Saturday. Miss Emily called Lamont instead."

Pete turned his attention fully on her now. "But Mamie wanted Elmer to do her service."

"I know that," Brooke retorted. "And you know that. But I'm afraid that Letitia and Emily didn't believe that."

Pete's eyebrow slid north. "But Elmer's a licensed minister. What was their problem?"

"He wasn't *their* licensed minister. And he happened to only be licensed in the Church of the Cosmic Consciousness." She shrugged. "I just think they were afraid he'd allow some of the...irregularities Mamie wanted."

"None of them?" he demanded incredulously. "Elmer, 'Laredo,' nothing?"

"I often met Mamie on the streets," Reverend Purcell offered, his hands flat on the pulpit, his head bowed reverentially, "and passed the good word with her...."

"Not unless that good word was 'Elvis lives,'" Brooke muttered under her breath.

"But she could never stand that man," Pete objected a little louder.

Brooke didn't bother to hush him up. The Renfields were doing a nice enough job of that. One gleaming smile from Pete neatly shut down the impending protest.

"Well, she wasn't around to argue the choice," Brooke retorted angrily. "And a certain close relative who's bigger than her two sisters put together, and who just might have prevailed, was busy somewhere in the Baltics."

"I did the best I could," he protested.

Brooke knew he had. She could see it in the bruised, drawn strain of his eyes. Pete survived jet lag better than most people, but it was a bet he was on the short end of it right now.

ISN'T IT ROMANTIC?

He'd been up for close to a week covering a hot-breaking story, and then flown home in time to get to the service.

"Besides," he offered in her ear. "You're bigger than they are, too. Why didn't you stick up for Mamie?"

Brooke whirled on him. "Why didn't I *what?*"

Three rows of mourners and the reverend turned her way.

"A...good, *good* woman," the reverend stumbled on, by now solidly entrenched in his favorite—his only—eulogy line.

Brooke was all set to pull Pete right out of the parlor by his ear. One look at the crooked, knowing grin he flashed her killed the impulse. They went back too far and knew each other too well. Pete knew just what would get her goat, what would snap the frustration that had been building for the three days since she'd called him collect on his network's money.

"I guess this means that the Elvis impersonator is totally out of the question," he added.

"A...*good*...woman..."

Laughter was building right beneath Brooke's sternum. Insidious, insistent, absolutely irreverent.

"Even when I asked if he could sing 'In the Chapel,'" she answered, her voice breathless with control. She was grinning back, a silly, wicked grin Mamie would have loved. An expression at the edge of crumbling, too close to exposure for the very well mannered group who'd gathered.

"The Hell's Angels couldn't make it, either?"

Brooke could do no more than shake her head.

"I'm going to read for you now a verse Mamie was particularly fond of..."

Pete's eyebrow cocked. "Not..."

Another shake of the head. "I think it was the man from Nantucket that spoiled it."

He just nodded and turned back to the front, the silliness escaping onto his features, as well. "Elmer would have read one."

The reading, in truth, was lovely. Or would have been if the Reverend Purcell hadn't been reading it. He tended to do everything as if he were imparting civilization to the natives. Mamie probably wouldn't have minded hearing Elmer read it.

But Elmer wasn't reading it. Elmer wasn't here. Or the Hell's Angels, or the New Orleans jazz band Mamie had wanted to lead the funeral procession. There were only very nice people who had considered Mamie a town eccentric instead of the only

ISN'T IT ROMANTIC?

unique being within a fifty-mile radius. They all sat silently, fanning themselves with available booklets and listening to the Reverend Purcell intone yet another familiar passage, only allowing their attention to stray surreptitiously to where Pete Cooper sat amid them for the first time in nigh on to five years.

And Brooke, sitting just as silently, fought the frustration of not being able to better represent her friend, of not successfully bucking the system like Mamie would have been able to do, of not having somebody else close by during those last few weeks to help defray the strain.

Brooke had loved Mamie so much. Never in that bright, sly little woman's life had she ever made Brooke feel "different," even in the years when Brooke had battled every convention in town, when a twelve-year-old girl hadn't known how to accommodate a five-foot-nine-inch frame and bright red hair. Brooke still felt like Clarabelle the Clown. She was still too tall, her hair too red, her face never as dainty and porcelain sweet as her sister's. But because of what Mamie and Pete had given her in those years, she'd at least finally learned to stand up straight and be proud of her differences. No matter what she looked like, then or now.

It was why she was dressed in bright blue, instead of gray. Celebrate yourself, little Mamie had always said. Always face the world like you got the better of it, and the world will believe you.

"And now," Reverend Purcell finally said after Miss Letitia's grandson serenaded his aunt with an accordion rendition of "You'll Never Walk Alone," "we'd like to invite Brooke Ferguson up to the organ to sing Miss Mamie's favorite hymn."

At least, she thought, they hadn't been able to keep her from doing that. She smoothed down the peacock blue material of her skirt and rose all the way to her feet, chin high, eyes bright, never letting the town know that she still felt like that gawky, unhappy teenage girl who had yearned so much to be accepted. And alongside her, Pete, her dearest friend and most stalwart supporter, gave her one of his patented smiles, sure to make her feel pretty, no matter how she really looked.

She looked beautiful. Pete hadn't expected it, not really. It had been so long since they'd really been in the same town to-

ISN'T IT ROMANTIC?

gether, carrying on their friendship over the phone lines of the world since he'd signed on as a correspondent.

Whenever he thought of Brooke, he thought of that thirteen-year-old girl who had always tagged along with David and him, an explosion of auburn curls and freckles and braces, so painfully shy that she turned the world on its head in rebellion. He thought of her dressing up for her senior prom, trembling on the edge of maturity, her great blue eyes wide and appealing. He'd known all along, he supposed, that she'd grow into her looks. He'd just never realized how well.

The people in the little chapel were mesmerized by her regal walk, her stately posture, her cool beauty that didn't have to rely on accepted fashion to compel. They smiled in delight to hear the sweet alto of her voice as she sank into the first notes of "Amazing Grace."

Mamie had known. She'd known all along. Pete remembered talking to her about it that first time, slamming into the house after walking home from the Fergusons'.

"You should see her," he'd said, munching on the apple he'd plucked from the Wilson's tree on the way home and plopping into the beanbag chair that crouched alongside Mamie's red brocade fainting couch. "She looks like a stork somebody stuffed into a burlap bag." He shook his head. "Poor Stump. Her first dance and she has a date who can stare straight up her nostrils."

Mamie had never looked over from where she was helping a TV detective solve crime over dinner. "Don't you dare talk about that girl that way, Peter," she demanded. Pete still saw Mamie as he always did, in her orange stretch pants and her red-and-green-and-blue painter's smock, feet bare, toenails a lurid pink, her wispy gray hair held back by rhinestone barrettes. "If you tell her she's ungainly, how is she ever going to understand how beautiful she is?"

"Beautiful?" he'd demanded, almost choking on his apple. "Mamie, you see her. She looks like Ichabod Crane!"

Mamie had turned very unamused eyes on him. "I'd have to say that's mighty thoughtless talk comin' from a boy who just spent my bulb money on pimple cream this afternoon. She'll be beautiful if she believes it," she informed him gently, those cagey old blue eyes pinning him in his place. "It's our job as her friends to help her do that. And mark my words, Peter Jackson Cooper. If we work hard enough, that little girl will be like

16   ISN'T IT ROMANTIC?

an amaryllis in a clover patch. She'll outshine this town someday—'' She'd waved her fork at him in punctuation and then
turned back to the television where gunfire sputtered and cars
screeched. "Mark my words."

You were right, Mamie, he couldn't help thinking as he
watched Brooke sing for her friend, eyes closed, body swaying
gently with the music, her audience rapt. More than a flower,
a jewel. A rare life and light in this little town of conformists.
He couldn't have been prouder of her if he'd found her and
polished her himself. It was no matter, really, that Mamie
hadn't had the send-off she wanted. She had the tribute she
deserved in the woman Brooke Ferguson had become.

Brooke stood by the food table at Miss Letitia's and watched
Pete with wry amusement. She hadn't seen that much humility
since Gary Cooper stepped up to the microphone in *The Pride
of the Yankees*. Local boy does good seemed to have been
playing big this season. All the old women doted and all the
young women simpered. The men nodded wisely and confided
that they'd known Pete Cooper had it all along.

Brooke just chuckled. They hadn't said that when Pete had
bought his first motorcycle. But then, they'd labeled Pete
Cooper a long time before that, and it had nothing to do with
his soon-to-be legendary charisma. Funny how they forgot.

"Isn't it lovely that Pete could get here?" Wilhelmina
Waverly gushed over her punch as the knot of people moved
with Pete toward the food table like moons following a revolv-
ing planet.

Brooke threw Coop a coy smile and nodded. "I think it's so
nice he could see his way clear to visit. This makes it twice in ten
years."

She knew he'd get over to her eventually. She held his drink
in her hand, old whiskey on the rocks. Pete reached for it with
an answering smile that said a lot more than anybody in the
crowd saw.

"Hey," he protested, hand to tie and tailor-shirted chest in
a show of sincerity. "I can't help it if world events interrupt my
life sometimes."

Brooke laughed. "Don't be silly. World events *are* your life.
You missed my graduation...."

He nodded. "Tiananmen Square."

ISN'T IT ROMANTIC? 17

She handed over the bourbon. "The baptism of your godchild..."

"Berlin Wall."

"Mamie's eightieth birthday party."

"I explained."

"Saying, 'Sorry, Aunt Mamie, I can't make the party' as you're donning a gas mask on international television isn't exactly hearts and flowers," she teased.

He took a sip of bourbon and nodded. "How was I supposed to know that the press secretary really meant get out of Baghdad?"

"I think the pleading note in his voice would have tripped a few instincts."

"She understood."

Brooke laughed. "Are you kidding? She ate out for six months on that story."

"She did dote on you so," one of the other ladies assured him.

For just a moment, Coop's eyes clouded over. "It was mutual," he assured the woman, and then took a good slug of whiskey.

"What are you going to do now?" Millie Bell asked, her eyes fluttering. "With the house and all, I mean."

"Oh, I haven't decided," he allowed. "I haven't even had a chance to sit much less think about that kind of thing."

No less than four women patted his arm and murmured, "Of course, dear," just as if he were their nephew.

Brooke took a sip of her own drink to keep her silence. Across a sea of upturned female faces, Coop shot her a glance that begged rescue. He was looking a little more frayed at the edges. Too much flattery on an empty stomach would probably do it to her, too.

"If you'll excuse us for just a moment," Brooke immediately spoke up, setting her drink down. "I need to discuss something with Pete. About Mamie's animals."

She got him away from the crowd, but it was like pulling a foot out of wet sand. She could almost hear a sucking noise as they let go of him. Pete gave her his arm, which seemed quaintly appropriate in this, Miss Letitia's shrine to Southern hospitality where she'd never asked her younger sister to attend. The two of them headed right for the front door.

18   ISN'T IT ROMANTIC?

They didn't make it. Harlan Willoughby intercepted them halfway across the front parlor.

"There you are," he wheezed, a large asthmatic man with a penchant for white linen suits and silk handkerchiefs. "Couldn't get to you through all them titterin' females. Good to see you home, boy."

Pete clasped the man's ham-size hand. "Harlan."

"Since you're here, and the little ladies are here, thought we'd dispense with the will right now. Mind?"

Harlan, Rupert Springs's most senior lawyer, cherished his reputation as a good old boy. He also liked to play the role of crafty Southern politician, a wily mind behind a slow Southern accent. The problem was, most days the only part he got right was the accent.

"Couldn't it wait?" Pete asked. "I just got in from a long flight, Harlan. I'm beat."

"It's all pretty cut-and-dry, boy. I just figured I'd get things movin' so Miss Letitia and Emily could start arguin' about the furniture." He gave Brooke his best crocodile smile. "Pretty crafty little girl here," he allowed, even though he had to look up to the "little girl." "Movin' right into Miss Mamie's house and changin' the locks so the old girls couldn't sneak in and cart off the best stuff."

"I just didn't want to worry about burglars who read death notices," Brooke demurred. Or about sisters who spoke often and emphatically about what a waste it was to have Great-Grandmother's chifforobe in that horrible little house. And Great-Great-Aunt Esther's tea service. Things like that belonged in a civilized home, not one given over to strays.

"Fifteen minutes," Harlan announced with that same knowing smile and a pat to Pete's arm.

"Might as well get it over with," Brooke told Pete. "I'll wait for you." She smiled. "That way I don't have to worry about your virtue with that crowd out there."

Pete scowled. Harlan came to a kind of attention.

"Oh, no," he argued. "You, too. Didn't I say that?"

Brooke turned on the man. "Me? What for?"

Harlan looked at her as if she were a couple of sandwiches shy of a picnic. "Because Mamie made it a special point to mention you, of course. Be there."

Harlan lumbered off and Brooke stood there, mouth open a little, stunned. "Oh, no," she protested.

ISN'T IT ROMANTIC?   19

Pete was laughing. "I wonder what it'll be?"

Brooke just shook her head. "God only knows."

Besides being acknowledged as the town eccentric, Mamie was also the state's most prolific collector. And not of normal things like butterflies and ceramic animals. Brooke wondered if she had been left Mamie's collection of doorknobs or the clown paintings. With her luck, it would be the license plates. All six thousand of them.

"You still want to go in and face that?" Pete asked, downing the rest of the drink he'd had the foresight to hang on to.

Brooke shook her head. "Might as well. I'd never be able to work up the courage to come back."

They held the meeting in the library, just as in all the old movies, with Harlan settled behind the great mahogany desk and the family members scattered over straight-back chairs. Pete and Brooke shared the couch at the back of the room so they could be both participants and observers. Letitia and Emily fanned themselves in identical fashion, with Letitia's daughter Ella Sue pacing the carpet.

No one actually *read* in the library, just as they didn't really play music in the conservatory. The books that lined the shelves had never suffered the injustice of a stretched spine, nor had the pages been smudged with fingerprints. They stood, row upon row in the floor-to-ceiling shelves, in silent splendor to accent the hunter green-and-leather decor of the room where Miss Letitia's latest late husband, the Colonel, conducted his used-car business.

"First off," Harlan announced, picking up one of the sheets of paper in front of him, "Brooke, I think you wanted this. It's the list of things Miss Mamie wanted at her funeral." His smile was companionable. "Didn't have much luck, did you?"

Brooke got to her feet and walked over to take the handwritten sheet back. After all the fighting, she didn't really need it. She knew the list by heart. She'd asked for it anyway rather than lose even the memory of Mamie's request.

"I'll save it for my funeral," she assured the older man with a smile.

When she got back to the couch, she handed the list to Pete, who was nursing his refilled glass.

20 ISN'T IT ROMANTIC?

"Now then, all," Harlan began, settling his glasses on the edge of his rather bulbous nose and resettling papers. "You've all heard the lingo before. It's too hot for that today, so I'm just going to hit the high points."

"Duck fast," Brooke advised Coop under her breath, knowing where Mamie's largess would rest, and therefore, her sisters' resentment.

Coop just settled a little more deeply into the leather and gave his tie a yank. "I can handle Letitia," he assured her out of the side of his mouth. "I'm counting on you to take out Emily for me."

Brooke gave her head a definite shake. "No way, bud. I've already done my time."

"Gone with the Wind?" he demanded suddenly, looking down on the paper. "You didn't tell me that one."

Brooke just shrugged. "We couldn't have found enough costumes to dress everyone in town anyway," she allowed.

"Now then," Harlan announced, looking over his glasses, much as he'd seen Burl Ives do in the movie of *Cat on a Hot Tin Roof.* "Here it is." He looked back down at his work. "'To my loving sister Letitia, who has always been so concerned with my appearance, I bequeath all my jewelry. You can finally throw it all away, just like you've wanted to do since you were eighteen.'"

Brooke stifled a chuckle with her fist as Harlan handed over a shopping bag of jewelry she'd helped him collect, each piece more gaudy and outrageous than the last. Letitia was not amused.

"I still think we should have fought for the Elvis impersonator," Pete murmured, his attention obviously not on the business at hand.

"We did," Brooke retorted. "We lost."

"'To Emily, guardian of the family name and history,'" Harlan continued, "'I leave a sigh of relief. You don't have to worry anymore about including me in the family tree. But remember, a family's no fun at all without a black sheep or two. So I also leave you Pete, whom I hope follows in my footsteps.'"

At that last sentence, Pete looked up from his aunt's list and smiled. Brooke could tell he didn't even notice the startled little gasps of outrage from his other aunts.

ISN'T IT ROMANTIC?

"'And to Ella Sue, I leave my collection of salt-and-pepper shakers. Maybe it'll help your cooking a little, child.'"

This time Brooke couldn't contain her laughter. Nor could Ella Sue contain her fury.

"How dare she!" the very prim woman demanded.

Harlan just shrugged. "Her property," he said with just a hint of delight. "'To my lovely Brooke Ferguson, I leave all the memories of our rides together. Those long, soft spring evenings when we drove up through the Ozarks and dug up dogwoods and redbuds for my yard....'"

A silly thing to make a person cry, but it was doing it to Brooke. The deep, shady yard behind Mamie's house looked like an Ozark forest for all the trees they'd transplanted.

"'...and I leave the car.'"

"The what?" Ella Sue demanded, whirling toward Brooke.

"The what?" Brooke echoed in a choked little whisper.

Harlan's smile was broad and delighted. "The Thunderbird, girl. Mamie said that aqua would go so well with your hair, she knew you had to have it."

"But that's a classic!" Brooke protested.

Harlan nodded. "You know where the keys are."

"The rest all goes to Pete. 'All I ask,' she says, 'is that you love it like I did.' And that's all."

"It can't be!" Letitia protested, leaping to her feet.

"She can't have that car!" Ella Sue shrilled. "That car was to be saved for little Lyman's sixteenth birthday."

"She shouldn't have left it to me," Brooke murmured to Pete, truly overcome. That car had been Mamie's pride and joy, an original 1957 two-seater that shone like a new penny.

"Of course she should," Pete retorted. "Now all you have to do is enjoy it."

"But how can I take that?" Brooke protested. "I let her down. She thought I was going to arrange her funeral for her, and I couldn't get anything."

He shook his head, oblivious to the firestorm that was raging around Harlan not ten feet away. "Nobody here would have really appreciated it anyway. Can you really see this town highstepping through the streets behind a jazz band, or reading their favorite limericks at sunrise?"

"But dammit, she deserved to have the funeral she wanted."

"Tell you what," he offered. "If you let me ride in your car, I'll let you sit on my couch, and we can read limericks by ourselves. We can even go on up to the mountains and pick up another dogwood or two."

Brooke wasn't sure where the idea came from. Maybe the result of all that fruitless arguing over the past few days, maybe the fact that now that Mamie was gone there wouldn't be any more spontaneity in this town. Maybe the fact that the sisters who should have mourned her were already picking over her things after denying her the send-off she wanted. Whatever it was, the minute the impulse struck, Brooke knew it was pure gold.

"No," she retorted, snatching the paper from Pete's hands. "That's not good enough."

His expression was dubious. "I guess you'll tell me what is."

She grinned now, suddenly happier than she'd been since the day Mamie had calmly announced that she was dying. "You bet your cute butt I will, boy. We're going to give Mamie the send-off she deserves."

Pete looked a bit bemused. "Brooke," he reminded her, "Mamie's already been sent off."

But Brooke shook her head. "Not really. Not officially. I say we hop in that little car of hers and take off in search of her funeral."

Pete still stared at her. The din of the room was rising. Harlan had both hands up trying to fend off female outrage, but neither Brooke nor Pete paid any attention.

"Come on, Coop," Brooke urged. "Do you really think she had the send-off she deserved?"

"Of course not. There weren't even any party hats."

Brooke nodded, her own hat tipping precariously toward Pete with her enthusiasm. "Then let's do it. You and me. Let's go find everything Mamie wanted. It'll be kind of like a cosmic scavenger hunt."

Pete stopped staring long enough to finish off his drink. "You're nuts."

"I know. But isn't that just what Mamie would have wanted?"

It took him a moment. First he looked at Brooke, then over where his aunts and cousin were circling Harlan like an Indian scalping party. Finally he turned back to Brooke, and that old challenge lit his eyes. "Yeah," he admitted, "it is. Let's go."

Two

IBN, EVENING NEWS AT 6:30 P.M.

Marsha Phillips

Good evening, this is the news for May twenty-third. I'm Marsha Phillips, and this is Brian Thorn, filling in for Pete Cooper, who is away on assignment. And now for the top stories tonight...

"**I**'m not so sure about this."

Twirling her hat on the edge of her index finger, Brooke scowled over at Pete where he sprawled in the beanbag chair that had been too small for him by the time he was fifteen. Pete's shoes were off and his tie was draped around his neck like a scarf. There was a fat tabby cat curled up on his stomach and another dozing between his feet. "Don't be silly," Brooke said. "It's a great idea. Mamie would definitely approve."

He gave his head a slow nod. "Oh, she'd approve all right. It's Parischell I'm not so sure about. I'm supposed to be back at my desk tomorrow night smiling out on the masses."

24 ISN'T IT ROMANTIC?

"Oh, your boss will understand, won't he?" she asked. "After all, you just buried the woman who raised you."

Pete's expression didn't improve any. "That bastard? He wouldn't let me take off if I'd just buried *me*. All he cares about is audience share and Q rating, and my being out of town during sweeps is not going to make me any friends."

"But you've *been* out of town," she countered. "In a city I can't even pronounce."

He raised a finger in exception. "Ah, but one that had a satellite feed. I don't think you can say the same for Rupert Springs."

"We're not staying here. I mean, when was the last time a New Orleans jazz band strolled down Main Street?"

She spun her hat a little wide and it sailed like a saucer right over to land on Pete's lap. The cat never moved. Picking up the offending millinery, Pete spun it right back at her.

"Besides," she added, flinging the hat right back again, "I thought you doted on the linoleum that Parischell walks on. He's the inspiration behind the network, the spiritual leader of all that media trendsetting, isn't he?"

"He's the man who signs my paychecks." Pete gave up tossing the hat and just settled it onto his own head like a bright blue sombrero and nestled his head back against the vinyl. "I'd call him Mother Teresa as long as he leaves me alone."

Brooke shook her head in mock sympathy. "Tsk, tsk. The great Pete Cooper having work troubles just like every other slob in the universe. Imagine that."

Pete's answer was nonverbal and succinct enough to make Brooke laugh. "It's good to have you home, Coop."

With one finger, he tipped her hat up like a cowboy checking out the competition. It wasn't steely eyes Brooke saw beneath the brim, but gentle eyes. Familiar eyes, comfortable eyes that still, even after all these years, had the power to take the stuffing out of her knees. "It's good to be here, Stump. I missed you."

Brooke flashed him her own retort and the two of them settled back into their state of semisomnolence.

"Besides," Pete continued into her hat. "Who's going to watch the house? You know damn well that the minute I turn my back Letitia and Emily are going to come right in and snatch every license plate on the kitchen wall."

ISN'T IT ROMANTIC? 25

"Well, what were you planning to do with the house when you went back?"

"Have you live here."

Brooke came to a kind of attention. "Oh, Coop, I couldn't..."

He didn't even bother to lift the hat again. "All those trees in the back are yours anyway. Not to mention the car in the garage."

"But what about all her good things? The furniture, the crystal, the family things."

He shrugged. "Wouldn't fit in my apartment right now anyway. I thought maybe you'd watch over it until I got a real vacation and we could sort through it all together."

"But I'm living in *my* house."

"Which you've wanted to put up for sale ever since your mom died. There's plenty of room in here for your good things, and nobody'd take better care of Mamie's treasures than you."

"Coop..."

He lifted a hand. "I'm fading fast here, Stump. Let's argue later."

"When are you going to call your boss?"

"I can't leave this house open for the vultures."

"You're not," she assured him. "We have reinforcements."

He wasn't moving at all now. Brooke watched him, splayed over that chair, all arms and legs, and thought of the evenings they'd sat in this living room watching *Hawaii Five-O* with Mamie. Popcorn fights and endless teasing and the first, shy realizations of puppy love on her part. Coop and Chick and Stump, two friends and a tagalong who had, in the end, become closer to her brother's friend than her brother. David was in Greece now with the consulate there, a family man, an upright citizen. Brooke's sisters had moved, too, one with a husband, another with a job, leaving her alone in the town where they'd been raised.

And the funny thing was, even though she was close with them all, visiting holidays and exchanging letters about children and old hometown gossip, Brooke still felt closest to Pete. Pete had been the one who'd known what it meant to feel different. He'd faced that small-town narrow-mindedness before her and cleared a kind of path. And then he'd gone off to the world like everyone else and left her behind.

26   ISN'T IT ROMANTIC?

Funny how just the sight of too-long arms and legs and shoeless feet could put a knot in a person's throat.

"Good Lord, I'm too late. Emily shot him and then tried to dress him like Letitia."

Startled, Brooke looked up to see the uniformed officer on the other side of the screen door.

"That's it, Sergeant," she said with a grin. "It was all over the salt-and-pepper shakers."

"I heard about that." Her friend giggled as she pulled open the door and stepped inside. "The entire town is abuzz. Congratulations. I hear you cheated Lyman out of his rightful T-Bird."

"Nothing wrong with the news-gathering capabilities in this town," Pete muttered, still not moving. "That's not Allie Simpson on the other side of this fashionable hat, is it?"

"This guy must be a journalist," Allie retorted dryly, pulling off her police ball cap and running a quick hand over her jet black braid.

Coop finally lifted his hat and then dropped it completely. "Good grief. What are you doing in that outfit?"

Allie looked down to where her generous curves gave new dimension to the navy blue uniform she wore. "Keeping the peace in these parts, boy. The Fillihue ladies asked me to check on a potential disturbance over here. They're planning one. From what I hear, you two are invited."

Pete actually made it to his feet, displacing the two cats and towering over the town's law enforcement. "Come on," he retorted, hands on hips. "That's not really your uniform. You're too short to be a sergeant."

Allie's scowl was impressive for someone who hadn't grown since sixth grade. "You sure got a lot of nerve saying that to a woman who's licensed to use a gun."

Pete's grin was purely salacious. "Tough women turn me on, baby. Can I play with your nightstick?"

Allie chuckled. "I was about to ask you the same thing. Welcome home, Coop. You look like you've just gone a round with your aunts."

"Two rounds," Brooke said, climbing to her own feet and thinking better of it when her feet protested still being in heels. The offending attire ended up in a tumble alongside Pete's as she wiggled her stockinged feet against the cool hardwood of

ISN'T IT ROMANTIC? 27

Mamie's floor. "Do you have time for refreshments, Sergeant?"

"As long as Bill Thompson thinks I'm down at the Donut Drop, sure. What kind of sedition are we planning? I have my overnight case in the cruiser."

Pete turned to Brooke with a bemused expression. "*She's* your protection?" he demanded.

"I wouldn't sound quite so outraged if I were you," Brooke suggested as she led the three of them out to Mamie's sparkling white kitchen that had been decorated with hanging flower baskets in the windows and rectangular representations of every state in the union and quite a few countries covering the walls. The room looked like a cross between an upscale restaurant and a body shop. The refrigerator was still stocked with plenty of beer and lemonade, and the cupboard hid away a few of Mamie's more exotic cold remedies.

"Well, why aren't you staying here, Pete?" Allie asked, accepting a glass of lemonade as she dropped her cap onto the table and slid her nightstick from her belt so she could sit at the lace-and-clear-plastic-covered table.

"Because we're off to give Mamie a funeral," Brooke informed her, pulling over the maps she'd dug out when she'd first returned to the little clapboard house. Out the window the dogwood leaves looked as lacy against the light as the good tablecloth Mamie had tatted.

Allie momentarily forgot her lemonade. "Wasn't she there today?" she asked Pete with a motion to Brooke.

He nodded, rubbing at his eyes with a weary hand. "She's decided that it wasn't enough."

"Even with the accordion?"

"You ever heard Lyman play that thing?"

Allie winced. "I live two houses down. That's why I agreed so quickly to stay here for you."

"And I appreciate it," Brooke conceded, pulling open the Arkansas map and spreading it out between them. "All you have to do is keep the Fillihues out and the animals in."

Pete finally gave up and joined them, his own glass of lemonade rapidly disappearing. "What do you have in mind?" he asked.

Brooke shot him a bright smile, the exhilaration beginning to bubble again. She'd just give him the basics. He was look-

ISN'T IT ROMANTIC?

ing much too strung out for details. Besides, details only got in the way, anyway. At least, that's what Mamie always said.

"Well, what do we have to find?" she asked.

Pete shrugged and rubbed at his face again. "I don't know. Limericks, jazz bands, Elvis..."

"He's in Minnesota," Allie informed them all. "Working in a fast-food joint with Princess Grace. I saw it in the *Daily World* at Hanson's store when I picked up coffee."

"Someplace we can find costumes to dress up as our favorite characters in *Gone with the Wind*," Brooke added, "and a place to pay tribute to the Fillihue ancestors."

"Don't forget about the Hell's Angels," Allie said. "And somebody to sing 'Streets of Laredo' and 'Joy to the World.'"

Brooke snorted. "You should have heard the arguments about that one. Letitia couldn't imagine why Mamie wanted Christmas songs at her funeral. She never did figure out what the bullfrog had to do with it."

"So, where are we going?" Pete asked.

Brooke stared at him, much the way Harlan had stared at her. "Come on. You're the famous journalist, here. You should know where to find this stuff."

"I'm a journalist, not a booking agent for sideshows. I mean, we have to find an Elvis impersonator."

"Well, how many can there be out there?"

"There were two hundred at the reopening of the Statue of Liberty."

Brooke shot him a sharp grin. "Got lost in the crowd, huh?"

Pete had the good grace to chuckle back. "My jumpsuit was at the cleaners that weekend."

"So, where do you have to go?" Allie demanded.

Brooke took a moment to think about it. "Well, where would be the first place you'd look for Elvis?"

"I told you. Minnesota."

"When he's not with Princess Grace."

"Oh. Well, Graceland, I guess."

"Exactly. Are you keeping up with this, Pete?"

He nodded, his chin in his hands, his eyes half-closed. "Anybody know what time it is in Belgrade?"

"This will only take a minute more, and then I'll even take your socks off myself so you can go to sleep."

"Are you going to call my boss and tell him why I'm not going to be in for a while?"

ISN'T IT ROMANTIC? 29

"Sure. Would you like an indictment or a disease?"

His scowl was pure Coop and made both women laugh.

"The question is," Brooke said, "do we go to New Orleans by way of Memphis, or Atlanta by way of Shiloh?"

All Pete could offer was a groan.

"I'll take that as a yes." She challenged him, eye-to-eye, knowing damn well that he'd never forgive her if she let him back out now. Pete Cooper had been seen at every society function Atlanta had put on in the past four years. He'd been dressed up and buttoned down and as respectable as Sunday service. And in all that time, he hadn't had a decent vacation, or just kicked back and done something silly or given in to whim. Brooke knew, not only from his letters to Mamie, in which he never really admitted his growing frustration, but in his calls to her. He was aching for this trip, and he didn't even know it.

Well, it was up to her to make sure he didn't get back on that plane in Little Rock without a bit of insanity. If she had to use Allie's gun to achieve it, then that's just what she'd do.

"Okay," she finally acquiesced with a huge smile, never taking her gaze from Pete's as she got back to her feet. "You win. Straight down to New Orleans first. Now all we have to do is figure how we're going to pack everything into that little car."

Outside, the sunlight flickered through the young trees and baked the dark police cruiser in the driveway. Brooke had forgotten how bad the humidity was. It hit her like a wet rag the minute she stepped outside to walk Allie to her car.

"Thanks again for offering to stay," she said, picking at her dress.

Allie waved her off as she replaced her nightstick and pulled out her keys. "I told you. It's my pleasure. I haven't seen Letitia that color since they found out Ella Sue was pregnant without benefit of a wedding band. Just let me know when you're ready to go...." She shook her head with a wondering little grin. "I still can't believe you're doing it."

"Why not?" Brooke asked, staying to the grass to protect her feet. The dogwoods weren't much shade. "Can you think of anything better for Mamie?"

30   ISN'T IT ROMANTIC?

"No," Allie admitted, coming to a stop by the car. "But even for hanging around with her all these years, this is still a little abrupt. What about your job?"

"Oh, I'm due for a vacation. Besides, I have a feeling that if I don't do this now, I'll never take the time to later."

Allie just nodded, then grinned. "Out on the road alone with Pete Cooper. My, my."

"My, my, what?"

Allie's black eyes sparkled with mischief. "What would the *Daily World* say?"

"Nothing. They're all up in Minnesota buying burgers anyway."

"Somebody's going to find out."

Brooke shrugged. "It's just Coop, Allie. He needs to get away."

Allie took a moment to look in toward the house. "Yeah," she admitted. "He does. I didn't realize it until now. It's sure good to see him."

Brooke followed her gaze, as if she, too, could conjure sight of Pete beyond those clematis-covered walls. "Yeah, it is. Too bad it was to bury Mamie."

"I'm gonna miss her."

Brooke nodded, Mamie's loss still too big for words. "Me, too."

For a little bit longer, the two women simply stood where they were, enjoying their own memories. Then Allie straightened and opened the car door. She was about to climb in when she suddenly stopped.

"Oh, darn, I almost forgot. Harlan asked me to pass this on to you." Reaching into her shirt pocket, she pulled out a small envelope and handed it over. "In all the excitement yesterday, he forgot to give it to you. It's a personal note to you from Mamie." Brooke had her hand out for it, but Allie held back for a moment, a cautionary smile lighting her eyes. "To be opened in exactly ten days."

Brooke let her eyebrows rise. "Ten days?" What in heaven's name would Mamie want to say to her in ten days? And how in heaven's name was she going to wait to find out?

Allie waved the intriguing little envelope at her. "Promise?"

Brooke made a snatch at it. "Yeah, yeah."

"You're making that promise to an officer of the law, now."

ISN'T IT ROMANTIC? 31

Brooke fingered the envelope, the sight of Mamie's spidery handwriting igniting a bittersweet ache in her chest. "Thanks."

Her mission accomplished, Allie slid into her car and started the engine. "Well, give me enough notice to give you two an official bon voyage."

"Thanks again, Allie."

As she slid into her seat, Allie dispatched one last smile. "Just remember where I am if you need to talk."

Brooke lifted a quizzical eyebrow.

Allie smiled. "You look really great in that color. See you later."

And with no more than that, Brooke's best friend since sophomore year of high school slammed the door shut and departed. Brooke just shook her head as she tiptoed through the stubbly grass and back across the cool smoothness of the front porch.

Good old Allie, as comfortable as old shoes, as tied to this town as a homing bird. Allie, who had never sought to reach beyond her arm's length, who never needed to wander farther than the horizon. Allie had been Brooke's watermark for reality, but Pete had taught her to dream.

Speaking of dreaming, that was just what he was doing when she walked back inside. Head in arms, gently snoring, facedown at the table. He'd mumbled something about a shower when Brooke had gotten up to show Allie out. Brooke had a feeling that idea was a nonstarter.

She grinned down at the tousled head, the broad, strong back, the lanky frame she would have recognized anywhere in the world.

"Come on, big boy," she coaxed, slipping the envelope into her own pocket before settling her hands to his shoulders. "It's time for bed."

"Not tonight, honey," he muttered into his shirtsleeves. "I have a headache."

Brooke chuckled, her hands comfortable where they were. "I prefer my partners to participate, thanks. Come on, let's get you into bed. We have a big day tomorrow."

She got him to his feet, where he swayed like a young tree in the wind, his eyes bleary, his smile crooked. "Happens like this," he admitted. "I can go so far, and then I drop like a rock."

32   ISN'T IT ROMANTIC?

Brooke slipped her arm around his waist and turned him toward his old room, where the Cardinals posters still vied for space with NASA charts and a very nice shot of Cheryl Tiegs. "Then it's a good thing you're doing it around a girl big enough to keep us both from ending up on the floor."

Coop answered by sliding his own arm around Brooke's waist. It was a position they'd perfected over the years, close, comfortable, so at ease with each other that Pete didn't think twice about letting his head fall onto Brooke's shoulder as he stumbled back to the bedroom, the cats following with two smaller, black-and-white friends.

Brooke did take his socks off. She threw a cover over him, closed the curtains in his room and hung his jacket in the closet. By the time she turned to leave, the cats were curling up atop the spread, purring like car engines on the highway. Flung out on the bed, Pete was snoring softly, his hair tumbling over his forehead, his face still strained. Brooke allowed herself a real smile. It was good to have him home. She hadn't realized how much she'd missed him until she'd seen him again.

Closing the door gently behind her, she headed for home and those chocolates he'd brought.

"My God, Coop. What happened to you?"

Pete stretched out the kinks left from his sixteen-hour sleep and gave way to a window-rattling sneeze.

"Cats," he snarled, his voice barely a rasp. "I forgot."

Beyond the film that blurred his vision and the itching, burning irritation in his nasal passages, Pete could see the real concern in Brooke's eyes give way to a certain amusement.

"Perfect," she crowed, clapping her hands together.

Pete rubbed again at his eyes with no noticeable results and gave in to a very miserable-sounding sniffle. "Perfect for what?" he demanded.

She just shook her head. "Listen to you," she marveled, stalking to the phone. "You sound like hell."

"It's only fair," he retorted with another sneeze that made her flinch. "I feel like it. I'm going to take a shower. Then I'm calling Doc Levin."

She spun on him. "No. Not yet."

Pete saw now that she had a phone receiver in her hand. Even as she grinned at his distress, she punched buttons.

ISN'T IT ROMANTIC? 33

"Why?"

She waved him off. "This is the Rupert Springs General Hospital calling Mr. Evan Parischell," she intoned with nasal precision into the receiver.

"Brooke!" Pete protested without any success. With what was left of his voice after sucking in cat hair over sixteen hours, he didn't sound impressive.

She waved him off again, her smile growing into a huge grin. "It's about Mr. Cooper," she told the person on the other end of the line. "Wait? I think not. I have other patients to attend to."

Pete couldn't do much more than roll his eyes and sneeze again. Just what he needed, an accomplice. Well, since there seemed to be nothing for it, he headed on past Brooke to pull a can of soda out of the fridge. All that mourning and sneezing had stirred an appetite. Now, if he could only taste his food...

"Ah, Mr. Parischell," Brooke all but sang into the phone. "This is Dr., um, Patterson. I'm an ear, nose and throat specialist here in town, and I need your help."

Pete pulled out a kitchen chair and sank into it, eyes again rolling at Brooke's impersonation. Someday Parischell would make a pilgrimage to Rupert Springs and find out that the town wasn't big enough to sport a doctor who specialized in one organ, much less three. Then Pete would be in for it.

"Well, yes, he *is* sick," she informed the executive. "*Very* sick. I'm not sure what the man was doing before he came home for his dear aunt's funeral, but he has absolutely no voice left. He keeps insisting that he has to get back to work. Doesn't want to let you down, you know..." Pete gave her another grimace, which she blandly ignored. "Well, now that's precisely the point. If he tries to use that voice right now, he might lose it entirely. And you wouldn't want a news anchor who sounds like Louis Armstrong, would you?"

"He'll know," Pete muttered. "I'll get my voice back tomorrow as soon as the cats go."

"Would you speak to him?" Brooke asked the man. "He simply won't listen to me."

Pete tried shaking his head. He wasn't even in the mood to put up with Brooke right now, much less Parischell. It didn't do any good. Brooke simply walked the phone over to him and substituted it for the soda he'd been about to taste.

34   ISN'T IT ROMANTIC?

"Two weeks, Mr. Cooper," she informed him with stern voice and outrageously laughing eyes. "You can't go back any sooner. Now, after you've talked to Mr. Parischell, not another word."

"Pete? Pete?" Parischell's voice floated free of the mouthpiece, the tone bordering on incipient panic. "Are you there?"

Pete did his best to stifle the next set of sneezes as he turned to answer. "Yeah, I'm here."

There was a pause, and then a stricken gasp. "Oh, my God, man. What happened? You sounded perfectly all right yesterday."

Pete heaved a sigh of capitulation. "I don't know, Evan. I woke up like this."

"Don't say another word! I want you right back in Atlanta where there are specialists who can look at you."

Pete almost smiled. Instead he reached over with his free hand and retrieved his soda. "It's just old-fashioned laryngitis, Evan—" The sneeze that punctuated that statement could have been heard in New Orleans. "And a cold, I guess. I'll be fine."

"Two weeks, that doctor said, huh?" Evan's voice kept rising, like a small child seeing his best bike being backed over by the family station wagon. "You couldn't have done this in January or March, could you?"

"Sorry."

The magnate sighed, a huge, frustrated noise that displaced almost as much air as Pete's sneezes. "All right. Get some rest. Lots of fluid, that kind of thing. Brian will have to cover for you."

"He won't mind."

"Shut up! Not another word! Just take care of that voice."

By the time Pete handed the phone back to Brooke, he almost believed he really was sick.

"And how are we going to explain the jaunt to New Orleans?" he demanded.

Brooke grinned like a pirate. "Just because you can't talk doesn't mean you can't travel."

He ran his hand through his hair, trying to pull some kind of order together. "What time is it?"

"About eleven in the morning. Boy, kid, you should see your eyes. They really look terrible."

ISN'T IT ROMANTIC? 35

Pete snorted. "Thanks, they look bad enough from this side. You haven't been here all night, have you?"

"Don't be silly. I ran over when the Fillihue early-warning system went off. Allie will be here in twenty minutes, my bags are in the living room and the car is gassed and ready to go."

Pete made it a point to look around him. "Now?"

Brooke just smiled. "As soon as you get a shower and I get some antihistamines from Doc Levin. Otherwise we're in for round three with Letitia. She's coming to complain about the will."

Pete stood stock-still for a minute, in the shirt and slacks he'd worn to the funeral, facing down a terminally bright Brooke in her blue chambray shirt and tan cotton twill slacks, her hair pulled up in a knot that spilled copper curls down the back of her neck. Her eyes glittered like sunlight on water, equal parts glee and anticipation, and Pete suddenly realized that he couldn't resist them. He couldn't resist her. As miserable as he felt, he found himself actually looking forward to two weeks in a convertible alongside her with nothing more to do than look for Elvis.

"I'd appreciate it if you'd get the cats out back in the barn while I shower," he conceded.

Brooke's smile exploded into laughter. "We should probably hang on to one. Just in case Mr. Parischell shows up."

Not only did Brooke take care of the cats while Pete was doing his best to beat some life into his flagging body, she took care of the medicine. Antihistamines, eye drops, nose drops and about a case of tissue all waited on the kitchen table when he walked back out of the bathroom. Brooke was sitting in the living room, sharing sodas with Allie.

"He looks terrible," Allie was saying, her feet up on the table, her sunglasses on, her attention on Pete.

"He looks better," Brooke answered, in similar position, her feet up on a suitcase.

Pete scowled at them both. "He appreciates the sincere concern. Is that your luggage, or are you setting up a refugee camp?"

Brooke didn't seem particularly offended. "I'm waiting for you to bring yours out so we can get the car packed."

Pete just lifted the beaten, dusty duffel already in his hand.

That brought Allie's glasses up and Brooke's feet down. "Coop," she admonished, standing up. "This isn't a quick jaunt to a war zone."

He motioned to the matching softsider luggage clogging up most of the floor space. "It's not the grand tour, either. What the hell do you have in those things?"

Brooke looked down at the various bags and scowled. "Accessories. You men are so damned spoiled. What do you need for a trip? One suit, three ties and a razor. Try scooting through Europe with four pairs of shoes, makeup, jewelry, panty hose, and enough hair equipment to start a salon."

Pete made it a point to look over at Allie. "Has she been this way long?"

Allie grinned. "Since she started traveling on business."

He returned his attention to Brooke. "This is Aunt Mamie we're remembering, Brooke. Not Coco Chanel."

Brooke huffed at him and bent to pick up the bigger bag. "You remember her your way and I'll remember her mine."

Allie never moved from where she was slouched on the couch, her drink balanced on her flat belly. "Well, this is sure shaping up to be the trip of the century. I'm just sorry I have to stay behind and guard the fort."

"No, you're not," Pete and Brooke answered simultaneously.

Allie's grin was delighted. "No, I'm not."

By the time the sleek little aqua Thunderbird backed out of Mamie Fillihue's garage, Brooke had left two of her bags behind and Pete forgot the nose drops. They had maps, though, and a vague idea of where south was. The day was going to be cool, with high puffy clouds chasing the sun and just enough of a breeze to demand the customized top be put down. A good start for a quest. A good day to begin a vacation. Even though Brooke resented having to leave behind her best dress and Pete was still sneezing and wheezing, they were looking forward to the next few days.

Standing out in Mamie's front yard, Allie just waved, laughed and shook her head. And then she went back to prepare for the disasters she knew were coming.

Three

There was a young man of St. Kitts,
Who was very much troubled with fits;
The eclipse of the moon
Threw him into a swoon;
When he tumbled and broke into bits.

"**W**here are we headed?" Pete asked, yanking yet another tissue from the box. His head was back against the seat, the wind tunneling through his hair, the sun gleaming against his face, his sunglasses hiding the worst ravages of his allergy.

Brooke shot him a look and turned back to her driving. "I don't know. What looks like a fun road to follow south?"

He turned his head toward her. "You sure planned this out to the letter, didn't you?"

Brooke laughed and turned the radio up so she could hear Genesis a little better.

"Impulsive behavior's good for the soul sometimes," she admitted, the sudden, unexpected freedom swelling in her chest. She hadn't said anything to anyone, even Mamie, but work had been wearing on her. A good job, solid career lad-

38   ISN'T IT ROMANTIC?

der, but with no option for variety, no chance ever to do the work she'd been educated to do. The kind of real life that needed escaping every once in a while.

"Impulsive behavior is what gets nations into wars and young women into diaper service," Pete intoned, his voice not sounding appreciably better.

Brooke laughed at him again. "Are those your words of wisdom for the day?"

"Depends," Pete retorted, "on where we end it."

"Live dangerously, Coop."

"I thought I did that in the Gulf."

"You had the biggest army in history keeping an eye on you. This little jaunt's solo. What do you want to do first?"

The houses were thinning now into pastureland and a few industrial parks. The sky opened up beyond the trees, and the wind sang in Brooke's ears. Off to the right she could see Parson's Stables where she used to take lessons, and beyond that the twin silos of Allie's parents' place. Familiar, unchanging, as predictable as sunrise. Falling behind her with the memories of the hard past few weeks, the sense of desertion, the sudden, sharp loneliness when Mamie had left her behind.

"I want to go," he mused slowly, "to a little town where nobody knows who I am, and I can order a beer and a hamburger at the tavern and watch a ball game."

Brooke contained her sense of satisfaction. "I don't think that's in the will."

"Executor's fees."

She nodded. "I know just the place."

He shot her a quick look. "They won't recognize me?"

She grinned. "Not looking like you do now."

His grimace was telling. His sneeze was even more so. "Damn cats."

They drove that way for a long while, sating themselves on the silence, the isolation, the unique freedom of the American road. The land folded into hills as they sped by Little Rock and then flattened into farmland, emerald green in the sunlight, trees burgeoning with new leaf and the sky an aching blue. Where they were going didn't matter so much right now, the going did. The getting away from not only the funeral, the fighting, but everything that had led up to it.

"Did David get ahold of you?" Brooke asked.

"We talked for an hour and a half."

ISN'T IT ROMANTIC? 39

"It killed him not to be here."

"Well, I told him that it was a legitimate payback. I was in Central America when your dad died."

Brooke nodded, her eyes on the ribbon of road that stretched east and south toward the Mississippi, her attention on the music that throbbed from the old radio that had first played Dion and the Platters. It was a great car. She and Mamie had spent some wonderful afternoons in it, top down, sun in their faces, purloined trees sharing the passenger seat. Mamie couldn't have given Brooke a more lovely gift to remember her by.

"I wish I could have been here for her," Pete said suddenly, as if privy to Brooke's thoughts.

She never looked away from her driving. "You were," she assured him. "Every night. We'd sit in her room and watch the news and she'd complain that you obviously weren't getting enough sleep, and that your prissy station had ruined your sense of fashion."

Pete's laugh was wistful. "I'm on most of the best-dressed lists."

"It was all those suits," Brooke confided. "She liked you much better in your bomber jacket and chinos. And the Hard Rock Cafe T-shirt she sent you."

"Well, that look's okay at the Dahran Hilton. It's not the same at the evening news desk. Besides, I don't wear all of the suit."

Now Brooke did look over to see Pete's smile. "I always knew you were an exhibitionist," she accused with an answering grin.

"Jeans," he defended himself. "It saves on wear and tear. Those suits are expensive."

"Poor baby."

He reached across to take hold of her hand for a minute, and Brooke was suddenly afraid she was going to have to fight tears.

"Thank you, Brooke," he simply said. "You made sure she wasn't alone."

Brooke gave his hand a quick squeeze, doing her best to keep her eyes on the flat, unchallenging road ahead. "Come on, Pete. We made a promise to each other. You know I wouldn't let Mamie down."

40 ISN'T IT ROMANTIC?

Finally he took his hand back and turned his attention ahead. "Yeah, we made a promise all right. Only one of us kept it, though."

Brooke's answering smile was wry. "Only one of us was home."

"You've always been there, though. First your dad, then your mom and now Mamie. Everybody else has been gone from that town for years."

"Everybody else had someplace else to go."

She could feel his gaze on her, bemused, intense, and suddenly she didn't want to deal with it.

"We'll be in town in another half hour or so," she said, turning the station up a little louder, interfering with Pete's concern. "They have the best greasy spoon in four states there."

For a moment Pete didn't answer and Brooke was afraid he meant to continue his previous line of conversation. But she hadn't come on this trip to discuss her prospects or her future or the sacrifices Pete thought she'd made over the years to stay where she was. She was here to cut loose, to share the sun with an old friend and maybe dredge up some silly memories to honor Mamie by. And that's just what she meant to do.

Badger, Arkansas, consisted of one street, two stop signs and a grand total of ten buildings, three of which had something to do with the buying and consumption of liquor. Pete found himself in the second such building, Bud's Badger Bar, where he and his antihistamines shared a chipped, scarred table with Brooke.

She should have looked as out of place here as a crystal vase in a box of bowling balls. She was taller than most of the denizens and certainly had better taste in apparel. Her hair shone like burnished copper in the fluorescent lights that provided Bud's ambience, and the easy, fluid grace of her movements would have settled her comfortably into any fashionable party in Atlanta.

Much to Pete's amazement, though, she was greeted like a long-lost friend, clapped on the back with greasy hands and challenged to any number of games of pool, which she turned down in favor of lunch. For the first time in about three years, Pete went completely unnoticed.

ISN'T IT ROMANTIC? 41

"There's obviously something you've been leaving out of your letters," he accused with a grin, wondering if the bar was really this dim and grimy without the sunglasses he still wore in deference to his red, swollen eyes.

Brooke's laugh was like music. "It's been too long since you've mingled with the common folk, boy. I'm here at Bud's at least once a month."

"The pool's that good here?"

"It's on my way to most of the sites I have to examine. Besides, a lot of drivers for Amex eat here. I can catch up on what the street says."

Pete gave his head a slow shake. "You have a degree in art history. How did you end up repping for a trucking company?"

"Hard work," she allowed with a severely straight face. "And the best set of legs in the shop."

Pete's scowl was quick, a lot more instinctive than he'd remembered. "You'd better not be putting up with any funny stuff there."

He must have surprised her. For a moment she just stared at him, eyes wide, head tilted a little in a position of consideration. Finally she laughed again. "Those old protective instincts die hard, huh?"

Pete scowled, chagrined. Truth be told, it had surprised him, too. Any person walking into this place would know without a word being exchanged that Brooke was a woman who could take care of herself. He imagined that it was no different in that trucking company. She had truly matured into her potential. Except she'd matured in a direction none of them could have predicted.

"Well, somebody has to keep you in line," he protested with a self-effacing grin. "Especially now that Mamie's gone."

That delighted her. "Are you kidding? I spent all my time keeping *her* in line. She was the most outrageous flirt to hit the streets. The truckers ate her up like candy. You saw them all at the service, didn't you?"

"Hey, girl, what you doin' here on a Saturday?" a new voice demanded.

Pete looked up to see a behemoth in leather and chains looming over the table. Pete had done a piece inside Folsom once. He could have sworn he'd eaten lunch with this guy there.

42   ISN'T IT ROMANTIC?

The tattoos and forest of facial hair were a dead giveaway. This probably wouldn't be the time to bring it up, though.

Brooke was beaming at him as if they were related. "Barney," she greeted him. "Where have you been?"

Barney actually looked abashed. The old biker's cap he'd been wearing was now in his hands as if he were presenting himself to the Queen, and his head was bent. "Oh, I had a little disagreement with the state police a couple of months ago. This time they won."

Brooke just nodded her head. "Uh-huh. What have I told you about mescal?"

All she got was a shrug. Now Pete was really curious. Like any good reporter, he simply sat there and waited for the next chapter.

"Barney used to drive for Amex," Brooke said to him. "Until he had a disagreement with his next-door neighbor and used his rig to redesign her bathroom."

Barney looked up, contrite. "Mescal," he said. "Makes me a touch cranky."

"Barney, this is my friend Pete." Brooke introduced them. "Pete, Barney Little."

The men nodded at each other, Barney's expression even more guarded than Pete's.

"You work with her?" he demanded.

Pete almost laughed out loud, his own prejudices coming out of lips that couldn't even be seen behind all that growth. For a minute he was tempted to tell the man that he was running a white slavery ring and was considering giving Brooke a position. Pete knew, though, that broken ribs would not endear him to Parischell any more than the laryngitis.

"We grew up together," he managed, wondering what else he could say. Wondering just how he felt that old Barney didn't know who Pete Cooper was.

"Pete is Mamie's nephew," Brooke allowed.

Immediately Barney's posture changed. "I heard," he said to Pete. "She was a real little spitfire, that one was. I was real sorry to see her go."

Pete couldn't think of any better answer than a nod.

The burgers came and Barney ambled off—back to the poolroom where Brooke was still expected. Left behind, Pete slid off his glasses and took a long, considering look at her.

"I should have kept a closer eye on the both of you," he said.

ISN'T IT ROMANTIC? 43

Brooke waved away his assertion with the catsup bottle she was pounding. "We were fine. Mamie got to be a hell of a pool player."

Pete snorted. "I'll just bet."

"Don't sound so outraged," she advised. "I've never had to change a flat tire or worry about getting stuck on the road. And Mamie was much too old to be corrupted."

"Well," he retorted, "I guess those dates with the bikers back when you were in high school finally paid off."

She'd been just about to bite into her hamburger. Pete's words stopped her short, and she laughed. "Maybe I shouldn't have invited you along after all. You have a much too well-defined knack for digging up indiscretions I'd much rather leave in the past."

Pete lifted an eyebrow. "You mean nobody remembers?"

Brooke shot him a challenging glare. "Just like nobody remembers your foray into locker room navigation. You have to have been the only boy in Rupert Springs High who set out to catch a glimpse of the cheerleaders in the showers and ended up with a full frontal assault from the Mad Bomber herself."

Pete shook his head with a groan. "I still swear that woman was an Eastern bloc track star."

"It would have explained the mustache."

"And the penchant for quaint little tortures. For a phys ed teacher, she was a great drill sergeant."

Brooke laughed. "She always spoke highly of you, too."

Taking Brooke's lead, Pete spent a while concentrating on lunch. The antihistamines had begun to work—not to mention the distance from Mamie's cats. He was beginning to get his sense of taste back, which was fortunate, since not only was he starved, but Brooke had been right. Nobody made hamburgers and fries like this anymore, dripping with grease and seared on a stove that was probably just packed in carcinogens.

In the past six years Pete had eaten at some interesting places, from foreign street vendors whose products had probably been somebody else's pet to the finest five-star restaurants in the world. He couldn't say he'd enjoyed one more.

It was the sense of homecoming. The smells and tastes of his childhood, his teen years when he and David had cruised Rupert Springs's main drag on a Friday evening looking for cute girls and bad food. For a minute he experienced the oddest

44   ISN'T IT ROMANTIC?

sensation of dislocation, as if he were sitting in two places at once, here in Bud's Badger Bar, and Burgerland, where the last carhops in America had cruised among cars on roller skates and a date could still cost under fifteen dollars.

Brooke had been there with him, always there in the back seat, where sisters who were being allowed along were exiled, often too loud and too uncertain, always fierce in her loyalty, more comfortable with older boys than peers of her own sex. A middle child out of place, a rebel with a child's heart.

It was funny. He'd been home for over twenty-four hours, walked the streets of Rupert Springs, shaken enough hands to run for office, caught up on gossip and family and settled into the bittersweet familiarity of Mamie's house. And until this moment he hadn't hurt, not really. He hadn't ached for all that he'd left behind.

Suddenly he missed Mamie. He missed David and Brooke and the carhops who used to roller-skate with loaded trays in their hands. He missed the certainty of childhood, the breath-taking ambivalence of possibility and responsibility that had been his teen years, when the world was still out there for the taking.

He'd taken it. He'd gone out and made a place for himself that no one in Rupert Springs—with the exception of Mamie and Brooke, maybe—could have foreseen for him. And yet, suddenly, briefly, he wished for more.

"Hey, Coop?" Brooke asked, her voice soft, her own eyes introspective.

He looked up to see some of the memories in her gaze. Some of the same longings and regrets. "Yeah, honey."

She set down her hamburger and leaned toward him, suddenly intense, inspiration sparking fire in her eyes. "Let's start now."

Pete frowned. "Start?"

She nodded. "The memorial. I mean, what better place? Everybody here knew Mamie. They really liked her and, once we get to New Orleans and Memphis, we won't have that."

Pete finally set down his own half-finished lunch. "What do you suggest?" he asked. "I can't really see old Barney dressed up like Ashley Wilkes."

She was alight now, her mind tumbling to possibilities. Pete found himself grinning at her enthusiasm. It exploded into the

ISN'T IT ROMANTIC?

dingy room like a sunburst. She sat up, reached out a hand to lay on his arm, her posture intense, her mind made up.

"Where were we going to do the limericks?" she asked.

"Don't ask me," he countered. "You're the one organizing this party."

She shrugged off his retort. "I didn't know. A park, maybe. Mamie always liked to watch the sun come up over the river. I thought that might be nice. But, think about it. What could be a better place than the poolroom at Bud's Badger Bar?"

Maybe someday Pete would consider what an odd question that was. For now, though, he couldn't help but succumb to Brooke's unholy excitement. "Do you know any?"

She laughed, then. "Don't be ridiculous. Who do you think taught Mamie?"

Pete lifted an eyebrow then to match his scowl. "I *have* been away too long," he accused. "You're completely out of control."

The minute the hamburgers and fries were dispatched, Brooke led the way back into the smoky, claustrophobic poolroom where ten or twelve players battled with a battered old pocket pool table, a couple of cast-off chairs and a cigarette machine for space. Evidently all the decorating money had been spent on the front room. Back here it was bare walls and the hollow echo of linoleum. Brooke walked in the way a socialite commanded a charity ball.

"Finally come back to earn some of that money you lost, little girl?" one of the men asked. Straightening from where he'd been setting up a shot, he brushed the low light fixtures. One of the few people who could really call Brooke a little girl and mean it, Pete imagined.

Brooke's greeting was familiar and easy. "You mean, let you earn money back, Bud. Seems to me I was the one who ran three racks last week."

Bud snorted, the sound not unlike a train letting out steam. "I was bein' nice, seein' as you was in your good dress and high heels and all."

Brooke never gave an inch. "You were distracted. Why did you think I wore that dress?"

The room erupted in pleased laughter. Standing behind Brooke in the doorway, Pete watched with hands in pockets and judgments in abeyance. Even two days ago when he'd thought of Brooke, he'd thought of her crouched in that back seat, tee-

46   ISN'T IT ROMANTIC?

tering on the edge of open revolt. Endearing, frustrating, ingenuous enough to need saving.

She didn't need saving anymore. Not from him or anyone else. He wasn't quite sure how he wanted to come to grips with this new Brooke, this woman who should have carved out her own path in the world, who should have taken command of New York or Los Angeles, not Badger, Arkansas.

"Bud, I need to ask a favor," Brooke was saying. "It's for Mamie."

Every head in the room nodded.

"When they buried her yesterday," she said, "none of Mamie's wishes were honored. Pete and I have set out to rectify that, and you guys can help."

Curious eyes swung toward Pete and back to Brooke. No one ventured a protest.

"What can we do?" was all Bud asked.

Brooke smiled. "Mamie wanted us to read limericks at her funeral. I want to do it here."

Bud took to scratching his head. "Limericks?" he countered, giving the room a quick glance to get other reactions. "Well, sure, for Mamie. But I don't know any clean ones."

Brooke's smile was delighted. "Bud," she said, hands on hips. "Why do you think I'm asking?"

An inspiration. A stroke of genius. Perched on the edge of the pool table, orchestrating the crescendo of bad taste in the room, Brooke decided that Mamie would have been proud. What had begun as a stop for lunch was turning into a first-rate Irish wake, with all the Badger Bar regulars showing up to share in beer and memories and outrageous rhymes.

It had started simple. A few Ogden Nash, a tribute or two to towns everyone knew, salacious puns that had provoked heartfelt groans from the audience packed into that little poolroom, beer in hand, imaginations stirred and challenges laid out. And then, because it was his right as the heir, Pete had really gotten things going with Mamie's favorite, the man from Nantucket. Pete, the world-famous newsman, whose face was more familiar than the president's, whose name appeared on the same lists as actors, statesmen and magnates, stood slouched in the corner in a rolled-up oxford shirt and chinos, with Bud's arm around his shoulder, laughing until his eyes

ISN'T IT ROMANTIC?

streamed, matching and calling every bad limerick with a worse one of his own.

After all, Brooke might have taught Mamie, but Pete had first taught Brooke.

"He's real good at this," Bud admitted, topping off Brooke's beer.

She was glad Pete wasn't drinking. She'd been obliged to hold up the Fillihue honor amidst all those toasts, and it was making her just a little giggly.

She shot Pete a look as he launched into the woman from Nance, and grinned. This was what Mamie had wanted for him, this comfort, this ease. She'd bet her last donut that he didn't get a chance to do stuff like this in Atlanta.

"That's the man who taught me everything I know about pool," she admitted, pointing to Pete.

Bud's battered, ex-fighter face betrayed his respect. "No kiddin'. He teach you that little trick with the short skirt, too?"

Brooke laughed. "You think my legs look nice in heels. You should see his."

"He looks familiar. He drive through here or something?"

"No. This is his first time." It never occurred to Brooke to lie to Bud. After all, this was the man who had proposed to Mamie on six different occasions.

"That's the nephew who does the news," she admitted. "Pete Cooper."

Bud's face folded into surprise. "You mean it? That guy all the women go pantin' over like he's just reinvented chocolate candy or somethin'?"

Brooke nodded dryly. "Surprising, isn't it?"

"You're tellin' me. I figured him for somethin' a lot more...artsy-fartsy, ya know? In Eye-talian suits and gold chains."

Brooke shook her head. "Nah. Mamie trained him better than that."

"He get all her collections?"

"All except the salt-and-pepper shakers."

Bud nodded and drained his own beer once again. "I'd give a lot to have some o' them license plates. To decorate the front room, ya know."

Brooke was tempted to giggle again. "You could name it the Mamie Fillihue Memorial Lounge."

48   ISN'T IT ROMANTIC?

Bud grinned with all ten remaining teeth. "She woulda liked that, wouldn't she?"

Brooke nodded. "Except I think the Miss Mamie Fillihue Memorial Poolroom would be much more appropriate, don't you?"

Bud's expression actually took on a hint of anticipation. "Think he'd do it?"

Brooke smiled and gave Bud a reassuring pat on the arm. "I'll work my womanly wiles on him."

She was surprised to see Bud roll his eyes. "Poor sucker don't stand a chance. I'll get the nails tomorrow."

She'd been joking. Brooke Ferguson had no womanly wiles; everybody knew that. All her life she'd waited for somebody to call her sexy or provocative. She'd wished for that natural little sashay her sister Annie had that would draw boys in a line behind her like ducks after a seed truck. But instead, her mother had always said, Brooke had inherited stature. Brooke was a good friend and a better shoulder to lean on, someone you could depend on for a joke and a ride home.

Which was why she knew that Bud was joking. Especially when it came to Pete Cooper.

"There was an old man known as Buck...."

They'd left a lot closer to sundown than Brooke had anticipated. The early summer sky was carmine and peacock, the sickle moon hanging just above the horizon, the trees dark, lifeless shadows in the heat that had gathered in the afternoon. Brooke and Pete tumbled out of the tavern on each other's arms, laughing, with the uproar of the party they'd left still in their ears as their shoes scrunched over the gravel parking lot.

It had been a perfect afternoon. A perfect tribute. They'd even capped it all off after everyone was awash in beer and bonhomie with four verses of "Streets of Laredo." Glasses held high, voices warbling more than a hair off-key, not a dry eye in the house for the little lady who had held court in Bud's like an elfin Queen Victoria.

"'So bang the drum slowly and play the fife lowly...'" Brooke sang out into the dusk, her cheeks still wet from mirth and mourning, her head reeling from hops and brewer's yeast, her bad sense of pitch even worse.

ISN'T IT ROMANTIC?

"You're waking up the roosters," Pete complained, tightening his hold as they swayed toward the car.

"I'm brilliant, Coop," she crowed, patting his belly with her free hand. "Absolutely brilliant. I wish Letitia could have been here."

Pete laughed. "Letitia would have had a hemorrhage."

"Exactly."

His laughter was as breathless as hers.

"Wasn't I brilliant?" she demanded. "Don't you think Mamie would have approved?"

To answer, Pete stopped where he was, ten feet from the car, and turned Brooke around to face him.

"Yes," he answered, his eyes glittering and sweet. "She would have loved it. *I* loved it."

Brooke smiled, a smug smile born of long acquaintance. "Mamie was right," she told him. "You've been fading like a cheap shirt in that job. You needed a little real insanity."

His expression softened, the neon from Bud's flickering from his eyes and the sunset tinting his skin a golden hue. Brooke had never seen such a handsome man, even with swollen eyes and red nose. She'd never known one with more life, more courage. It was good to see that glint of mischief back in his eyes.

"What next?" he demanded.

She tilted her head, her own arms around his neck, fitting into his hold as easily as an old pillow. Too comfortable where she was to move, too happy to be back to question, "Who cares? Isn't that the whole point of this?"

For a minute he didn't answer. He just watched her, familiar emotions skittering over his features, new exhilaration joining old memories. Brooke felt his hands around her, hands she knew better than anyone's, hands she'd held when he'd hurt, when he'd celebrated. It was good to have them back. To have him back in her reach where she could feast on his cool exuberance.

"Yes," he finally admitted, letting go of her waist. "It is." Before Brooke could move away or let go, he lifted his hands to cup her face. To lift it to him. "Thanks for making me come along."

And as naturally as friends do, he kissed her.

Except it wasn't a friend's kiss. Not by a long shot. It began simply, a meeting, an instinctive expression of delight, of gratitude. Within a whisper, though, it changed. Deepened. Softened. Pete's thumbs began to move, to stroke the sensitive skin at Brooke's jaw. His mouth stopped greeting and began inviting. And Brooke, who had first dreamed of a kiss just like this on her eleventh birthday, pulled away.

Four

WMJM RADIO, 1420 AM, THE COUNTRY VOICE:

And now, for the weather for southern and central Arkansas. Continued fair and warm today, with the temperatures heating up again tomorrow. Expect a cold front to be rolling through here tomorrow afternoon, producing possibly severe thunderstorms....

"I thought you weren't drinking in there," Brooke accused, her head down, her voice shaky. She'd already shoved her hands into her slacks pockets so she couldn't get herself into more trouble, and had turned a little away toward the car just in case Pete didn't get the message from everything else she did.

"I didn't," he answered, sounding just as uncertain. "I guess antihistamines make me a little . . ."

"Strange," she provided for him. "Are you too . . . strange to drive? I sure can't."

"No, I can drive. Where do you want to go?"

Home. Her heart was still skittering around inside her ribs like a ricocheting bullet, her lungs struggling to maintain oxygen levels. It had been just the way she'd always dreamed.

52   ISN'T IT ROMANTIC?

Warm, sweet, nourishing. As thick as honey and dark as a dream. Brooke could still remember the long nights spent curled up in her dormer window, eyes out to the trees that hid Pete Cooper's house, when all she'd wanted was for him to look at her like a young woman instead of a pesky little sister. When she'd have given anything for a kiss like this.

But she'd been twelve years old then. She'd needed a knight in shining armor, a buccaneer to sweep away the tedium of small-town normalcy. She didn't need a knight now, she needed a friend.

She flipped him the keys. "I was hoping to make the Louisiana border tonight. I don't think we're going to do it."

"Well, let's at least give it a shot."

Brooke nodded and headed over to the car. The top was still down, so when Pete started the engine and pulled back out onto the road, the wind caught Brooke's hair and tumbled it behind her. She wanted to lay her head back on the seat, much the way Pete had done, her stomach still in more of a turmoil than the beer should have left it.

"Which way?" Pete asked.

She just pointed and busied herself with the radio.

"Y'know," Pete was saying, "that was the first time in a while I haven't had to sign autographs and give informed opinions on world affairs when I was in a group of people. Do you know any other places like that?"

"Why, do you want me to avoid them?" she teased, trying very hard to distance herself from the sudden delight he'd unleashed.

He chuckled. "It's nice to know I can always get support from my friends, Stump."

They were deep into farmland now, the night air smelling like plowed earth, wet grass and manure. Rock and roll floated on the breeze and the cares of the world were hidden beyond the horizon. And Brooke's head still fizzed with celebration.

"Which reminds me," she countered. "You never told me. Who did you end up taking to that awards banquet a couple of weeks ago?"

He looked over briefly, the light shuddering across his face so that his eyes were hidden. "You mean the Peabodies? I thought I told you."

"The last I heard from you, you were torn between the corporate lawyer and the teen queen model."

ISN'T IT ROMANTIC?

Brooke was relieved to see the good old Coop scowl. "She is not a teen queen," he protested. "She's at least twenty-one."

"Well, your bail bondsman can breathe a sigh of relief," she retorted gleefully. "Just what would you two talk about on a date anyway? New Kids on the Block?"

"Do I detect a small note of jealousy?"

Brooke snorted. "Of what? Big Bambi eyes and a vocabulary that only includes the adjectives 'awesome' and 'fabulous'? I just guessed you'd wait until at least your fortieth birthday before you succumbed to Mid-Life Crisis."

"She's a nice kid," he retorted.

Brooke gave way to a triumphant grin. "Exactly."

That at least got her a laugh. "Like I said, it's always nice to have the support of my friends."

"And what would you have said if I'd taken a nineteen-year-old college jock to the company Christmas party?"

"That's younger."

"So am I."

"Oh, well, in that case, I'd say that you were a frustrated old maid."

"There. I knew you'd be just as enlightened as I was. So, I imagine she looked wonderful in a teeny tiny spangly dress."

"She did not. The corporate lawyer did."

"Well, hallelujah, there's hope after all."

There was a pause punctuated by the rush of wind and the chirrup of insect armies massing in the trees. "Who did you take to your Christmas party?" he asked.

Brooke's smile was sly. "A nineteen-year-old college jock."

By the time they found a motel with a vacancy sign they'd made it over the border after all. It was late by then, cool enough that they'd had to stop to put the top up and so long past dinner hour that the grumble of empty stomachs punctuated the heat lightning that flickered along the horizon. They were right down by the river, in a town of seafood shops and tug-repair services. When they finally climbed from the car to stretch out the kinks from driving, they could hear the plaintive hooting of barges on the river and a train somewhere in the distance. Country-western music spilled from the open door to the Bayou Café, and the smell of frying grease battled the cloying perfume of magnolias for predominance in the night

54 ISN'T IT ROMANTIC?

breeze. Next door a pink neon sign proclaimed that the Riverside Motor Court had a vacancy. Actually it said the Ri*ersi** Moto* C**rt, but Brooke was good at filling in the blanks.

"I don't know about this," Pete demurred warily, his eye darting between the peeling, disheveled one-story building beneath that sign and the dusty pickup trucks in the neighboring parking lot.

"Oh, the Riverside's okay," Brooke said as she reached over to yank her purse out of the car. "I stayed here once when my car went bad on me."

Pete shot her a frown. "Don't you ever go to places that have carpeting and room service?"

Brooke swung her purse onto her shoulder and turned for the front door. "Coop, you're turning into a snob, you know that?"

Shaking his head mournfully, he followed. "Self-preservation has become an instinct after all these years on battlefronts."

"Well then, you'll be glad to know I'm carrying a gun."

That stopped him dead in his tracks. "What?"

Brooke grinned. "All licensed and legal. The company arranged it. I'm a pistol-packin' momma, baby, so don't get fresh."

For a minute it looked as if Pete were going to manage an answer. Finally he simply gave his head another dismal shake and headed on past Brooke.

Inside, the front office consisted of a closet-size vestibule leading to a Formica-paneled wall that held both sliding window and closed door. Brooke suspected that the glass was bulletproof. She waited while Pete punched the bell.

"Yeah?" The glass slid back to reveal a woman in housecoat and curlers, a sandwich in hand and the TV on behind her.

Pete fought hard to keep a straight face. "We need a place to stay tonight."

She glared at them both as she finished dispatching whatever was in her mouth. "Well, I already figured that. You don't look like no Girl Scouts wantin' to sell cookies."

That obviously delighted her, because she broke into a wheezing, purple-faced laugh that didn't look or sound very healthy.

"Got a nice double room right by the road," she said.

ISN'T IT ROMANTIC? 55

"No," Pete countered easily, his eyebrows still up but his face admirably passive. "We'd prefer two singles if you have them."

It took another bite of sandwich to figure that one out, but they finally got a nod. "Jimmy'll show you down. Got luggage?"

Brooke nodded.

The woman handed over keys, got signatures and chewed on contentedly. Brooke was wondering just what was in store for them when the door alongside the window opened up and the aforementioned Jimmy stepped out.

Brooke promptly stopped breathing. He was probably eighteen or nineteen, dark, sleek and powerful, with eyes the color of a moonlit night and hair like raven's wings. And he had a smile that lit for her like an invitation to sin.

She smiled right back. "Why, I think we were just talking about you," she offered with a delighted glance at Pete, whose face was folding right into astonishment. "Are you going to help me with my luggage?"

Jimmy nodded and stepped close. He wasn't wearing anything special, just a white T-shirt and jeans. But on Jimmy they looked the way God had meant them to look, just shy of illegal. "Yes, ma'am," he said in a voice like smoke. "You haven't been around here lately, have you?"

Brooke slid her arm into his and headed right back for the door. "Oh, no," she answered. "I would have remembered."

An hour or so later Brooke managed to knock on Pete's door to see about dinner. He gave her a look like David used to when he'd have to pick her up from some of her more questionable outings.

"What's the matter?" he demanded. "Is it past his bedtime?"

Brooke enjoyed a good chuckle. It would have been a lot less fun to betray the fact that Jimmy had stayed in her room just long enough to deposit her luggage, and that the past hour had been spent repairing some of the ravages of a day out in the humid wind.

"Meow, Coop," she accused. "I thought you'd be a gentleman about this. I mean, maybe you and Bambi could double-date with us."

"Her name is not Bambi," he snapped.

Brooke answered with widened eyes. "What is her name?"

56   ISN'T IT ROMANTIC?

He actually flinched, a tiny movement most other people would have missed. "Buffy."

Brooke let go a hoot that could have been heard on the river. "Come on, old man. I still have enough energy to eat dinner with you."

Pete grabbed his jacket from a chair by the door and followed her out into the night. "Are you sure you want to be seen with someone who has more than a third-grade education?"

Sliding her arm through Pete's, Brooke sashayed back toward the street. There was a pole light to illuminate the way, but great, thick old trees kept most of the parking lot midnight dark. Those magnolias grew right alongside her unit, their waxy leaves shining faintly and the white flowers smelling seductive. It was pleasant in the late evening.

"Actually," Brooke admitted with delight as she plucked one of the flowers and settled it into the curls behind her ear, "Jimmy's home from Tulane. Pre-med."

"You're lyin'."

She shrugged. "Ask him. He has the most wonderful way with Latin."

Pete just shook his head. "No wonder I spent so much of my life pulling you out of scrapes."

Pete shouldn't have been the one to wake up with a hangover. He'd seen the way Brooke had put away beer the afternoon before. She'd topped it off with some of the hottest chili he'd ever tasted at the Bayou Café and then managed to keep him up until almost two in the morning talking about the Peabody Awards.

And yet, he was the one who felt as if he'd fallen off a very high wagon.

Maybe it was because he hadn't gotten much sleep the night before. Maybe it was the aftereffects of the antihistamines, or the fact that the Riverside air-conditioning was a matter of wishful thinking. Whatever it was, it left him tired and frustrated and irritable, wrapped up in itchy sheets, sweating and subjected to dreams that made no sense to him. Dreams that obviously reflected his recent bout of celibacy, but which seemed to betray a troubling dislocation. The very willing partner in his dreams hadn't been the nubile Buffy or the sparkling, sharp Eloise, but Brooke.

ISN'T IT ROMANTIC? 57

Brooke. He couldn't figure it. That was like dreaming about your little sister. Like finding yourself kissing your math teacher. Those kinds of things just didn't happen. Stump was his buddy; she was his alter ego, his conscience. She kept him in his place, just as he did for her.

That simply wasn't the kind of person a man should be having erotic dreams about.

But he was. Vivid dreams, troubling dreams. Dreams that had left him in the shower before dawn and sitting out on the front porch in a rickety folding chair, watching the morning mist burn off from over by the river as the streets came to life.

It was the change in her, he decided. The realization that she wasn't a child anymore. No matter how close they'd been over the years, never more than a phone call away, he hadn't seen her. Not since her mother's funeral, and he had to admit that that wasn't the kind of time you judged a person's attraction. She'd been drawn and pale and silent then, a dim wraith in that big old house where he'd spent so many Friday nights.

But now, he couldn't ignore the fact that good old Stump wasn't a stork stuffed in a burlap sack anymore. The more appropriate analogy would have been the ugly duckling. Well, the duck had matured into a swan, and the rest of the world was still quacking in comparison.

If only he could have just been proud of her, it would have been all right. But damn, she'd also learned to kiss.

"What are you doing up? You're not a morning person."

Pete turned to see Brooke stepping outside her door. She was in a dress today, loose white cotton that swirled lazily around her legs and left her throat bare. Her hair gleamed in the sunlight like a fresh fire, its curls tied into order with a scarf. Pete wondered if he could really smell the soap from her shower on her, or whether it was just residue from his dream. The kind of residue that had him thinking of what those long legs of hers would feel like in his hands.

"Sneaking off to help Junior eat his oatmeal?" he asked with a wary eye, unaccountably surly.

Her grin was mischievous as hell. "I thought we'd concentrate on those all-important clothing fastener techniques. Today's lesson is the zipper."

Pete pushed himself to his feet. "I'd better get you out of town before his mama hurts you real bad."

58 ISN'T IT ROMANTIC?

Brooke tilted her head. "We're not having breakfast at the Bayou?"

"Are you kidding? They probably put Tabasco on their eggs. I'm more in the mood for grits and gravy."

Brooke took a moment to consider the sky beyond the meager overhang. "It's going to be really hot today, isn't it?"

Pete scowled at her. "It's already hot today, Brooke. Let's get going."

She chuckled. "Now do you know why I told you not to accept any of those morning-show offers? You would have committed murder in a week." Reaching over, she straightened the collar of his shirt. "I guess you're not going to let me meander down to the river and watch the barges."

"Not till I've had my coffee."

She nodded, those emerald sharp eyes much too knowing and amused. "Okay. Let me get packed. Why don't you just sit here and snarl in peace for a few minutes?"

Stuffing his hands into his jeans pockets, he turned to follow her. "It'll go faster if I help."

"Pack your own stuff."

"It's already in the car."

She laughed. "Of course it is."

Pete had just reached her open door when he came to a sudden halt. "Don't move," he commanded, grabbing hold of her. "I've seen terrorist attacks before."

"What do you mean?" she demanded, shuddering to a stop alongside him.

Pete considered the scene beyond the half-opened door. "Your room. The question is how they got the bomb in through a closed window."

Brooke pulled out of his grip and stalked over to begin picking up the articles of clothing that lay scattered around the room like flowers after a tornado. "Oh," she countered, "and I suppose you're the Neatness Poster Child?"

Pete picked up a bra from where it had landed on the top of the mirror and handed it to her. "You can run a lot faster if you always know where your passport it."

"I know exactly where my passport is," she retorted, snatching the article of underwear from his hand and stuffing it into a brimming suitcase. "It's still in the unopened envelope it came in."

ISN'T IT ROMANTIC? 59

Pete rooted around for shoes and came up with cosmetics. "I invited you to visit when I was in Paris."

Brooke straightened from where she'd just located her nightgown wedged behind the television. "You were married then."

"Alicia wouldn't have minded."

"Alicia would have scratched my eyes out."

Pete aimed a curling iron at her. "You never did get along with her."

Brooke's smile was purely feminine. "I'm still not convinced she has a reflection in a mirror."

The laughter bubbled in Pete's chest, just where it always did when he was challenging Brooke. "Meow right back, Brooke. A bowl of milk, perhaps?"

Brooke offered him a sickly version of the same smile as she relieved him of his latest burden. "Well, you obviously got along with her."

Pete nodded and went after a nest of panty hose on the headboard. "I sure did. Especially when I was in Moscow and she was in Paraguay."

He must have let some of that old bitterness escape into his voice, because Brooke slowed her manic hunt to face him. "I was really sorry it didn't work for you," she said sincerely.

Pete couldn't do anything but smile in response. "I know, Stump." He collected the jumble of cosmetics she held in her hands and began to stuff them into her bag. "And what about London?" he demanded. "I remember calling."

"Right in the middle of finals."

"And Beirut?"

"Oh, thanks."

"Are you still on these?" He held out the round container of pills that he'd found on the sink.

Brooke snatched them from his hands. "I'd take arsenic and itching powder if it'd take care of my cramps."

He frowned at her. "Still?"

Her answering smile was not pleasant. "I enjoy being a girl, Coop. What can I say?" She turned back to her suitcase to stuff in her cosmetic bag. "Doc Levin says that things'll straighten out once I have babies, but I just figure it's not worth the savings at the pharmacy right now."

60   ISN'T IT ROMANTIC?

"But they do have other hormone treatments for that now. Our medical reporter did a story on it last week. You shouldn't need to blow up like a summer sausage."

That brought Brooke to a halt. She faced her friend and grinned with a sad shake of her head. "You know, it occurs to me that you know more about me than a man should tastefully know about a woman."

Pete grinned right back. "Meaning that there's no mystery?"

"Meaning that I can never sell the real dirt on you to the *Daily World*. You have much too much stuff you can blackmail me with, too. Especially if I decide to get involved again."

"Why haven't you?" Pete asked as they climbed into the car.

Brooke turned on him, thinking how very cool and handsome he looked in his pleated slacks and blue chambray shirt. The world-famous journalist, the self-effacing media star. The small-town boy who had spent too long away from home. She wanted to run her fingers over his face and curl up against his chest like she used to when he'd try to reassure her that she wasn't the only unhappy teen to make bad judgment calls about dates.

"Why haven't I what?" she asked.

Settling into the driver's seat, Pete slid his sunglasses on and fingered her keys. "Gotten involved again?"

Brooke concentrated on buckling the seat belt Mamie had gone to such trouble to get installed in the car. "Good taste," was all she said.

Pete turned over the engine and eased the car back out of the lot. "Well, that's a new twist for you."

"Thanks, bud," she scowled, positioning her own sunglasses. The top was staying up today out of deference to the heat and humidity that gathered outside like congealing gravy. "I always know I can come to you for unbiased support."

She'd dreamed about him last night, just like she had as a girl. Well, not exactly. When she was a girl, the dreams had been a girl's dreams, chaste and vague, the mysteries of passion still beyond her. She remembered that the high point had always been the kiss. The moment he'd wrapped her in his arms and bent her within his torrid embrace—torrid embraces seemed quite dangerous enough to an eleven-year-old girl.

ISN'T IT ROMANTIC? 61

She knew too much now to settle for that single, chaste kiss, the thrill of promise in his gray green eyes. After that exhibition on the parking lot, all stops had been pulled out in her subconscious.

That she should have less than pure thoughts about one of the ten most eligible men in the States couldn't have come as a surprise. She'd known how attractive Pete was a lot longer than the television viewing public. If Pete had ever given her the slightest encouragement as they'd grown up side by side, she probably would have risked her morals on him.

But Pete was a buddy, a best friend who had seen her at her worst and not held it against her. He'd salved her hurts and shared his own, night after night out on the front porch where the crickets had kept them company. He'd set the rules early and never seen the need to change them, and Brooke had been comfortable with it. Until last night.

Last night, for the first time in a very long while, she'd lost her firm hold on pragmatism, and ended up tossing and turning without getting any sleep. All those silly old dreams had bubbled to the surface in her sleep and danced with the imagination of a grown woman, leaving her short-tempered and frustrated. And, suddenly, more physically uncomfortable near him than she'd ever been.

"Well, the dating pool is a bit limited in Rupert Springs," Pete admitted. "During the time I was there, the only eligible males I think I saw under Social Security age were the Tanner twins, and they're still paperboys... of course, give them six months or so and they should be just the age you want."

Brooke allowed a wry grin. "At least I've never been seen in public with someone who wasn't even alive when I hit puberty."

"And given the chance, you'd still turn down the opportunity."

She chuckled. "Well, that's another story entirely."

"Then why jump on my back with hobnail boots?"

Brooke sighed, teetering between sincerity and levity, wondering which would serve better. "You've become hotter than the flag since that little jaunt in the Gulf. I don't want to see it go to your pretty head."

Pete looked over then as he idled the car at a stoplight in the center of town, and Brooke could see the real surprise behind

ISN'T IT ROMANTIC?

those glasses. "Hey, Stump, no kidding. You really see some kind of problem?"

Brooke did her best to hold his gaze, even lost behind two sets of colored glass. "Mamie didn't just leave me this car, bucko. She left me you. She wanted to make sure there was somebody around to remind you who you are when all those tabloids are seating you next to aliens and Princess Grace on that big celestial bus ride of fame."

The light changed, and the car behind them honked. Pete turned back to business, but Brooke saw the new creases between his eyebrows, right where he carried his concern. She'd seen them when she'd hurt herself as a kid, and most lately when she'd seen him report on the homeless.

"Mamie never said anything to me," he said, his voice tentative, as if reassessing his actions since hitting the celebrity jackpot.

They headed down a country road that paralleled the river. For a minute Pete did little more than concentrate on his driving as they passed patches of rice, their sweet green bright even through the fug of humidity.

"Luckily," Brooke offered, "a severe reprimand had never been in order. But I thought a nice trip down South might help prevent problems."

Pete shot her a rueful scowl. "You're as sneaky as Mamie was."

"Oh, worse," Brooke assured him with a real smile. "Much worse."

He looked over her way, the creases easing, laughter folding the edges of his features. "I can count on you at the studio door the very second I overstep the boundaries of good taste."

She grinned back and felt the weight lift from her shoulders. "While you're still fantasizing about it," she assured him.

He grimaced. "Then where were you when I married Alicia?"

Brooke just shook her head and pulled out the map they'd follow. "I said I'd be there. I didn't say you'd listen."

The scenery stretched out flat and listless before them, the humidity sapping color, the sky vague and uninspiring. Brooke found a station that played zydeco and flipped up the volume, singing along through her nose just to see Pete wince. They stopped for breakfast when they saw the water tower with a black bat painted on it. They ate grits and gravy, and bought

ISN'T IT ROMANTIC?

several souvenirs in the form of rubber bats—the kind that fly—and skull earrings courtesy of the imaginatively named town of Transylvania, Louisiana. Later, they headed on south, back out toward the rich farmland of Madison County and its pecan groves and pastureland.

Brooke smiled with the sense of escape, the easy familiarity of having Pete next to her on the drive, the delight of having him back in her life.

It had been too long since she'd seen those now-famous chiseled features, since she'd ruffled the perfectly groomed mahogany hair. Phones were nice and telegrams sometimes even better, but best friends were meant to be in the same town, the same street. They were for calling on impulse and dropping in on. It was hard to drop in on a guy two states away.

If only she could forget that kissing business . . .

They were singing along with Randy Travis at the top of their lungs, humoring Pete's secret passion. The man who looked as if he'd invented the tux, who graced every classical music function in Atlanta and New York, really yearned to just sit in with his guitar on a Nashville session and wail. Something else Evan Parischell would have a seizure over.

"So, where are we staying when we get to New Orleans?" Pete asked.

"I don't know," Brooke answered, resettling in her seat, an eye drawn suddenly to the horizon. "I think it's your turn to scout out a location, don't you?" She leaned further over and pulled her glasses down her nose, to get a better look.

Pete actually nodded. "I was hoping you'd say that. I'm not in the mood for another Riverside."

"And what was wrong with it? Seems to me I heard worse notices about some of the places you stayed in Central America."

"That's called ambience, Stump," he advised her. "Riverside was called cheap."

She shrugged, distracted. "The only difference was a couple of whirring overhead fans and a banana tree in the corner. Do you think we'll get down there tonight?"

"I don't see why not."

"What about that weather coming in?"

Pete squinted over at the black line of clouds quickly piling into the southwestern sky. "A little rain isn't going to stop us."

64 ISN'T IT ROMANTIC?

But Brooke was shaking her head. "You've been in Atlanta too long. That looks unpleasant. Especially as hot as it's been."

The trees along the roadside were already bending before the first whispers of wind, and the morning shuddered with approaching lightning.

"Oh, come on," he chided. "Since when have you been bothered by a storm?"

"Since one took off the roof of Allie's house last spring. We were crouched in the basement at the time."

"It's too early in the day for a real storm," he said. "Didn't the weather reports say the front was going to move through this afternoon?"

"I think it decided not to wait."

And they were driving right into it. Within the space of fifteen minutes the sunlight disappeared and the first fat raindrops were splattering against the little windshield. Pete flipped on both wipers and lights.

"Well," he philosophized as the first real bolt of lightning sizzled across the sky, "at least we don't have to worry about traffic."

They were the only inhabitants on the narrow country road. Brooke could see neat rows of pecan trees on one side and crinkled fields of soybeans on the other. The trees at the edge of the field and along the small bayous had begun to dance and writhe. The car bucked in the sudden wind and slid a little as it sailed through the driving rain.

Brooke just closed her eyes and hung on to the door handle. "I don't like weather like this," she moaned. "And don't give me that stuff about it being a sight safer than dodging the enemy fire in Afghanistan. At least they were aiming."

"Yeah," he countered. "At me."

"Didn't you tell them to just turn off the TV like everybody else if they didn't like you?"

"I never got the chance."

Thunder cracked and bellowed. Lightning seared the edges of the sky and snaked down to seek out the trees. Brooke could only see the scenery in the shudder of failing light, and it pushed a lump further up in her throat. Those trees were bending almost in half.

ISN'T IT ROMANTIC? 65

"This is happening all too fast," she protested, leaning forward for a better look. "Pull over."

"Oh, we don't have to—"

"It's my car, Coop, and I'd really rather not lose it this soon. I promise I'll never tell another newsman in the world that you didn't drive right into a hurricane with the top down."

He made rude noises, but he pulled the car over to the side of the road to wait out the storm. "See?" he demanded, motioning to the solid stream of water pounding the windshield even at a stop. "It's not so bad. Open your eyes and watch the show."

She did. Just in time to see the show stop.

Completely.

"Oh, Coop," she breathed, looking out into the suddenly still landscape.

Pete leaned forward, eyes widening. "I may have just changed my estimates."

Brooke pointed, not even aware that her hand was shaking. "Is that what I think it is?"

He squinted to get a better look. "If it is, we'd better get out."

Brooke forgot the swirling green sky, the sudden, eerie stillness in the storm-ravaged morning. "And leave the car here?"

"This isn't a house," he snapped. "If we go up, we're not just going to fall back down on a wicked witch."

They looked around just in time to hear the first howl from the southwest.

Car doors were thrown open and feet hit the asphalt. Pete headed for the ditch at the side of the road. Brooke ran the other way. Skidding to a stop by the trunk, she unlatched it and threw it open.

Expecting to find Brooke on his tail, Pete looked over his shoulder at the same moment he pulled to his own three-point halt. "What are you doing?" he demanded at full yell over the howl that was now a roar as he retraced his steps.

Brooke was tugging at one of her suitcases. "I'm getting the hell out of here!"

Pete yanked her away from the car, leaving the suitcase to thump to the asphalt. The sound effects were now deafening and the morning a dark, livid green. Both Brooke and Pete

66 ISN'T IT ROMANTIC?

leaned over to reevaluate the situation. Then they turned to each other.

"Run away!" they both yelled and dived headfirst into the nearest ditch.

The tornado swept over them not more than thirty seconds later.

Five

A Vanishing Breed; the Family Farm, an IBN Report with Pete Cooper:

"No single symbol has been more central to the self-image of America than its farms, no occupation more romanticized, no life-style more eulogized. And yet, as America moves into the twenty-first century, this symbol, this life-style, might go the way of buffalo and boom towns...."

"**H**ey, Toto," Pete muttered in the vicinity of Brooke's ear. "If I lift my head, do you think the world will be in Technicolor?"

Brooke squirmed enough to get her face out of the drainage water that was already dripping into her eyes, and managed to sink her nose into Pete's chest hair. "It will if you don't get your elbow out of my back, Dorothy," she snarled.

She was shaking, rapidly coming apart at the seams, her teeth chattering and her knees the consistency of Silly Putty. The tornado had sucked out her breath, pummeled the ground beneath her like an artillery attack and peppered her and Pete with

68   ISN'T IT ROMANTIC?

debris, and then headed on its merry way. Left behind, Brooke felt battered, a little deaf and incredibly giddy.

Pete was already repositioning himself. "Uh-oh," he was saying as he got his head up.

"The car?" Brooke asked, trying to follow.

"Is right where we left it. Your luggage, however," he informed her, plucking a pair of panty hose from the top of his head and handing them over, "is not."

Brooke managed to get to a sitting position, still hip deep in water and soaked right through her lightweight dress. With still shaking hands she pushed her hair back out of her eyes and made her own evaluation. And offered her own groan.

"After all the trouble I went to, to pack that stuff," she mourned, taking in the bright bits of cloth that littered nearby fence, shrub and tree. It didn't seem worth hanging on to the panty hose since she had nothing much left to wear them with. Unconsciously she stuffed them into her belt.

Pete considered the scene with a calm eye. "Looks just like your hotel room," he admitted.

Brooke gave him a jab that should have knocked the breath out of him. "What am I going to do?"

He didn't bother to turn around. "Auction off the privilege of climbing the trees for your panties."

She elbowed him again. "You could do it for me."

That produced quite a laugh. "And find out that the next helicopter that passes has a *Daily World* photographer in it? I'd really love to see the story of my scavenger hunt all over the front pages."

"Well, *I* can't get it."

He considered the situation for a minute, still calmly seated in the same muddy, rather aromatic water as Brooke. "Did you sew your name inside the waist or anything?"

Brooke shot him an arch look of disbelief. "I wasn't headed for camp. The only name in that underwear is Diane Von Furstenberg."

He nodded and shot her a crooked grin. "Then whoever retrieves it will think it's hers. Leave it where it is. It can be on the next episode of *Unsolved Mysteries*."

Brooke couldn't believe it. She wanted to laugh. She'd just ridden out a tornado in swamp water, seen her personal belongings tossed around the countryside like bunting at a political rally, lost her wardrobe for the rest of the trip, and she

ISN'T IT ROMANTIC?

wanted to laugh. It was all Coop's fault. He did it to her every time.

"Thanks, Coop," she acknowledged dryly. "That would have been my second idea."

He laughed even before she could, which was when she realized that he was shaking, too. His eyes glittered like polished jade, and he looked thoroughly disreputable, wet and disheveled. It was a look Brooke missed on him since he'd become the nation's most respected anchor. She'd liked him in his bomber jacket, too.

"Damn, Stump," he crowed, taking her by the arms and pulling her along to her feet. "We won. We beat the big guy again."

Brooke couldn't take her eyes from Pete's. Couldn't pull herself away from the sudden spark in his grip. He was thrumming with life, with sensuality, potent and devastating. Water slid down his temples and beaded in the hollow of his throat. His shirt was torn and his slacks sodden. It would take a good shower before anybody recognized him as a good credit risk, much less Pete Cooper, but caught in his grip, Brooke suddenly couldn't get her breath, and it wasn't from terror.

"Again?" she demanded instead, grinning back, the force of him swelling in her chest along with the relief, the exultation. "I think once is more than enough for me, thanks."

But Pete wouldn't have any of it. "Aw, come on. We weren't in any trouble. And we got a ringside seat to one of the greatest phenomena in nature. Don't you even think it rates a toast?"

"I think it rates the whole damn loaf," she countered, infected by him, drawn to him, standing there shivering with the sudden wind that knifed through her, the dawning realization that they had just very narrowly cheated a very big time death...with something even more primal. "Is this what it feels like when the Afghani rocket misses you?"

He nodded, still holding on tight, still hot and taut, his hands the only things warming her. "It's a terrible feeling," he assured her. "One I'm sure I won't go looking for again. Certainly nothing that would ever tempt me away from my news desk to cover a war close up."

Brooke did laugh then, because even before this she'd known better. "Coop, your eyes should be brown."

70   ISN'T IT ROMANTIC?

"I think they are," he retorted, inspecting the damage the dip in the creek had done. "Along with my shirt, my socks and my undershorts. And," he added, swinging his gaze her way, "your dress. Do you realize that right now you're breaking obscenity laws in about fifteen states?"

Brooke took a quick look down and gasped. "Oh, my God."

He was right. She was so soaked that her dress was all but transparent, clinging to her like a second skin. Even her once-white lacy bra was as good as invisible. If Pete had ever had any misconceptions about just how well or otherwise endowed Brooke was, or how sensitive nipples tended to react to both cold and shock, he had them no more.

She lifted her gaze back to him, ready to throw off a quick line about the proper attire in which to be caught in a tornado, when she bumped right up against the sudden, surprising heat in his eyes.

Recognizable heat, fantasized heat. A sweet, sleek languor that made old daydreams pale in comparison. His eyes had darkened, deepened, widened. His mouth was parted in surprise. He let his gaze return from his perusal of all her worldly charms, and Brooke slid right into their depths.

She froze, burned, crumbled.

"You look like a drowned rat," he accused, his voice suddenly raspy as he lifted a hand to push back a straggling strand of her hair. His jaw had tightened, and his fingers trembled against her skin. It unnerved Brooke even more than storms.

"A very large—" she managed, terrified and mesmerized at once "—rat."

Pete's hand strayed down past her ear to curl around her neck, back where her skin was so sensitive. Just the feel of his fingers there sent fresh shivers through her, showers of sparks like a misfired rocket at a Fourth-of-July exhibit.

Still she couldn't move. She couldn't pull away or ease closer. Old reservations battled with older dreams and stilled her right there within the grasp of only his fingers.

And then, she was caught solidly by the delicious warmth of his lips.

A kiss, she thought distractedly even as he began to deepen it, to demand more, the exhilaration of survival shimmering from him, the thunder of arousal stunning her. It's just a kiss, a toast to life, a challenge to its precarious hold.

A kiss.

ISN'T IT ROMANTIC?

If it had just been a kiss, she wouldn't have moaned. Wouldn't have folded herself into his embrace or threaded her own hands through his hair. She wouldn't have opened her mouth to his greedy tongue or allowed him to cup her breast in his hand. She wouldn't have felt the fear melt into anticipation, nor forgotten that she was standing out in the open with her clothing scattered about her.

"Hey, you two okay?"

Brooke bolted upright as if a sheriff had just shone his flashlight in the front seat of the car. Still shivering, still woefully short of breath, she dipped her head, not able to pull away from the support of Pete's arms, suddenly not comfortable in them anymore, either.

Pete, his heart still thudding against his ribs, pulled her close enough to his chest that she was at least partially protected from general view.

"We're fine!" he shouted over her shoulder. "How 'bout yourself?"

Brooke couldn't even open her eyes to put a face to the gravelly voice asking after her welfare. She couldn't still her heart enough to feign nonchalance.

Then the voice returned, closer this time and definitely awed. "Well, sit me on a tree stump and slap me silly."

Above her, Pete suppressed a chuckle. "I think we have our first bidder for the auction."

Brooke moaned again, this time out of mortification. She could just imagine what the man thought stomping across his fields to find all her finery in his trees.

"Real nice lingerie, ma'am," he offered, his voice a bit subdued.

Brooke couldn't even lift her head from where it was wedged against Pete's chest. "Thank you."

"You two look just a mite bedraggled there. Why don't you come on back to the house and get cleaned up and changed . . . that is, if you have anything left."

"Sure do," Pete acknowledged. "I left *my* underwear in the car."

Brooke gave him another quick jab. Behind her, their mysterious benefactor chuckled. "You're not hurt or anything, we can walk on over."

"I can't," Brooke muttered.

Pete looked down at her. "You can't walk?"

72 ISN'T IT ROMANTIC?

"Not until I get covered."

The assessment he made of the situation was much too protracted and produced a return of those sparks she'd been fighting.

"Keep your eyes to yourself, you jerk," she snapped, "and get me a shirt or something."

Pete just chuckled. "I never knew tornadoes could be so much fun. Don't move."

She lifted her head then to glare at him. "Hustle, bud. I'm freezing."

His smile was purely salacious, sending even more chills through her. "I'll bet."

By the time she finally turned in Pete's raincoat to introduce herself to the gentleman who owned the soybeans, Brooke saw that he was blushing, his own head dipped uncertainly. It made her wonder what kind of picture she'd presented from the back. Oh well, she thought. It can only get worse.

"Thanks for the hospitality," she acknowledged. The farmer was a good-looking man, about forty with sandy hair that was graying at the temples and a chin that looked hewn from granite. She thought he had blue eyes, but they were still firmly cast down, so she couldn't quite be sure. "I hope your home wasn't damaged?"

"Nope. Just a lot of noise and a few shingles goosin' the cats. Lost an old apple tree that made some of the best pies in the parish, but it wasn't gonna last much longer anyway." His eyes finally came up, the shy eyes of a quiet man. Brooke liked him on sight.

"My name's Brooke," she introduced herself. "Brooke Ferguson."

His head dipped again in salutation. "Martin Bishop."

His hands full with the clothing he could manage to pluck from low-hanging branches, Pete joined them by the back of the car.

"Pete Cooper," he offered, instinctively reaching out a hand.

Martin probably would have taken it, except that it had one of Brooke's filmier undergarments dangling from it. Martin shied away from it as if it could burn him. Scowling at Pete's cavalier treatment of her personal belongings, Brooke stalked up and snatched the lot from him and stuffed it into the trunk. The suitcase her clothing had been packed in was missing in action.

ISN'T IT ROMANTIC?

"How 'bout if we just drive over?" she asked pointedly.

Neither man could come up with an objection other than the fact that they just enjoyed standing there watching the lace and silk fluttering in the wind like pastel pennants, so they all piled in and headed for Martin's house.

Martin's wife knew who Pete was. She knew even before her still-stammering husband made the introductions. Brooke had just climbed out of the car when the woman opened up the screen door to see Pete walking her way.

To say she was stunned would have been an understatement. She turned to stone. A once-pretty blond woman in jeans and work shirt, she opened her mouth to exclaim but never made it any further.

"Emma?" Martin said a bit uncertainly.

Brooke was tempted to just stay where she was and watch. Even though she'd heard about this phenomenon, she'd never actually seen it happen. Two natural wonders in one day. It could be some kind of record.

"It's all right," she assured the man. "It'll wear off in a few minutes."

His wife didn't even blink. Just stood on her own front porch step, a hand still on the open door, another caught on the way up to check her hair at the sight of a strange car in her driveway, her mouth gaping a little wider than her eyes.

Brooke turned to see Pete acknowledge the reaction with only the most minute of facial expressions. He waited for his host to make the first move.

"Woman," Martin was saying as he loped up to his house, his voice more astonished than when he'd first seen Brooke's secrets, "you look like the president just asked you for coffee."

That seemed to snap her out of it. "Do you know who that is?" she demanded as if Pete weren't really standing there.

Her husband turned to consider the man he'd just ridden next to. "Name's Pete Cooper. He and his lady friend were caught in the twister, and I told 'em they could wash up here before they headed on. You got a problem with that?"

"A problem?" she retorted, her voice raising. "A problem? I swear, Martin Bishop, you wouldn't know what was goin' on in the world unless it fell on your head."

74 ISN'T IT ROMANTIC?

And without another word for her husband, she turned a beautiful smile on Pete that completely transformed those tired features. "It's a pleasure to have you, Mr. Cooper. I watch you every night. Meant a lot to me, that piece you did on the plight of family farms."

They were all beginning to coalesce toward the door. At his wife's words, Martin shot Pete a look and squinted. "That you?" he demanded.

Pete nodded.

Martin nodded back, answer and judgment. "Pleasure havin' you in my house."

Brooke watched as Martin headed on in, obviously feeling that everything that needed to had been said. On his heels, Pete stepped up to Mrs. Bishop and took her hand in his.

"It's awfully generous of you and your husband to take a couple of strangers in like this," Pete said, and Brooke knew just what kind of look he was giving that poor woman. Back in high school the girls had dubbed it, "The Killer," because any girl on the receiving end might as well have dropped dead for all the breathing she could manage for the next five minutes.

Mrs. Bishop didn't seem any more immune. Brooke fought a groan as she stepped up in her turn and prepared to be ignored.

But Mrs. Bishop came to life again just as Brooke reached the porch.

"And you are?" she asked with real sincerity.

"His babysitter," Brooke said with a grimace.

She knew Mrs. Bishop was going to make it when she laughed and rolled her eyes. "He needs a police escort, you ask me."

Proper introductions were finally made, coffee put on the stove and both bathrooms put into service. Pete and Brooke weren't simply afforded courtesies, they were made guests. The Bishops insisted they take advantage of the two working showers in the house and then bundled up their dirty clothes in a laundry bag for them to carry on with them.

By the time Brooke walked back into the kitchen in a pair of rolled-up wheat slacks and T-shirt she'd stolen from Pete, Emma was serving lunch. She tolerated no arguments and served her guests along with herself and her husband. The four ended up sharing a quiet, comfortable meal and cementing a surprising friendship.

ISN'T IT ROMANTIC?

Emma had never been out of Louisiana. Martin had been born in the house, which had been built before the turn of the century, and planned to hand it to his children if farming survived that long. They were straightforward, unpretentious people who embodied the last of what had made hospitality a byword of the South. Brooke found herself grateful that a tornado had blown Pete and her off their intended path.

It was when she was enjoying a delicious apple pie and coffee that she realized that the visit to the Bishops was more than just pleasant serendipity. It was a sign from God.

"Coop," she breathed, nudging him where he sat at the trestle table that took up much of the kitchen. "Look."

Seriously involved in his own dessert, Pete took a minute to look up. What Brooke had noticed was the coatrack by the back door. Seed caps and a Stetson, jean jackets, children's slickers, a jumble of boots beneath. One special garment stood out.

Pete saw it, too.

"Martin," he said, motioning with his fork. "You ride?"

Seated across from them, Martin had to turn to find out what Pete was referring to. "Used to," he admitted. "That's a memento of my misspent youth, as Emma calls it. Sowing my wild oats and all."

Brooke raised an eyebrow. "With the Hell's Angels?"

Martin's shrug was self-effacing. "Sometimes you just need to get the road out of your system before you settle down to the land."

Brooke turned to Pete. "It's perfect. It fulfills another requirement."

Pete scowled. "I'm not so sure," he demurred. "I mean, she wanted a whole gang of them."

"And where are we going to find a gang of Hell's Angels on forty-eight-hour notice? Don't you see? Martin's symbolic."

"Symbolic?" Martin echoed uncertainty.

Brooke flashed him a rueful grin. "Sorry. It's the reason Pete and I are on the road."

"You're looking for motorcycle gangs? What for, another story?"

"No," Pete admitted. "A will."

By the time they finished explaining, Martin and Emma had officially joined the wake. Martin not only donned his jacket

76   ISN'T IT ROMANTIC?

but all his riding leathers, and pulled his old hog, still pristine
and shining, out of the barn for a trial spin.

The apple tree lay out in the yard like a drying skeleton, and
shingles and debris littered the yard. Martin had a farm to run
and Emma three children to collect at the bus before starting
her rounds of Scouts and piano lessons. Even so, they spent a
good hour taking turns on the passenger seat roaring up and
down that country road where Brooke's unmentionables still
fluttered bravely in the wind. The sky cleared again, the weather
service marveled at the low damage estimates from the fast-
moving storm, and the young soybeans glistened with the rain.
It was another beautiful day to hold a funeral. Martin and
Emma even knew the correct version of "Joy to the World,"
and when the children came home, they all gathered to sing it.

"We're not going to get to New Orleans tonight," Brooke
observed as she and Pete stood out on the back porch, watching the sun gild the remaining clouds off to the east.

Pete took another sip of coffee. "It'll still be there tomorrow."

"Do you think we should call home just to make sure everything's okay?"

He shook his head. "I think we should take the Bishops out
to dinner."

They did, to a restaurant that made up for every intestinal
cramp the Bayou Café had provoked. And then Pete slept on
the couch and Brooke slept in Sally Bishop's bottom bunk bed.
When they left in the morning, she was already missing a family she hadn't even known twenty-four hours earlier.

Emma Bishop clutched Brooke's hands like a mother. "Take
care of him," she commanded, a wistful glint still in her eyes.

For a minute Brooke wanted to point over to Pete and say,
"That man? Take care of that man who has survived ambush,
political campaigns and network television without me?"

She didn't, though. She knew just what Emma meant. And
she smiled.

In return, Emma squeezed again. "And let him take care of
you."

Brooke didn't have any answer for that at all.

Six

IBN 6:30 World News report

Marsha Phillips

... and that's the news for this Tuesday. Before we sign off, I'd like to thank everyone on behalf of Pete Cooper for the letters, telegrams and home remedies that have been pouring in. As we said before, it's a simple case of laryngitis, and we hope Pete will be back next week.

"**W**here did you learn to kiss like that?"

Brooke looked over from where she was trying her best to read the New Orleans street map. "What?"

Pete never took his gaze off the rush-hour traffic on Highway 10. The rain the day before hadn't cooled things off at all. There was a fine sheen of perspiration on his forehead, even with the air-conditioning on, and Brooke could tell he was battling a headache from the glare that was getting worse as the sun settled toward the city.

"I said, where did you learn to kiss like that?"

"Like what? Are you sure your friend's expecting us?"

ISN'T IT ROMANTIC?

"Alex was delighted. There's plenty of room, and we go back a long way."

"So do you and I, and I'm not sure I'd put you and a strange woman up in my house on four-hours notice."

Pete's grin was enigmatic. "Which is probably why I've never asked."

Brooke snorted unkindly and went back to trying to draw a line from their position to Saint Charles Avenue in the Garden District. "That's because you never had the nerve to take your own medicine."

This time he did turn. "My own medicine? What are you talking about?"

Brooke slid her sunglasses far enough down her nose so he couldn't possibly miss her expression. "The gauntlet."

"The gauntlet?" he retorted with outrage. "Oh, come on. That was great stuff. You loved it."

"I had four dates run screaming from the house never to be heard from again."

"Just as well. They couldn't stand a little friendly interest . . ."

"Interrogation."

"David was being protective."

"You two were being jerks. I'll never forgive you for my first formal."

Now his expression was the soul of sincere confusion. "What did we do then?"

"There I was," she answered, "dressed up for the first time in my life. I had my hair done down at Luella's shop and my mama bought me my first long dress—you remember, that flowered thing with the hoopskirt and the ruffles. And I walked down those stairs like Cinderella to the ball."

"And we were there for support."

"Oh, really? Is that why you said, 'You don't mean to tell me you're going out dressed like *that?*'"

Pete ventured one look over at Brooke. Then he burst out laughing. After a proper pause, so did Brooke. It had been funny, the kind of teasing only close siblings and friends inflicted on each other. Her date had damn near picked her corsage apart from nerves after having to stand down in the living room with those two and two of their other friends lobbing questions at him like artillery shells, but Brooke would have missed them had they not been there to send her off.

ISN'T IT ROMANTIC?

"You haven't told me yet."

Her eyes were back on the grid of names. "What?"

"Where you learned to kiss like that."

"Just because my relationships didn't work doesn't mean they didn't have some good points," was all she'd say. Brooke hoped that Pete didn't notice that her fingers had suddenly begun to tremble. She didn't want him to bring up what had happened right now. After the wonderful afternoon they'd had with the Bishops, and the long drive down through Louisiana spent playing Name That Historical Figure—any competition was better than none—she'd thought he might have, well, not necessarily forgotten what had happened out on that road, maybe just misplaced it.

She sure hadn't. She'd spent the night before sweating through more sleeplessness, caught between the innocence of a six-year-old's room and the frustration of a twenty-six-year-old's very neglected hormones.

If she were completely honest, Brooke had to admit that the experience wasn't exactly a novel one, even though twice in two nights was a bit much. After all, she'd wanted Pete even before she'd known what it meant, back when his sharp smile was all it took to send her heart skidding and her imagination into overdrive. But Pete and Brooke were meant to be best friends, the kind who shared history without needing to share life-styles. They could forget to call each other for months, and when they picked up the phone, the other was expecting it. No hassle, no ritual, no muss. The right words, or no words at all. A soft shoulder and a strong back.

But not a lover. That would have been asking too much. It would have shattered the fragile equilibrium of their relationship and sullied their implicit trust. Lovers had other agendas, and Brooke knew better after all this time than to want that.

Or maybe she wanted what she had so much that she could think of very little that was worth jeopardizing it. Even being Pete's lover.

Especially being Pete's lover.

It didn't stop her from sweating.

"You surprised me," he admitted, his voice curiously serious.

Brooke fought the urge to look over for verification. "*I* surprised *you?*" she demanded. "I do not believe I was the perpetrator of surprises yesterday, Mr. Cooper."

ISN'T IT ROMANTIC?

His chuckle was rueful and dark. "Oh, yes you were, Stump old buddy. You grew up."

That brought Brooke's heart almost to a dead standstill. "Don't be silly, Coop. I've had breasts since I was twelve. You were still in town then."

"You didn't have *those* breasts," he accused.

She actually looked down, as if to verify the truth. "Well, whose breasts did I have?"

Again he shook his head. "Having breasts doesn't make you an adult. It doesn't mean you've learned those . . . those things that make a man . . ." But he didn't finish.

Brooke was sure she didn't want him to. This conversation was not one that should be held in a small sports car on another hot, close day. It put her suddenly too close to Pete, so that she wanted to squirm, to scoot away from the memory of how good he'd tasted and felt. How she knew he'd taste right now, with that tang of salt on his upper lip.

So she laughed away her discomfort. "I never learned those things," she protested. "If I had, I'd have fewer pals and more suitors."

"If you never learned those things," he retorted, his attention ostensibly on driving, both hands tight around the wheel, "why did I spend last night dreaming about you? Very vivid dreams, I might add."

Those words caught in Brooke's throat like bad food, like the queasiness of sudden dislocation. This wasn't the way the trip was supposed to happen. They were supposed to tease and abuse each other, just like always, physical and easy. They weren't supposed to be rewriting the ground rules only three days past seeing each other again. They weren't supposed to change.

Especially like this.

"Because I have breasts," she suggested dryly, hoping he didn't hear the awful catch in her voice. "Whoever's I've managed to abscond with. And if there's one thing I've learned about you over the years, you'd follow a decent set into a spitting volcano just to introduce yourself."

"Brooke—" He looked over, his own thoughts protected behind his mirrored glasses, those creases of concern back. She wasn't sure what he was about to say, but she saw the impulse die. "Where do we exit to get to Alex's?"

ISN'T IT ROMANTIC? 81

What had he wanted? she wondered. What had he been about to say? Brooke wiped damp palms against her slacks and picked the map back up, wishing her chest would clear, her heart slow. Wishing most desperately of all that the whispers of those old dreams would die, would fade right back into puberty where they belonged.

"We have about five miles left to the city," she said. "After that, I'll have to keep an eye on exits. Does Alex have a wife? Maybe we'd better stop for flowers or something."

Finally Pete managed a smile, and Brooke felt the surprising tension ease. "No," he admitted. "Alex doesn't have a wife."

"Well," she said, "I hope they live near a women's store. I need some underwear."

"*That* is Alex?" Brooke demanded an hour later as they pulled to a stop inside the wrought-iron fence that surrounded the Bellermain home on Saint Charles.

Pete pulled off his sunglasses and stretched a little before reaching for the door. "Don't sound so surprised. You'll like her a lot."

Beside him, Brooke made a very rude noise. "You could have at least told me she looks like a beauty contestant."

"Miss America runner-up, 1978," he allowed, just to hear her groan. She hit him instead.

It was amazing to Pete, especially after seeing Brooke handle herself at the funeral, at the Badger Bar. She'd developed the most instinctive grace, a dignity that simply couldn't be taught—and he'd been around some newswomen who had tried their damnedest. She had taste and style and a tongue that would have had William Buckley in tears. And yet she still had a miserable self-image.

Why should she have been so surprised that he'd be physically attracted to her? She'd grown into a beauty. Not a classic beauty, certainly, like Alex with her award-winning cheekbones and sloe eyes. But a serene strength, an intangible that composed those great blue eyes and overripe mouth into a whole package worth more than the sum of its parts.

He'd known his share of women. He'd married one of the most beautiful. But he couldn't remember ever feeling the warm comfort he had out in that field, wrapping his hands into

82   ISN'T IT ROMANTIC?

Brooke's sodden, limp hair and sinking into her mouth like a familiar bed.

"Peter, sugar," Alex greeted him with outstretched arms, a leggy African-American with flawlessly elegant features, legendary figure and a comfortable job with one of the local television affiliates, negotiated from the strength of her swimsuit scores from '78. Alex had been Miss Congeniality, beating out even Miss Texas with her bubbly personality. A canny woman rather than an intellectual one. Today she must have decided to assume her Voodoo Queen persona, dressed in a flowing purple-and-gold caftan, bare feet and huge hoop earrings, her hair pulled back into a severe bun to accentuate her features.

Pete climbed out of the car and smiled for her, an eye always to Brooke's reaction. She was standing a little behind him, quiet and passive. Observing. Marshaling forces.

"Alex, you poor starving waif," he answered, and gathered the woman into a hug, as always enjoying the scent and feel of her. Suddenly, surprisingly, he realized that marshmallows weren't really his craving after all. He was more in the mood for something tart. Something that demanded more than shut eyes and an empty stomach.

"Alex," he announced, pulling back far enough to include Brooke in the picture, "this is Brooke Ferguson. Brooke, Alexandra St. Claire. Alex and I go way back to my New York days when we were news virgins together."

The two women assessed each other with bright smiles and careful posture.

"Pete, darlin'," Alex said with great satisfaction. "You know how I feel about having a beautiful woman under my roof."

"The competition's good for you," he assured her, dropping a final kiss on her forehead before stepping away from her to go for his bags. "Did you manage to get the funeral arranged?"

Alex turned her full attention on Brooke, who still stood a bit stiffly beside the car. "Course I did. Would Alex disappoint you? Now, Brooke, I have to say, darlin', that's an intriguing outfit you're wearin'. I haven't seen a woman wear men's pants so well since Hepburn, darlin'. How do you do it?"

Pete saw that Brooke's smile was a shade cautious as she instinctively drew herself up to full height, making his faded blue T-shirt stretch quite nicely over her figure. "I got caught in a tornado and lost all my own clothes. These are Pete's."

ISN'T IT ROMANTIC?

Alex threw back her head and laughed with sincere delight. "Doesn't it figure?" she demanded, hands on hips in mock outrage. "I'd work a week to try and look that good. Now then, have you ever been to the Big Easy before?"

"Not in a few years," Brooke replied, the tone of her voice and her posture reminding Pete very much of the funeral. On exhibit. Putting on the facade, just like Mamie had taught her, that almost regal grace wrapped around her like a cloak to protect her from the threat of Alex's exotic beauty.

Pete caught himself wanting to shake his head. He was going to have to talk to that girl. The first thing she had to realize was that Alex never would have gone to the trouble of teasing him about bringing a beautiful woman if that hadn't been what she'd seen. It took a lot to impress Alex, who wasn't even impressed by her own looks.

Almost as if she'd already forgotten Pete, Alex floated right over to Brooke and slid an arm through hers. "In that case, we must make the most of however long that skinflint lets you stay. You like to go to Galatoire's, or Antoine's maybe?"

"We can't," Pete immediately protested, head popping up from where he was emptying the trunk of its remaining contents. "I'm supposed to be sick in bed in Rupert Springs, Arkansas."

Alex waved him away. "Oh, pooh. Rene will be home soon," she announced, still to Brooke, who followed along in a silence Pete couldn't interpret. "Now, mind you, don't steal him away from me. He goes all weak-kneed for redheads, that one does. Especially ones with legs as long as yours..."

Pete finally found Brooke again about an hour later after the maid had guided him to the upstairs rooms to deposit the luggage. The home Alex shared with Rene Bellermain was a big old Victorian with high, echoing rooms and colonnaded balconies in the back that overlooked a lush garden complete with magnolias, oaks, fan palms and rhododendrons. Even set along the Saint Charles trolley line, the house was private, well shaded and as elegant as its owners.

The temperatures still hovered in the damp eighties, but Pete found the women already in the garden, the setting sun striking fire from Brooke's hair. She and Alex were lounging on the patio with tall, very cool looking drinks in their hands.

"I hear you still have the kiss of death, darlin'," Alex greeted him as he stepped out into the lengthening shade.

84 ISN'T IT ROMANTIC?

He decided not to answer until he'd taken a good taste of the third drink that waited on the wrought-iron table between the two women.

With the bite of rum and exotic juices washing away some of his headache, he settled into a chair and tilted his head back a little. "You heard about the tornado, huh?"

Brooke was squinting over at him. "Alex says you're notorious for this kind of thing. That there was a pool going in Saudi Arabia that the Hilton would get hit just 'cause you stayed there."

Pete shrugged. No use denying the infamous.

"You never told me these amusing little stories," she admonished. "It might have been a thoughtful thing to do before you offered to go on this jaunt with me...especially considering what's happened so far."

Pete did his own squinting. "I didn't offer anything," he retorted, thinking that Alex was right. Brooke shouldn't have looked so cool and pretty after driving around all day in his clothes. "I was kidnapped and threatened."

Alex's laugh was deep and musical. "What threat could possibly work on Pete Cooper?"

Brooke's smile was not in the least charitable. "Two elderly aunts. Alex has been telling me some very interesting Peter Cooper stories," she said, obviously to him.

He deliberately closed his eyes, ignoring them both.

"And Brooke," Alex countered, "has been doing quite the same. I wish I'd known you while you were still a bad boy, sugar. You have always been too much of a gentleman around me."

"That's because Rene's meaner than I am."

"Not meaner," a sleek baritone offered from the doorway. "Just better looking."

All three of the garden's occupants turned to find the voice's owner striding out to join them.

Another person who looked too cool and collected on a day straight out of a sauna, Pete thought, climbing to his feet to greet his host. Rene was holding out a tanned hand, his smile sharp and sincere.

"I might have known I'd find you here with the women," he greeted Pete with the original article in French accents. Born and raised in Paris, Rene had met Alex in New York and moved with her to New Orleans, content to follow her career, since his

ISN'T IT ROMANTIC? 85

moved with him. A slightly built man a good four inches shorter than his lady love, Rene embodied everything that was French style and charm.

Pete was genuinely glad to see the businessman. "Call me a glutton for punishment," he acknowledged easily, shaking Rene's hand. "How are you, Rene?"

He got a Gallic shrug, another smile and the kind of handshake that betrayed the Frenchman's power. Pete would have made introductions. He was turning to do it, as a matter of fact. Rene beat him to it with one wave of his hand, as if words would only interfere with his attention as he turned his gaze on Brooke.

The smile that lit his face was genuine and heartfelt. And purely, fatally, French. Reaching out both hands to a stupefied Brooke, Rene pulled her gently to her feet and then looked at her the way a museum attendee would examine a Rembrandt.

Pete saw the blush start at the base of Brooke's throat and creep higher the longer Rene looked. Pete knew she would be helpless with this kind of scrutiny. Far more experienced women than she had admitted to finding themselves weak-kneed with Rene's singular attention. Brooke looked very much like a baby bunny caught in the approach of a bright light.

Pete was surprised by his own reaction. He wanted to protect her, to pull a supportive arm around her.

He wanted to belt Rene, and that had never happened before.

"Bonjour, ma jolie fille," Rene finally greeted her, her hands firmly in both of his, her cheeks pink with the scrutiny, her eyes wide. "It is a rare pleasure to welcome you to my home." And then, his gaze never leaving her face, he bent to kiss the knuckles on her hands. "Has Alex told you that I have a weakness for beautiful redheads?"

"She also told me you're a wonderful liar," Brooke managed with a humor that defused every bit of tension.

Rene threw back his head and laughed. Alex smiled like a mother. And Pete, easing back into his chair as the four of them settled in for drinks, saw Brooke turn suddenly brittle and look at him with exhilarated eyes. He smiled for her, amused by her surprise, reassured by her presence of mind. Jealous as hell that his best buddy would look like that after one lousy compli-

86 ISN'T IT ROMANTIC?

ment from a slick Frenchman with a thousand-dollar suit and lifts in his shoes.

Pete hadn't thought much about what he'd expected from this trip, other than settling Mamie into her next life. He realized as he watched Rene monopolize Brooke's conversation and attend her like an acolyte, that he was going to have to change that situation. That, actually, the situation had already changed on him sometime during those years he'd been away. He was just going to have to decide what the hell to do about it. And soon.

"Coop?"

Pete rolled over on his back at the tentative whisper. It was well toward morning, the moon up and the traffic slowed to a mutter along the street. Pete had said good-night to Brooke at her bedroom door next to his at about one and had then gone on into his room to toss and turn in yet another futile attempt at sleep. She evidently wasn't having any more luck than he.

"Are you awake?" she whispered from the open doorway, the moonlight that spilled in through the long window washing her legs and leaving the rest in shadow. Pete did see that the T-shirt he'd lent her until she could replace her own nightie skimmed the tops of her thighs and gently hugged the rest. It made him wonder why she'd never looked like this all the times they'd gone swimming and she'd strolled around in similar attire. If she'd looked like this back then, they never would have made it to the pool.

"Yeah, Stump," he answered, pulling himself into a sitting position. "I'm up. What's wrong?"

Her arms were wrapped around her belly and her head was down a little so that her hair tumbled around her shoulders, the frail moonlight gleaming on it like a dark waterfall. She padded barefoot across the floor. Pete made room for her on the bed, but she walked by as if she hadn't seen him, to stand by the window.

"I can't sleep."

The moonlight again. This time it found her throat and kissed it, a sleek, soft wash of silver that drew Pete's eyes like a prospector's. He wished suddenly that she wouldn't stand like that, that she'd move her arms. She was pulling the material of

ISN'T IT ROMANTIC? 87

his old, soft Hard Rock shirt across her breasts, outlining them in too-familiar detail and making his fingers itch.

Quickly he looked away, back down to where his hands still lay atop the sheet.

"Would you tell me something?" she asked, and suddenly, because he couldn't see her, he heard the thirteen-year-old Brooke. Uncertain, shy, chin out in blind challenge.

"Sure," was all he could offer, still unsure what she wanted.

"Is Rene serious?"

That brought his attention back around to find that she'd turned her gaze on him, her eyes hidden in the shadows, her brow pursed, the line of her arms tight.

"About what?" he asked, wishing he knew what she wanted. Wishing like hell she didn't look so damn vulnerable asking for it—especially when she also looked so beautiful here at the whispery edge of morning. "His cooking? His career? The position of France in the world?"

She actually flinched, a small movement, no less intense. And then she dipped her head even further, unable to face him. "Me."

So that was it. Good old Stump, her insecurities let loose in the dark, her self-image still at odds with her actions.

Sighing, Pete climbed out of bed. It didn't really occur to him that he was clad only in his gym shorts. Brooke had seen them before. Pete's first thought was simply that she looked much too forlorn standing there with only the moonlight to keep her company.

"Stump," he admonished, taking her shoulders in his hands. "What am I going to do with you?"

She didn't lift her head, but she smiled, a soft, tremulous smile that no one else would have been privileged to. "I just can't stand the idea that I'm being made fun of."

Pete actually gave her a little shake. "Do you mean that the entire time Rene was playing seek out the pulse points with your wrists, you were thinking he was setting you up?"

She shrugged. "It's happened before."

"In Rupert Springs, Arkansas. When you were fifteen."

"And sixteen and seventeen. I get propositions from truckers on parole, Coop, not internationally situated French businessmen. Not . . ."

"Not me?"

88   ISN'T IT ROMANTIC?

Her head came up, and Pete saw that he hadn't been the only one spending sleepless nights. In those beautiful eyes of hers, he saw the miserable uncertainty she never would have allowed anyone else to witness.

"You'd better not proposition me," she tried her best to tease, her voice tremulous, her chin out.

"You'd better be surprised if I didn't," he retorted, his fingers tightening around her arms, his anger surprising him. "Didn't you listen to *anything* Mamie taught you?"

"Mamie loved me," she argued, and suddenly Pete saw tears in her eyes and didn't know what to do about them. "Just like my mom and dad. Only Mamie insisted that I could be beautiful if I believed I could. Mom and Dad just settled for 'You'll always be stately, Brooke.' Well, stately's nice if you're a historical home. It stinks when you're looking for somebody with the guts to take you to the movies."

"Stately," Pete snarled with a shake of his head. "Stately."

She lifted her face, thrusting out that old belligerent chin at him. "Yes, damn it," she snapped.

Pete couldn't even form the words to tell her how patently ridiculous she was. He couldn't begin to explain to her why her blossoming into womanhood would have intimidated every living soul in Rupert Springs, those sweet, sincere, straightforward people who wouldn't know an original work of art if it were handed to them by Michelangelo himself.

He couldn't convince her that what she had become far outshone anything in her experience—in *his* experience, damn it, and he'd had a sight more than she had.

Finally all he could do was drag her along when he turned for the door.

"Coop—"

"Shut up," he commanded, swinging the door closed and then turning her before him so that the two of them faced the mirror at the far end of the room. They reflected in it like phantoms, Brooke's face wide open beneath his, his almost ferocious in the half-light. "I'll show you stately," he said, letting go of her shoulders to take hold of her wrists.

"What are you—"

"I said shut up." He pulled her hands straight up over her head. Never giving her the chance to protest, he reached for the hem of the T-shirt and swept it right up and off, leaving her in nothing but a scrap of panties.

ISN'T IT ROMANTIC?

"Pete!" she protested on a rasp, her arms already moving to cover herself.

He grabbed them. "Look," he commanded, trapping her between his hands, forcing her to face herself in the mirror where she stood, her back against his chest, her head down.

"I can't."

He didn't waste words on her, just let go of one arm enough to cup her chin in his hand and force it up. "I said look, damn it. We'll start from the top down, and I am going to show you exactly why Rene was speaking French in your ear all during the salad course."

"Oh, Coop, he didn't..."

"Your hair," he said, the hand that had held her chin lifting to the dark treasure of curls that framed her face like a midnight sun. "Your hair is gorgeous, Brooke. It's a color I've never seen before, a dark, rich auburn that reflects sunlight like copper ore. It makes a man want to touch it, to run his fingers through it and get all tangled up in the curls."

She tried to squirm, but he held her still. "Please don't..."

He anchored his fingers in her hair and kept her face to the mirror. "Your eyes," he went on, reacquainting himself with them. "You have eyes like a lake. They're so deep and blue that a man could blind himself on them. And you laugh with your eyes so that you have a couple of crow's-feet. Very sexy. You have skin the color of pale cream and a mouth that's damn near as soft as down. Kissing you is—"

"You've already demonstrated that, thanks." The tone of her voice was dry, but there was a tremor in it. She'd stopped squirming to get away.

Pete swept her hair back from her neck. "Your throat. Long and graceful, a good hand's width so a man can slide his fingers right down it, and the skin's so soft it's like losing yourself in silk."

He showed her, just to make sure she knew. He kept his eyes on her, forcing her to see herself for what she was, for what he knew she was capable of. Mamie hadn't been wrong. And he'd been hotfooting it all over the world rather than taking two days out to go home and find out.

"Your breasts..."

His voice had unaccountably begun to tremble, as well. His hand, so at ease against her throat, had stilled atop her shoulder. His eyes hadn't.

90 ISN'T IT ROMANTIC?

"Now you say they're mine?" she asked, her eyes finally following his, her skin suddenly just a little damp.

"Look at them, Brooke," he commanded, his voice a rasp, his hand beginning to slip. "They're enough to make a man ache. Full and high, with nipples the color of fresh roses. You might have had breasts at twelve, but they weren't enough to make a man fantasize about what they'd feel like in his hands."

Her nipples had hardened to tight buds with just his words, his gaze. Full, firm breasts that beckoned even more without the barrier of covering. Pete saw them in the dimness, an impression of lushness and responsiveness, curves and shadows and aching invitation.

He accepted.

"I don't think—" Brooke managed, her eyes wider still, her body suddenly very still as his other hand crept up to capture her other breast "—that a...a demonstration is necessary...."

"You're twenty-six," he answered, his attention torn, wondering what he'd set out to do, wondering if he'd thought about it. Knowing that if he had, he never would have risked temptation like this. She was so warm against him, her body so lithe and supple and sweet, her breasts heavy and full in his hands. "You still don't believe that you're beautiful. I had to do something."

"I'm not beautiful."

His smile was taut with control. "Then I'm not finished, am I?"

She swayed in his hold, her eyes briefly closing, opening, impossibly dark and deep. He ached suddenly to kiss those eyes closed, to taste her skin and tangle himself in those molten curls.

His hands slid farther, down her flat torso, to her belly, to where he pulled her back against him to discover in the most graphic terms just how beautiful, how desirable she was.

"Rene would have been blind, deaf and dead to not have tried to hit on you," he whispered just before he dipped to kiss the back of her neck. He'd caught her completely to him, his one hand wrapped around her hips, his other still cupping her breast, tormenting the nipple to even stiffer attention, his body seeking to surround her.

She was beginning to soften to him, her head up, her body supple and eager against his. He could smell her, soap and

ISN'T IT ROMANTIC? 91

shampoo and the faint musk of woman. He could taste the first tang of perspiration on her skin. He could imagine her tumbled on his bed, her hair a glorious riot against those once-crisp white sheets, her eyes languorous, her body dancing with his.

And then, suddenly, she pulled away. Her breathing shallow, her heart racing, her expression wild and haunted, that little rabbit on the run. Facing him with accusation in her eyes.

"What's the matter?" he asked, allowing her her distance.

She shuddered, not remembering now to cover herself with her arms, tears glinting in those great, deadly eyes. "Don't do this to me."

"Do what?" he asked. "Want you?"

She drew herself up tall, obviously not realizing how much more alluring it made her look. "Yes."

"Why, because you don't think you deserve it? Because I've known you since you were in braces and Clearasil?"

"Because you're my *friend,* damn it. You're the last person I can depend on, and that—" she flung an arm out in an uncertain direction, as if nailing his arousal to a point on the floor. "That would change everything."

Pete allowed an eyebrow to rise, since she obviously wasn't ready for anything else to. "How would it change it?"

Her eyes filled again, glittering in the darkness, stark and lost. "It would ruin it. It would bury it under hormones and expectations and regrets."

"How do you know we'd regret anything?"

She impaled him on the truth. "Have you ever had a lover you could really tell the truth to? Did you tell Alicia the things you told me you wanted to say to her?"

Pete knew there should be an answer to that, a sharp, succinct retort that would put that kind of logic right into its proper place. Maybe if Brooke hadn't been standing almost naked in front of him, half temptress, half child. Maybe if he hadn't been as surprised by their mutual attraction as she.

Maybe if she hadn't been telling the truth.

"You're the only person," she said, her voice soft with hurt, "the only person in the world I can really talk to. The only one who knows just where all my warts are and doesn't give a damn, who doesn't expect more of me than I can give, and is always there with a soft shoulder and a wisecrack to make me feel better. And maybe I haven't had quite the experience as you, but I've found that trading that in for sex usually isn't worth it."

Before Pete had a chance to answer, Brooke scooped up her T-shirt from the floor and dropped it over her head.

"Damn it, Coop," she demanded, eyes glittering. "How can I talk to you about my lousy love life if you *are* my lousy love life?"

She left him to the moonlight and silence without letting him vent his frustration or challenge her accusation.

Which was probably just as well. After all, she was right.

After that, the jazz funeral the next day was something of an anticlimax.

Seven

New Orleans, Let the Good Times Roll:

What better place to celebrate good times, good food and good friends, than in the French Quarter, or Vieux Carré, the heart of beautiful New Orleans, where everything goes. Stroll the streets, listen to the jazz, taste the cuisines that made the city famous . . .

Mamie would have loved it.

The French Quarter was alive that morning, swarming with tourists and shop owners and restaurateurs, the flowers brilliant in the heat, the buildings quaint and just a little seedy with their wrought-iron balconies and French doors open to the streets. As she passed, walking solemnly along next to Pete, Brooke could see the lush foliage of courtyards beyond plain facades and hear the chatter of water from hidden fountains. She could hear the ever-present wail of music and smell the river and the fillet of gumbo. A dozen different languages floated across the narrow streets, and a hundred different pitches of laughter danced on the heavy air like helium balloons.

94 ISN'T IT ROMANTIC?

The Vieux Carré was celebrating life by honoring death. Clad in gaudy satin cutaway coats, their gaily decorated parasols over their heads, their fans attached to their belts, their top hats cocked just so, the official marchers followed the band that was giving forth the proper dirge for one so recently departed. Slow, solemn steps and downcast faces, white-gloved sympathy for the bereaved.

And then, from one step to the next, from somewhere inside a single note, the band swung into jazz, into celebration. Into dancing and laughter and joy. The music ricocheted off the old buildings and provoked smiles from the sidewalk audiences. Children danced along with old men, and strangers ran from shop entrances and restaurants to join the impromptu parade. And right in their midst, Pete and Brooke and Alex and Rene joined in, giving Mamie the tribute she really deserved. Because if anyone would have understood why these old men danced down a hot street in New Orleans swinging their parasols and clapping their hands and prizing miracles from battered old instruments, it would have been Mamie.

"Beats the hell out of the accordion," Pete offered with a delighted grin.

Brooke shook her head, wishing yet again that Mamie could have been there to share the event. "I still can't figure out how Alex arranged it. These are only held for black jazz musicians anymore, from what I've heard."

Pete held her hand as they high-stepped their way behind the band. "Her grandfather was Little Sweet William Thibidaux, one of the best clarinet players that ever lived. She grew up with these guys."

"I'm really glad she could arrange it," Brooke admitted sincerely, and then added simply, "I'm glad I got to meet her."

Pete shot her a questioning look, but Brooke answered with a smile.

"She's a world-class shopper," was all she'd allow.

They'd had a wonderful time that morning hitting the shops Alex favored. Antiques, clothing, museums, they'd strolled through them all, until Brooke had glutted herself on the magic of New Orleans's past and severely dented her pocketbook in the present.

She'd gotten her necessities. She'd also let Alex talk her into some outfits she knew she'd never wear back in Rupert Springs, like the brightly colored gauze top and skirt that bared her arms

ISN'T IT ROMANTIC? 95

and shoulders and swirled around her legs as she kept step with the marchers. Perfect along with the ropes of beads and dangling earrings they'd added for an afternoon stroll through the sensuous, exhilarating streets of New Orleans, as out of place as a bikini in a church, back on Main Street.

But Brooke wasn't on Main Street. She was on Bourbon Street and, for just a moment, belonged there.

She still blushed to think of what Pete had given her the night before. Not just the praise, but the restraint. The understanding, the bullying, the patience. She'd returned to her room and pulled that old T-shirt back off again and looked in her own mirror, trying her best to see what Pete had seen. Still trying to find the swan hidden inside that duckling.

In truth, she couldn't. Her legs were too long and her mouth too big. She thought her jaw was square enough to do after-shave commercials, and she had shoulders like a halfback.

Maybe her breasts hadn't been so bad after all. She'd felt his hands on them—could still feel his hands, so big and gentle and protective around that most sensitive skin. She could still feel the way her nipples had tightened at his approach, unsure whether to anticipate or dread.

He'd wanted her. Maybe he hadn't set out to, at least last night when he'd yanked her shirt off. After all, she'd seen his eyes, and they'd reminded her of what he'd looked like the day he'd stormed into the waiting room at the county jail to pick her up from an ill-advised date. Angry and impatient and frustrated.

"Don't you know better?" that look demanded.

No, she thought on a stifled sigh. She didn't know better. She didn't know how to feel beautiful in the same house as Alex, whose looks and personality turned heads wherever she went. She didn't know how to seriously respond to Rene's outrageous flirtation. After all, the guys back at the Badger Bar were one thing. Their clumsy attempts at affection were easy to fend off and easier to dismiss. They'd become friends rather than potential dates, and that was fine. They weren't men who made romance a world-class art.

And just what did she do with a friend who had decided to do it the other way around? What did she do with the fact that everything she'd ever prayed for might have come true if she'd only had the courage to let nature take its course the night before?

96   ISN'T IT ROMANTIC?

Her palms were still wet, and it had nothing to do with the humidity. Her heart still raced unexpectedly, interfering with her ability to breathe correctly. Her gaze still strayed over to where Pete was watching the crowd like a kid at a circus, his sharp eyes bright and open, his face younger than she'd seen it in a long while on that national news show of his.

The sun gleamed like dark gold in his hair and warmed his skin. He wore an unstructured wheat-colored jacket over a green T-shirt and jeans, looking casual and elegant at the same time. Only Coop could exude that kind of cool sensuality submerged in southern Louisiana humidity like this. Walking in rhythm behind the band with a mesmerizing kind of step that mostly involved his hips, he was drawing more stares than the band, more comment than the entire city put together.

Last night, in the darkness, he'd turned that sensuality on her. For a brief moment, wrapped in moonlight, fantasy and possibility had been a handsbreadth away from reality. Alone, isolated, protected from what awaited each of them at the end of the trip. Unbelievably, unimaginably, he had asked in that silence to share with her the most beautiful of communications, the true expression of what they could feel for each other. And in the end, because she'd never known anything but disappointment from that kind of offer, Brooke had forfeited her chance.

There was no question this morning that the world had once again rushed back into the comfortable void they'd managed to create. Pete had been discovered. Women slapped hands against gaping mouths and men sucked in their pot bellies out of envy. And Brooke, whose hand he held, who received his delighted chuckles and shared the special bond that had brought them to this street, suddenly didn't know anymore how to be just his friend.

"*Bon Dieu,* if it ain't the best newsman in five feet, I'm thinkin'," a voice boomed out of nowhere, the lilt distinctly New Orleans.

Brooke turned to see a very short, balding man with hairy hands and wire rims reach up to clap Pete on the back.

"You came to visit me, did you, boy? And me, I have to go to strangers to find out 'bout it."

Pete's laugh was abrupt. "What the hell are you doin' here, Marv?"

ISN'T IT ROMANTIC? 97

Marv reclaimed his hand to place it over his heart. Except he had it on the wrong side of his chest. "Pete, my good friend, you don't like to see me?"

"I want to know what you're doing here." Without breaking stride, Pete included Brooke in the conversation. "Marv Gold, Bureau Chief for IBN," he explained more than introduced before turning back on the little man with a scowl. "What are you doing here?"

"You kiddin', no?" Marv demanded. "I love a good funeral."

"Only if there are surviving relatives to interview," Pete retorted.

Marv's considerable eyebrows lifted. "Are there?"

"Not if you want to make it to your next birthday, there aren't."

Marv gave up on Pete and turned to reach his hand out in Brooke's direction. "You know this scoundrel, eh? I'm still pleased to meet you, *ma jolie fille*. Eh, I hope you got a name."

"Brooke Ferguson," she allowed, briefly giving him her free hand over her shoulder. He almost had to reach over his head to get to it. "Nice to meet you."

"Pleasure's mine, *chère*. You enjoy yourself here?"

"It has its moments," she answered, ignoring Pete's scowl.

Marv nodded with a delighted smile. "Well, that good, that good. After all, you know what we all say down here in my N'Awleans, *Laissez les bons temps rouler*. Let the good times roll."

"What do you mean 'your New Orleans'?" Pete demanded. "Marv, you're from New York."

Brooke fought a bubble of laughter. "Interesting how well you picked up the accent," she said carefully.

Pete's scowl intensified. "When he was stationed in Dallas we almost ended up defusing a range war. Marv gets heavily involved with his area."

"So sue me," Marv retorted without noticeable heat. "I assimilate."

Brooke looked back over her shoulder. "Don't you get the bends when you go home?"

Marv's answering smile was delighted. "My mother won't speak to me for days. So, *chère*, where you know this scoundrel from, eh?"

98   ISN'T IT ROMANTIC?

Brooke knew better. "He picked me up down at the Pink Palace last night. This is his quaint little way of walking me home."

They'd just about run out of street, and when they did, it would be the end of the parade. Not the party, though. Alex had invited everyone to continue the celebration at one of the small jazz clubs that dotted the district like sequins on an Elvis jumpsuit. Brooke knew that Pete would rather Marv wasn't still around to join in the festivities. She also knew that it was going to be unavoidable. Marv had the same kind of qualities as the Reverend Mr. Purcell, that sense of sticking so close to somebody that you'd finally give in to them just to have some peace.

"Ya know, I be hearin' that Pete Cooper has laryngitis," Marv mused to himself, never missing a step. "Lotsa people, all over the country, they been sendin' in potions and poultices so he be okay. He sound pretty fine to me, all right."

That finally brought Pete to a stop so that Marv almost caromed into Pete's chest. "Okay, Marv. One drink. I'll tell you if you promise on your mother's matzo soup that it doesn't get back to Evan."

Marv lit up like Barney's Used Cars on sale day. "*Bon Dieu*, boy, you bet."

Pete's scowl was awesome. "And knock that off."

"You're going to have to call in," Brooke said.

Pete didn't look up from the café au lait before him. "Maybe Evan won't find out."

But Brooke laughed. "Are you kidding? That was the first jazz funeral in three years. There were three remote units there in five minutes. Even if Marv keeps his mouth shut, you've still been exposed like backside in an outhouse, son."

She earned quite a nice scowl herself for that one. "Don't you start getting all quaint on me, too," he threatened. "I had just about all I could stand from Marv."

Brooke chuckled, once again comfortable and familiar with Pete. It amazed her how quickly her hormones could flood and wane with Pete. It relieved her that no matter what else happened, the two of them could so easily return to honesty and humor. She could only hope it would continue.

ISN'T IT ROMANTIC?

The party had been over for hours. Brooke had shared tales and toasts with a dozen musicians, heard stories of Alex's grandfather and the times she'd ended up at Preservation Hall for baby-sitting. She'd sat among Pete's friends, the friends he'd made beyond her sphere of influence, and survived. Separate but not uncomfortable, watching more than participating, getting to know Pete through the people who knew him.

What she found out didn't surprise her in the least. Marv, a savvy and sharp newsman for all the unique ethnic charm, considered Pete one of the three reigning newsmen in the world. Alex recounted yet more tales of the year they'd shared airtime in New York, when Pete the gentleman had protected her from the sides of the city she hadn't been prepared for, and Pete the reporter had fought her tooth and nail for stories—and always won. Rene, world traveler and raconteur, respected Pete for his intelligence, his hunger for knowledge and his sense of fair play.

And Brooke, who'd known all this before they had, found herself loving her friend even more. Differently, with a delight that she'd been proved right all those years ago when she'd seen the potential in the boy others had miscast. When she had still been the only girl who had recognized the attraction of moss green eyes.

Even so, it hurt. Pete had moved on, grown beyond her into a place she didn't belong. He'd outdistanced even his own dreams, and until now, even watching that news every night and hearing the women from Little Rock to Memphis gush over Pete Cooper the way they would Mel Gibson, she hadn't appreciated it. Not really. Not face-to-face like this where she couldn't ignore the fact that Pete was internationally famous and respected, and she was a bean counter for a trucking company.

On the phone they'd been equals. In Mamie's eyes, in Brooke's, who had always seen her buddy as that twenty-four-year-old she'd seen off a final time for his big shot at New York. Before fame, before recognition. Before the gap had appeared that only now she appreciated.

She didn't know what to do about it. When they were alone, it was still Coop and Stump, still two kids who shared the same memories and had been raised to view the world from a compatible place. But when they walked into rooms like this, where people fawned and deferred, where they rightfully asked Pete's

100   ISN'T IT ROMANTIC?

opinion, she felt the difference and ached suddenly for it. She stumbled with the sudden knowledge that things had changed irrevocably, and she wasn't sure she belonged there anymore. And they still had to visit Memphis and Atlanta, where Pete was most known.

Brooke didn't know whether she was up for it. She didn't know whether they'd end the trip still friends, or as once-close acquaintances who'd managed to have their differences spelled out in irrefutable terms. After what had happened last night— what had almost happened last night—it could very well shatter her.

Once the last round had been shared that afternoon, and the last autographs had been signed for fans who'd been lucky enough to stumble onto the party, Pete had grabbed Brooke's hand and led her off for some privacy, some good food and some relaxation.

Only Pete could have walked into a top-notch restaurant like Antoine's and been immediately seated, even without a tie. Another little lesson in class differences, Brooke decided. She would have been standing out in the street for a week.

Brooke found that all of Mamie's coaching at least came in handy when she ended up as a satellite recipient of some of the fawning Pete collected. Pulling herself up to her most regal height, she flashed the maître d' her best smile, all the while wondering whether he knew that the fanciest place she'd ever entertained was the Family Steak House out on Route 3.

She must have handled herself without a major gaffe, because the waiters all smiled and bowed and murmured appreciation at her order. As the evening cooled with a susurrous breeze, she and Pete enjoyed their *estouffée* and blackened redfish beneath the sepia gaze of over a hundred years of Mardi Gras Queens.

"Let's not go on to the next city," Pete said suddenly, lifting his gaze back to Brooke, his fingers worrying the edge of his coffee cup. "Let's just head down toward the bayous."

Brooke was surprised by the sudden intensity in his voice, the dark edge to his eyes. "And miss Elvis?" she demanded. "What would Mamie say?"

The edge of his mouth crooked. "She'd say she'd understand that I didn't want to face the public again just yet."

ISN'T IT ROMANTIC?

Brooke's first instinct was to laugh, to throw off some caustic comment about fame being hell. But she heard the undercurrent in his voice and reached out for his free hand.

"You've never complained before," she said gently.

His expression grew wry. "I never took the time off to let it bother me before."

Brooke wasn't exactly sure what to say. "Coop, it's only been four days."

He nodded. "Four days with you," he retorted. "Four days when I haven't been expected to be anybody special, or do anything dramatic." He squeezed her hand. "Four days when nobody's reviewed the acceptability of my opinions."

"I never realized before how claustrophobic it must get," she admitted with a sly smile. "After all, I just see you on the news like everybody else in the country."

"Don't start that again," he warned. "I told you, I'd invited you."

"Oh, you're right," she retorted. "I should have come sooner. To think I've missed all these years of having other women just dying to see me pick my nose in public to prove I'm not worth sitting with you." To punctuate her point, she nodded and smiled to the icy blonde who was doing just that at the next table.

Pete's smile wasn't any happier. "Do you know how long it's been since I've been to a Three Stooges retrospective?" he asked quietly enough that the other diners wouldn't hear him and carry his problems back to the *Daily World*. "Or the last time I ditched the power suits and got on my roach-stompin' boots and just hit the kind of country bar where there's a grill between me and the band?"

Brooke shrugged. "Let's go now," she suggested. "If nothing else, I'm sure there's a good Cajun bar within driving distance we can get stupid at."

But he shook his head. "The bloodhounds are already out. I'd be spotted in a minute, and if there's one thing the sainted Mr. Parischell demands from his newsmen, it's respectability. He does not consider sitting in with Buddy and the Butt Kickers respectable."

Brooke scowled a bit, caught between this sudden revelation and the ones she'd been facing all on her own. Wondering what the best balance would be between Pete's need for isolation and her sudden dread of it.

102   ISN'T IT ROMANTIC?

"I vote we go on," she suggested diffidently, her gaze down to the dredges of mocha coffee in the delicate demitasse before her, her thoughts on the hand she still held, the familiar comfort of it, the sudden, disquieting promise of it. A person could hide among other people, even in a small town. She couldn't at all in the wild emptiness of the back bayous. "After all, it can't get much worse—and I think the bayous in early summer could. Besides," she added, lifting her gaze back to him, "we've been playing this whole thing by the seat of our pants anyway. Who says we have to actually go to Atlanta? Is Elvis *only* in Memphis?"

Coop didn't look appreciably happier. "Do you have to be so pragmatic?"

She smiled. "Just returning the favor. I know how crabby you get after a couple hours with a cat. I can't imagine driving in a small car with you after a whole night spent with a sampling from each entomological species on southern Louisiana sharing your bed. Can we come back in the winter?"

He tilted his head a little, and Brooke thought how winsome those eyes that usually faced the world with such authority looked. "Promise?"

That was all it took for the heat to rise in her. Heat Brooke was sure had been transmitted directly through Pete's fingertips—those same fingers that had trapped her breasts the night before and taught her with one caress what Mamie had been trying to with years of words.

She fought to keep hold of his gaze, to prevent the blush she knew was even now staining her throat. She tried her very best to answer him with even a few of the words that had been bouncing around in her head for the past twenty hours or so. Somehow, just the memory of what had happened the night before, the turmoil brought on by the past few hours, smothered her voice.

Pete understood and acted. "Let's take a walk," he offered.

Brooke nodded, and ten minutes later found herself being ushered back out into the sultry night by the maître d' himself.

"Do you eat in places like that all the time?" she demanded, slinging her purse over her bare shoulder as Pete wrapped his arm around her waist to walk her down the street. Without thinking about it, she returned the favor, settling comfortably against his hip.

ISN'T IT ROMANTIC? 103

"At least four nights a week," he retorted dryly. "The other three nights I have Nubian slaves feed me peeled grapes."

She chuckled. "Well, find your own on this trip, bud, 'cause I have trouble enough feeding myself." She shook her head, marveling at her first experience at a world-famous restaurant. "I'm not sure I could get used to that. I mean, every time I got up somebody grabbed my chair. I have the feeling that if I'd sneezed, one of them would have wiped my nose for me."

Pete looked down on her in amazement. "Don't tell me you didn't like that," he challenged. "You were the one who always talked about going to a real restaurant someday."

Brooke scowled as she sidestepped a rather gregarious reveler. "If memory serves, I made that statement sitting inside the booth at Burgerworld. I don't think that place even got a rating from the health department."

"So, you mean that if we did get to Atlanta and I offered to take you to the Dining Room at the Ritz, or Bone's or 103 West, where I have regular tables, you'd be forced to say no?"

Brooke grinned over at him, the memory of that dinner still fresh on her tongue, that shameful attention still warming her. "Don't be ridiculous."

He laughed, giving her a squeeze. "That's what I thought."

"You know," she mused, eyes up to the night sky and the throb of neon. "There is still quite a discussion on which is really the finest restaurant in New Orleans. And while Antoine's certainly has its supporters, there are those who favor Galatoire's. I, for one, would be loathe to even enter into the discussion without a fair sampling of some others." Fighting a grin, she turned an intent gaze on him. "Do you see what I mean?"

She looked over to find the laughter back in Pete's eyes, the easy outrage that passed between the two of them as friendship. "I've created a monster," he mourned.

She gave him the smile of her life. "You sure have."

For a while they strolled on in silence, just enjoying the New Orleans night. The Quarter came to life in the dark, with its gaudy neon and gaudier music. The clip-clop of mules drawing carriages punctuated the wail of clarinets, and laughter took on a sharper, more brittle edge. The air was still redolent with the spices of the river, the kitchens and the gardens. The night beyond these balconied buildings still carried the music of a

104 ISN'T IT ROMANTIC?

river port at night. But within those few blocks, life was as bright and playful as a circus at the edge of town.

The bad part was that drunks didn't obey the rules of the sidewalk, so that more than once Brooke ended up with alcohol cooling her dress and a blank, grinning face mumbling incoherent apologies. The good part was that those same drunks couldn't focus enough to recognize the famous Pete Cooper visage. No one gaped in astonishment or made stupid jokes about how the world was able to survive without Pete's reporting on it. No one made mention of the fact that this world-famous newsman, veteran inductee into the Bachelor-of-the-Year rolls, had his arm around an unknown woman as he threaded his way through the crowds.

Tonight amidst the anonymity of the Quarter, Pete and Brooke could be Coop and Stump again. They could walk along as unmolested as any other pedestrian. They could act like tourists and ride along in the open carriages, the driver offering advice, directions and general observations like any cabby anywhere, and then sit in a succession of clubs listening to sweating musicians batter the old walls with new music.

They could also, it seemed, be mugged.

"You've got to be kidding," was Brooke's first reaction.

"Shut up, Stump," Pete advised carefully as he faced the very nervous youth with the gun.

"He's right, lady," the boy echoed. "Shut up. Gimme your purse and wallet, we be even."

"But—"

Pete never gave her the chance to protest. Whipping her purse off her shoulder, he tossed it across at the same time he dug for his wallet. "I don't have much cash left," he said, his voice admirably calm. "Can I hang on to my driver's license?"

"Han' it over!"

That was about when it began to sink into Brooke that this guy really had a gun, and his hand was really shaky and sweaty as he pointed it first at Pete and then her. It was when she realized that if this kid was really as strung out as he looked, she and Pete could very well be balanced a millimeter or two from landing in a trauma center. If not sharing space in the crypt with Mamie.

ISN'T IT ROMANTIC? 105

All in all, she'd prefer to hold off on that option as long as possible. So she shut up, just as Pete suggested, and didn't even think of the extra gun that young boy was holding in her purse.

Pete was handing over his wallet when the kid's eyes narrowed. "I know you, don't I?"

"Now is not the time for this," Brooke muttered, her own hands sweating as they waved unsteadily in the air somewhere near her unprotected shoulders. The three of them were standing bare yards into a darkened alley where the boy had pushed them once he'd proved to Pete that the pressure against his kidneys was a Saturday night special. Of all the times for the Quarter to be its noisiest, its most unnoticing, this had to be it.

When Pete didn't answer fast enough, the boy jammed the gun in his belly. "I ask you a question, man."

Brooke was the one who flinched.

"My name's Pete Cooper," Pete allowed reasonably, still much too calm for having a pistol barrel shoved into his navel.

The boy seemed to jump a little, the gun digging deeper as a ghastly smile flickered over his features. "Man, oh man, now wouldn't that get me a name, poppin' somebody like you?" he demanded to himself. "I'd be in for sure."

This evening was definitely not taking the turn Brooke had anticipated. A serious discussion maybe, a reorganizing of the trip, maybe a nightcap out in the Bellermain gardens under the moonlight. Certainly not imminent murder.

"It's time for your gun now, Brooke," Pete said evenly. "Don't you think?"

Brooke whipped around on him. "What?"

"What?" the boy demanded in syncopated harmony, already turning to answer the new threat.

It seemed all Pete needed. When the boy pulled the gun far enough out of the way, Pete swung on him. One arm chopped down. Another swung across somehow, and then, from somewhere else, a leg, like ballet in the dark, sending the young boy tumbling back onto the pavement.

Standing no more than four feet away, Brooke watched in stupid silence, Pete's actions too quick and silent for comprehension, the violence over almost before it began.

Only the sudden explosion of the gun brought her back to life.

"Pete!"

106 ISN'T IT ROMANTIC?

But the gun was already clattering to the ground, skidding against the wall of the building to their right. Pete crouched over their assailant, who was scrambling to his feet. Urged by instinct, by the training she'd had and the knowledge that the last thing they needed was for that very unstable young man to get his hands back on the gun again, Brooke dived for it.

By the time she straightened, the slick weapon clutched frantically in her sweaty hands, the boy was already running back out the alley. Instead of giving him chase, Pete simply bent over to retrieve the purse and wallet that had fallen unnoticed to the ground.

"Why aren't you going after him?" Brooke demanded, her voice tremulous. She could hear footsteps pounding their way and the first wails of a siren.

Pete turned back on her and straightened. "I'm not James Bond," he reminded her dryly, taking the time to gingerly push the gun barrel in a different direction. "Why didn't you shoot him with that gun you're licensed to carry?"

Brooke giggled, the adrenaline finally pouring through her, not thinking to lower the weapon any further. "You never gave me the chance," she lied with a brash grin. "Finally got to use all those karate lessons, huh?"

His answering smile was smug. "A good newsman is prepared for anything."

He was looking down, his face creased in consternation, the purse still in his hand, when the police descended on them.

Brooke's attention was on Pete.

"All right, lady. Just hand it over," the first officer suggested. "I'm sure you two can settle it some other way."

Stunned, Brooke looked up to find two young officers braced about ten feet from her, guns drawn, attention all hers. That was when she remembered that she still had the gun in her hands.

"Oh, my—"

She would have dropped it onto the ground if Pete hadn't had a little more presence of mind. Grinning, he reached out and carefully plucked it out of her hands.

"She's just a little high-strung," he informed the officers with glee. "We've been mugged."

"Hey," one of the policemen said, stepping closer. "Aren't you Pete Cooper?"

ISN'T IT ROMANTIC? 107

Pete handed Brooke her purse. "And here I was thinking how maybe I'd make it through the rest of the evening without being recognized again."

Within an hour, not only every policeman in the city knew that Pete Cooper had prevented a mugging with some fancy footwork, but every news station. Pete and Brooke ended up down at the police station, filling out forms, drinking bad coffee and avoiding minicams. Pete was his usual affable self, composed and smiling and unflappable in the face of all the attention. Brooke felt as if she were going to crumble into little bits. Her coffee cup shook and one of the policemen had offered his jacket to help warm her, even though the air-conditioning wasn't anything to write home about. And as she sat there at the battered old desk listening to another war story being traded, she thought to herself that Pete was putting on a hell of a front.

She couldn't put her finger on it, but something bothered her. Not his smile, which was broad and easy, or his stance, which was comfortable. Not the fact that he refused interviews. The police knew all about his ruse to stay off work a few more days, and they were delighted to assist in the conspiracy.

But something.

She found out when Pete excused himself to head into the men's room. She followed.

"I really don't think you need protection in here," he protested with raised eyebrows, his voice echoing around the scuffed, aging tile walls. "The only guys with guns out there are on our side."

She glared at him, hands on hips, the blue nylon jacket rustling at her shoulders. She could suddenly see it under the fluorescents. He was sweating, a bit gray, and he was leaning up against the counter with a trembling hand.

"Give," was all she said.

He feigned innocence. "You law-enforcement types are all alike. No respect for privacy."

"I'll stand here until you blow up if I have to, bud," she threatened.

He grinned right back. "And I'll just attend to business while you watch. You forget, I've covered some pretty primitive places."

"You've also never fooled me once in your life. What's wrong?"

108   ISN'T IT ROMANTIC?

He sighed, and she saw those faint lines appear on his forehead, creases of weariness that had no business there. "Aftereffects," he admitted ruefully. "Usually if something big happens I can wait until I get back to the hotel room before I get the shakes, where nobody can see it happen." His quick, steely glare betrayed the fact that she was the first to witness the event. But then his expression folded again into weary resignation. "I guess getting shot moved up the timetable a little."

"Getting what?" Brooke demanded suspiciously, not for a minute believing him.

So Pete showed her.

She gaped. "You stupid son of a—"

"Keep it down, will you?" he demanded, pulling her closer in case he had to enforce his request. With his other hand, he grabbed some paper towels to wet. His hands were suddenly shaking so badly he dropped more than he collected.

"Pete, for God's sake," Brooke protested, "why didn't you tell anyone?"

There was an angry slash along his ribs, the blood now caked and dried to his shirt. Wetting the towels, he began to dab at it.

"Because the last thing I want is the notoriety."

"You *already* got the notoriety," Brooke retorted, yanking the towels from his hand and taking over the task. Pete conceded, his shirt bunched up in his hands, his features tensed in a tight grimace, his legs suddenly a mite wobbly.

"You know what I mean," he said, flinching at her ministrations. "I just want to go back to Alex's, Brooke. And then, in the morning, I want to drive off to find Elvis. Maybe get lost on the Natchez Trace someplace and not have to face Evan or the wire service or all that wide-eyed astonishment out there. Are the bayous still out of the question?"

Brooke gave him quite a glare of her own. "You have to get this taken care of," she insisted, realizing that they'd made a mistake getting it wet. They were making it bleed again.

"It's just a—"

She bolted upright, outraged. "You say it's just a flesh wound, and I'll smack you, I swear," she snarled. "You look like you're gonna pass out on me, and that's just what I need, to be found in the rest room at the New Orleans police station with an unconscious man with a gunshot wound. Then what am I gonna do?"

ISN'T IT ROMANTIC?

Amazingly enough, she made him smile. "You can nurse me," he taunted, that crooked cant of his mouth fatal. "Just like in all the westerns."

She gave him no quarter. "You're an idiot."

He nodded. "But you'll help me, Stump. Won't you?"

"How?" she demanded. "You're gonna get found out. Especially now." Frustrated, enchanted, furious, she shook her head. "Alex was right," she mourned. "You really do have the kiss of death."

Pete leaned right over and dropped the real thing on her lips. "Come on, Stump. Give a guy a break."

Just then one of the officers saw fit to answer the call of nature. Brooke being certainly one of the last people he expected to run into, he slid to an unceremonious halt, eyes wide, hands already at zipper.

She smiled, stepping in front of Pete so he could surreptitiously hide the evidence. "We're inseparable," she allowed brightly.

The officer couldn't seem to pull a sensible answer together. Finally giving up completely, he turned to Pete. "Lieutenant told me to let you know, your boss called again. He wants you to call him by eight tomorrow at the latest. Sounded really upset."

Pete nodded. "Yeah, thanks."

"In that case," Brooke announced, turning to give Pete an affectionate pat on the rib cage, "I have to go find a couple of cats."

She was satisfied to hear his heartfelt groan as she strolled on out the door.

Eight

New Orleans Times May 27—

Last evening at approximately midnight, IBN anchor Pete Cooper thwarted an attempted assault on himself and a lady companion in the French Quarter. The assailant escaped, but after facing Cooper's anger, left without the booty he'd sought. Cooper was unavailable for comment....

"Aah-choo!...ow..."

"Serves you right."

"Did you have to make it three cats? Three big cats?"

"I would have made it a leopard and a cranky puma if I could have. You're going to get this thing infected, and your rib's probably broken, and I'm gonna end up with a feverish anchor somewhere in a motel in Mississippi and have to explain to the local doctor that you were shot, but that I didn't do it...."

"You're blowing this all up out of proportion...aah..."

ISN'T IT ROMANTIC? 111

Busy squirting antibiotic ointment into the still-oozing slash along Pete's fifth rib, Brooke finally enjoyed a well-deserved smile. "Yes?"

After dispensing with yet another sneeze and moan, Pete scowled at her. "You're heartless."

She repaid his kiss of the night before. "You bet. What did Evan say?"

Pete took a second to answer as he held the new gauze against his side while Brooke taped it. She could see the discomfort on his features, and not just from the renewed attack of allergies. This damn thing was hurting him, and it was his own stupid fault.

It wasn't, really. It was just that Brooke still got weak-kneed when she thought how close he'd come to crumpling down to the ground in that alley and never getting back up, and the only way she could deal with that was to yell at him. Now, finally, she understood why her mother had yelled at her when she'd fallen out of the tree and broken her arm. She'd yelled and then she'd cried. It was exactly what Brooke felt like doing.

"Evan said," he rasped, his voice ghastly, his attention on her handiwork, "that he couldn't figure out how I could get into so much trouble on sick leave."

"He doesn't seem to know you very well."

"I told him that just because I couldn't talk didn't mean I couldn't mourn. That I was fulfilling the tenets of my aunt's will."

"Which he took well, I'm sure."

"Actually, having Alex get on the phone and swear that I really did sound this bad helped. Evan's never been able to argue with Alex."

"You're not going to tell her that you got shot, either?"

"She'll just worry."

Brooke looked up from where she was stabilizing the last piece of tape. "And I won't?"

He flashed her that same damn crooked smile that shot down all her protests. "Where are we going today, nurse?"

She scowled heartily, wanting very badly to grin, to chuckle back at his outrageous charm. "Straight to the sanitarium. You're nuts."

"But you love me anyway."

Brooke gave the tape one last little smack that provoked a predictable reaction and straightened. "Don't push it."

ISN'T IT ROMANTIC?

The car was all packed and ready to go. Rene had bid his goodbyes before leaving for the airport and a trip to Zurich, and Alex waited downstairs with a picnic basket she and her maid had packed for the trip. All that was left was getting Pete downstairs, too.

"Here," Brooke offered curtly as she flipped a prescription bottle at him. "Take one."

Pete took a good look at the name on the bottle. "Boy, you *are* prepared."

"I told you," she retorted, stuffing the rest of the bandages she'd bought that morning into her overnighter along with her toothbrush and maps. "I'd tap-dance naked down Wall Street to get rid of my cramps."

Pete looked up, amazed. "You always said they were bad. I didn't realize they were this bad."

Her smile was dry. "No man does."

"And the pill doesn't help?"

"Most of the time. I keep these handy in case I get thrown off." Her smile was not pleasant. "Like finding myself in a tornado and a mugging in the same week."

Pete grimaced as he flipped the bottle back to her unopened. "This ought to be a great trip."

Brooke glared at him, suddenly frustrated all out of proportion and not sure why. "I'm not going to spend ten hours in that car listening to you whine. Take the damn medicine."

Pete lifted an eyebrow, his mouth quirking again. "Shouldn't I be the one in the bad mood? After all, I'm the one who's bleeding."

Brooke huffed indignantly. "I'm the one who has to put up with you."

Very gingerly he got to his feet and tucked his T-shirt into his jeans. "Are you going to be this pleasant all the way to Memphis?"

"I don't know," she said, making great show of zipping up her bag. "I don't know what other disasters await, do I?"

That bright new dress she'd worn last night wouldn't stay put in the bag. Brooke tried stuffing it down further so the zipper would work. She didn't notice that Pete had approached until his hands were on her arms.

"You want to talk to me before we're all alone in that very small car where you won't have nearly enough room to get a good head of steam up?" he asked gently.

ISN'T IT ROMANTIC? 113

She refused to look at him. It didn't help that her hands were shaking, or that she hadn't gotten any sleep last night again. Every time she'd started to fade off she'd relived that moment in the alley, except that in her dream she'd seen Pete get shot. Except that Pete had died, right there in the puddle of blackness at the edge of the French Quarter, and she'd been unable to stop it.

What did he want from her after a night like that? After scrambling around to find cats to make him sick and then sneaking out to find a pharmacy to counteract all the discomfort. And now he was acting like John Wayne and refusing to admit that he even hurt.

And the worst part was, that wasn't even what was making her want to cry.

"I don't know," she admitted miserably, head down, eyes squeezed shut. "I don't know what's wrong. I just feel like hitting somebody."

"Can you make it somebody else?" he asked gently, his voice very close. "I'm already a little sore."

Brooke took a deep breath. "I've lived my entire life in Rupert Springs," she said. "Very orderly, very predictable. I know everybody, know how everybody sees me. No surprises, except the ordinary ones. And when I finally decide to throw caution to the wind and just take off for an adventure, the adventure takes off on me. I'm not sure I'm made for a life of excitement."

It seemed perfectly natural that Pete would fold her into his arms. After all, he'd done it when she'd been stood up for the spring dance, and again when she'd had her heart broken the first time. No, she thought, the second time. Pete had been the first to do that.

She laid her head against his chest and wrapped her arms around him, her arm resting against the fresh bandage, and thought of the changes in their lives, in their relationship. She thought of the life she'd expected and the one she'd ended up with. She thought of how she felt like crying because in a few days she was going to have to go back to that neat, orderly, unexciting life where Pete was only as close as a telephone. Where she couldn't hear the steady reassurance of his heart and feel the sweet warmth of his embrace.

Where she might never again be the one to conspire with him to escape the pressures of being Pete Cooper.

114   ISN'T IT ROMANTIC?

"Stump," he offered, a hand in her hair, "you're entitled to a few nerves. It's been quite a few days."

Brooke didn't want platitudes. What she wanted was silence and strength. She wanted Pete to just be there for her again.

"Don't patronize me, Coop," she threatened miserably. "Just hold me."

He did. For a few minutes they simply stood where they were, wrapped in each other's arms, closed off from the world, sharing the dregs of fear and exhilaration and upheaval. Behind them dust motes danced in the hot Louisiana sun that poured in through the tall windows where the moon had so recently visited. Traffic muttered and growled, and out in the trees birds chattered. But in that cool white room with its lacy four-poster and walnut armoire and hardwood floors and history a hundred-and-fifty years old, Pete and Coop reaffirmed their own. They fit in each other's arms with an ease neither thought to comment on anymore and reassured themselves with small pats and caresses. And when Alex called from the stairs, they parted with newly hesitant smiles that held the sum of their changing friendship.

Once past Pontchartrain, they stuck to the back roads again. Mississippi this time, great stands of pine forest, and lumber mills that smelled like powerfully rotten eggs, and small towns up and down the rolling landscape. And kudzu. If Brooke ever thought of the South again after that trip, she decided, she'd sum up the landscape in that one word. Blanketing the side of the road, coating the trees and hanging down like Spanish moss, thick green and glossy everywhere, it was the one pervasive symbol of Southern roadways.

By the time they stopped for lunch, Pete had chosen antihistamines over pain medicine and spent the better part of the morning dozing in the other seat, leaving Brooke to listen to country music on the radio and wonder what she'd gotten herself into. It was getting harder to watch him asleep and vulnerable like that. Her friend. Her buddy. The man she'd been in love with most of her life.

What was it she wanted? she wondered. She fought him when he tried to get close and then abused him when he moved away. She shrilled at him when he entrusted his secrets with her and yet protected him like a lioness.

ISN'T IT ROMANTIC? 115

Her friend. Her buddy.

She looked over at him, his hair disarrayed as if he'd been dragging fingers through it, his face drawn and pale, his eyes once again swollen. He couldn't have stayed in Atlanta, where both of them were safe, where status could have stayed quo. He couldn't have understood how fragile Brooke's state of mind was.

How was it that Pete Cooper, who had known so very much all these years, who had understood things about Brooke that she hadn't, still hadn't realized that she was in love with him?

Why was it that Brooke hadn't realized the same thing?

"Where are we?"

Switching off the ignition and looking around, Brooke shrugged. "I don't know. My navigator's been asleep."

Pete tried stretching and then thought better of it. "Unpredictable lot, those navigators. How long have I been out?"

Brooke scowled at him. "You've been watching too many Bogart movies. One asks a question like that after being hit on the head, not dosing oneself with antihistamines."

"You ever take antihistamines?" he asked.

"Nope."

He nodded. "There isn't much difference. It looks like a park."

"That's what the sign said when I pulled in. I figured we could stop for a little nourishment. That is, if the patient doesn't mind."

"The patient will even help you unload the food."

Brooke had found some pine trees, tall sentinels that whispered with the constant wind and flavored the air with their sharp tang. Nearby a stream chuckled, and small birds danced along picnic tables looking for handouts. After the humidity of the gulf, the air here seemed clear and sweet. Brooke eschewed the tables to spread their bounty out on the grass nearby where they could see the land roll away from them and hear the wildlife.

"How are your ribs?" she asked, passing across a plate of fried chicken and pasta salad.

"Actually, not bad," Pete allowed, stretching out on the ground. "How 'bout you?"

"My ribs are fine, thanks."

He squinted over at her. "How 'bout your temper?"

116 ISN'T IT ROMANTIC?

She gave him a sweet smile in return. "Greatly salved by watching you sneeze your way around that gunshot wound this morning, thanks. I always feel that those pipers have a way of getting paid, one way or another."

"You went into the wrong business," he scowled as he tested his lunch. "You should have been in corrections. Or motherhood."

It took Brooke a minute to answer. She was busy watching the sunlight play in Pete's still-tumbled hair, thinking of how very relaxed and peaceful he looked for having just survived a rather violent attack and the subsequent attention. Stretched out on his unaffected side, in jeans and his Hard Rock shirt, his arms sleek and powerful, his torso as tight as sculpted marble through the soft material, his legs strong.

For that moment, nestled in the sun's warmth, in the companionable silence of the forest, Brooke thought of how that body had fit against hers the other night, how the sudden heat of his arousal had damn near robbed all the strength from her resolve.

She'd dreamed about that, too, actually tumbling in Pete's arms, her imagination no longer limited by a child's dreams, really seeing that fierce desire in Pete's eyes, really knowing his hands on her, testing the force of his very real arousal.

For her. His desire for her.

For a brief moment longer, she allowed herself to suffer the sharp ache of yearning. Surrendered to the understanding that no matter how much she'd argued, with herself and Pete, it was something she'd dreamed of before. Something she'd dreamed of frequently. It was still something that would ruin what she had, and she knew it.

That didn't mean that she could so easily put it back in its place.

"Brooke?"

She obviously wasn't as sly about her fantasizing as she'd thought. Fighting the urge to blush, Brooke turned her attention to her food.

"Sorry," she admitted. "I was just thinking how mundane life's going to be once I'm not dodging natural disasters and jumpy muggers anymore."

Pete picked at his chicken, his own attention ostensibly on his food. "What are you going to do?" he asked.

ISN'T IT ROMANTIC? 117

Brooke looked up, unsure of his meaning, not trusting the offhand tone of his voice. "About what?"

Pete didn't quite look up. "Work."

She still wasn't following him. "Hope they didn't find out I was caught in the men's room in New Orleans, I guess. That tends to make truckers a little nervous."

Pete finally looked up, and Brooke was sure she didn't like the fact that she didn't find any humor in his eyes.

"You don't have to stay in Rupert Springs anymore, Brooke."

Now she was sure she didn't like it. "You make it sound like a jail sentence," she said carefully, her hand wrapped around the plastic fork, her back stiffening a bit.

Shrugging, Pete returned his attention to lunch. "Isn't it?"

She wanted to be able to smile. To throw off a quick line about one man's heaven. The problem was that this was something she didn't find very funny.

"For you," she admitted.

Pete looked up, a little surprised. "What about you? You've only stayed home because of your parents and Mamie. Well, they're all gone now. Isn't it time you got out of there and stretched your wings a little?"

She shouldn't be having this conversation here. She shouldn't really be having it anywhere. There were some things even Pete didn't know, truths she'd come to realize over the years that didn't reassure her much. Maybe if he knew now, he wouldn't be so anxious to torment her into taking her place in the kind of worlds he traveled. Maybe she'd just tell him and find out.

"Pete," she countered quietly, "I've stretched my wings about as far as they'll go."

"Don't be ridiculous," he retorted, now sitting straight up, the movement provoking a brief wince. "You have a degree in art history and more class than anybody else in that town. You have no business being there."

"I like it there," she said.

That brought him to a dead silence. Staring at her, his eyes betraying as much confusion as outrage. "That's not what you've been saying all these years."

She dipped her head, anxious to be away from the disappointment she knew was coming. Wishing that things could be different, that she could be different. "And how do I admit that I don't belong anyplace but a dot on the map in the middle of

118   ISN'T IT ROMANTIC?

nowhere?'' she demanded quietly. ''That I've finally come to the realization that a twenty-six-year-old has to come to grips with reality instead of living on wishful thinking?''

''What reality?''

She did manage to face him, then, and it hurt. ''Dreams are really nice at eighteen,'' she admitted. ''When you're that age, anything's possible. But then, life gets in the way. It makes you realize that at most you settle for what you get. You've made your way, Pete. You've done what only one in a million people manage to do. Well, I'm not one in a million people. I'm one of the people who had to settle for what came, because I just wasn't special enough to be singular.''

''Of course you're special.''

Her smile was wistful. ''I'm an office worker, Pete. Just like millions of other office workers. I do my job, I go home, and on a good night I get to watch an interesting movie on television with my popcorn. And the thing that makes that all bearable is that I have friends around me who might share my popcorn or call and talk about their day. I'm not Alex St. Claire, and I never will be.''

She knew she was frustrating him. Knew he didn't really understand, even after all this time. Pete had escaped. He'd won. He figured that anybody could.

''But, Stump, what about your education? What about the fact that nobody in that dead little town knows half of what you do?''

She could only offer a shrug. ''So I'm like a big percentage of the world with degrees. I love what I've had, Coop. I've never regretted taking those years for it. But I simply don't have the drive to storm New York and prove myself anymore.''

She'd been wrong. It wasn't disappointment that flared in those spring-soft eyes, but anger. Hot, sudden anger the likes of which Brooke hadn't seen in years. Frustration, fury.

She'd sure kicked over a tree stump that had memories crawling beneath it.

''And that's going to be it? Just settling into your place without a whimper? Disappearing into the mainstream because you don't care enough to fight it?''

She didn't know what to do, how to argue. She hadn't expected such ferocity from him. ''I guess.''

His plate hit the ground right before hers did. Pete grabbed hold of her by the arm, his fingers steely and unforgiving, his

ISN'T IT ROMANTIC?

glare as dark as damnation. Suddenly Brooke didn't recognize him. She didn't know this man who battled for the words she could almost see tumbling around beneath those glittering, feverish eyes.

"You little idiot," he accused, giving her a shake that almost hurt. "Don't you understand anything?"

"Understand what?" she retorted, too stunned to pull away, too shaken to protest. "The truth? That I'm not one in a million?"

He shook her again. "But you *are*, damn it. You're worth more than that entire town stood one on top of each other. You don't belong there any more than my mother did, and it's gonna kill you too."

Brooke's breath died. Her mouth opened, but nothing came out. Nothing forced itself through the maelstrom in her chest with which to challenge him.

They hadn't talked about this, not really, not ever. Brooke knew all about what Pete had faced as a kid, the censure, the looks, the assumptions leveled on a confused boy by a small-minded town. But in all that time, never once had Pete opened up about the cause.

"Coop. . ." Her voice was hushed, stricken. She could hear it. She saw it reflect in the turmoil in his eyes.

"Why do you think my parents drank?" he demanded harshly. "Both of them, right up till the day they died. It was because they were trapped in that place, forced to fit themselves into the mold the town demanded. Two brilliant, creative people stuck in the one place no one understood. And the more my mother hurt, the more she drank. And when my dad saw how she was dying, he did it too. Right up until that night the highway patrol called. Damn it, Brooke, do you think I want to see that happen to you?"

"It didn't happen to Mamie," she protested, his hold hurting her, his raw grief hurting her immeasurably more. She'd never met Coop's parents. They'd been dead by the time he was ten. She'd known how their tragedy had affected Coop. She'd seen it drive him through a troubled childhood and then away from the only family he had left. But she hadn't ever heard the acid that churned beneath all that determination. "She was exactly the person she wanted to be."

120 ISN'T IT ROMANTIC?

"And the only people who didn't laugh at her behind her back were your family. Mamie relished being as different from everybody else as she could. You don't."

No, Brooke thought, she didn't. She felt it right between her shoulder blades every time she walked down the street, right where Mrs. Walker watched her from the front window of the Shop'n Wash as Brooke walked by. She felt it settling like a weight on her shoulders each time she tried to explain the modern prints that decorated the old Fergusons' walls where only pastoral scenes and animal portraits had previously hung. She felt it each time she heard Pete's voice on the phone and thought of all the world events she wanted to discuss with him because no one in Rupert Springs would understand their importance.

But it wasn't as simple as that. "I'm twenty-six, Coop."

"So what?"

"So, what do I do? Where do I go? Maybe you've always been the kind of person to strike off for new territory without thinking about it, but I'm not."

"Then what's this all about?" he demanded, waving a hand behind him as if he could encompass the entire trip within it.

"That's different," she argued. "It's not my entire life. It's not forfeiting my entire support system just to test your theories."

For a minute, he just looked at her. Just unleashed a desperate yearning that Brooke knew was born back in those awful, sad years before he'd been sent to live with his aunt, back when his beautiful, fragile mother had spent her days on the couch and her nights down at the Rupert Hotel sharing "quality" time with her husband.

And maybe that was why she lost her fight. Maybe that was why every other protest she'd ever erected over the years to Pete's attraction, to his sudden admissions and invitations, crumbled, at least for a few minutes.

"Don't do it," he begged, his eyes as taut as his hands, pulling her closer. "Please, Brooke. Don't give in. You're better than that."

"How do you know?" she demanded instinctively, hearing all the cautions of her family rather than Mamie's cheerleading. Knowing that friends offered support even when there was none. "You've been away for the last ten years. It's really easy

ISN'T IT ROMANTIC? 121

to think whatever the hell you want when you're six hundred miles away."

That brought him to his feet. Glaring down at her, he stood there, the sun at his back, the wind plucking at his hair, frustration shimmering from the taut lines of his frame. And then he turned and stalked away across the grass.

"Coop?"

He didn't answer. He simply stood at the top of the small rise, hands jammed in pockets, head back, and looked out over the trees.

"Coop."

Brooke climbed to her own feet, the picnic forgotten beside her. Too much had been said in the past few minutes, too little. She could still see his face when he'd mentioned his mother, and it seared her through. Brooke had known all along about the Coopers. After all, they'd been the sort of town gossip that lived on forever. "Oh, those Coopers, yes. Quite a couple, weren't they? Neither one of them fit to drive a car, much less raise a small boy. Pitiful, pitiful."

Knitted eyebrows and clucking tongues. And never a hand held out in assistance. Brooke had known. But Pete had never once allowed his parents to be brought up to him. He hadn't spoken of them except to say he missed them, hadn't allowed what their deaths—and their short, tragic lives—had done to him. Even to Brooke. Even to his best buddy.

And now, in the space of a single look, when his defenses had finally fallen in an attempt to convince her, Brooke had seen. She'd understood where every barb had landed from those small-town judges, from his own aunts and cousins. She knew what it had been like for an eight-year-old boy to have to get his mother to bed and then to be left alone.

She wanted to hold him, to soothe away that old disillusionment. Instead, she'd chased him off again.

"You want to know how I know that you're better than that?" he finally said, turning back on her.

Brooke blinked up at him, thrown off balance yet again. He was smiling.

"Coop, I'm sorry—"

He strode back down to her. "You wanted to know," he repeated, and for the first time Brooke saw the determination right behind that smile. She backed up a step.

122 ISN'T IT ROMANTIC?

"No," she demurred, suddenly shaky. "Not really. Let's just drop it and get back to, uh, lunch."

But Pete was shaking his head. "You wanted to know." He walked up to her so that she couldn't escape, not his words, nor his gaze nor the hands he reached out to her.

Brooke flinched, shuddered. There was something more in his eyes all of a sudden, a fire that had no place here on a hill in a state park. That had no business anywhere in her life.

"You want the truth?" he demanded.

Shying away, her eyes down, she shook her head. "No."

"Oh, yes you do, Stump. You asked me." He'd moved closer, close enough that Brooke could smell the soap he'd used that morning, could feel the fan of his breath on her cheek. She could feel the heat begin to curl from his fingers where they held her once more—but differently. "Well, I'm going to tell you."

She shook her head again, her gaze caught by the sleek line of his thigh, by the taut betrayal of denim. "Don't."

Just like before, he lifted her chin. Captured her gaze, demanded her attention. Just like before, she couldn't deny it.

"I didn't," he admitted, his voice like dark smoke, his smile at once rueful and seductive. "Not really. Not until the minute I saw you again at the funeral. And again at the Badger Bar, and riding around on that Harley with your hair whipping out behind you in the wind."

As if to punctuate his point, he reached up to wrap a strand around his finger. A stab of alarm shot through Brooke like lightning—except that it felt delicious, which alarmed her even more.

"You never let me finish the other night," Pete was saying, and his eyes softened to the color of a deep sea, mesmerizing and powerful. Drawing Brooke in like a sailor beneath the waves. She wanted to protest, to protect herself from the spell he was weaving. She couldn't manage so much as a breath.

"I didn't get to the real reason Rene was hitting on you," he said, curling his finger into her hair and then slowly pulling it free again. Repeating the action, the sensation hypnotic and seductive. "Why I've been wanting to hit on you."

His hands paralyzed her. His gaze burned her, suddenly everything she'd yearned for, more than she'd ever expected. Hot, hungry, fatally sweet.

ISN'T IT ROMANTIC? 123

"Not just your hair or your eyes or your breasts," he whispered, his eyes never faltering, never retreating. "Something else."

His hand strayed again, to her throat, the throat he'd exposed to the moonlight, and now to the sunlight, whose heat seemed to burn Brooke. Or maybe it was his hand, resting there.

"Something more..."

He traced a line along her shoulder, down her arm. "You have style," he admitted, his voice almost surprised. His gaze still trapping Brooke into speechlessness, he bent to drop a quick, soft kiss on her lips. "Grace..." He returned, taking a longer taste, sharing the tastes of spices and heat, sampling her mouth like a delicacy on a pastry tray. "Passion..."

Brooke heard a small, helpless moan and realized it was hers. She didn't see Pete's eyes anymore. Hers were closed. Her world had shrunk to his touch, his scent, his sound. His hand as it eased its way along the hem of her shirt where it skimmed the top of her jeans. His arm where it held her up. His mouth where it plundered hers. Beside them the breeze played with their picnic, sending a napkin tumbling up the hill and a corner of the tablecloth flapping lazily. One of the small birds, its head cocked suspiciously, hopped up to pick at the grapes that had spilled from their container. In the distance, a train moaned low and mournful. Brooke didn't notice any of it. She only knew that her body had caught fire, and that Pete's hands and mouth were the tinder. She only knew that she'd begun to answer, suddenly hungry for the tastes and sensations he offered, already knowing the way in a thousand dreams and anxious to savor it.

His arms, corded and sleek, his shoulders, built up from all those summers playing baseball back in the county park when he'd hit homers into the duck pond over the rise. His chest, dusted in golden hair, as solid and sinewy as a carved maple, as warm as life.

Brooke didn't notice her misgivings flee or her reservations disintegrate. She heard no more from logic or sense or even the knowledge that she was forever changing that last true constant in her life. She only knew that she'd wanted this as long as she could remember, and suddenly, in the sunlight she forfeited any restraint she'd maintained in the moonlight.

ISN'T IT ROMANTIC?

"Remember what Mamie said all those years?" he insisted, folding her into his arms. "Well, she was right all along. You *are* beautiful . . . you're . . ."

When Pete eased her back onto the grass, she followed.

Nine

WTBS, Atlanta: The Dr. Lilly Show

Today, dear audience, I wish to discuss sexual fantasy.
This wonderful tool does much to enhance your love
life. It can be very fulfilling, almost a re-creation of the
act itself between loved ones....

Brooke had thought after all this time that she'd known what
to expect. She'd dreamed of it often enough, all the way back
from the time when fantasies were a tentative, forbidden thing.
She'd replayed Pete's touches, his kisses, his whispered urg-
ings over and over in dreams where censorship never inter-
fered, where the dance was choreographed by half-admitted
longing and unfettered desire, so that when it finally happened she should have known exactly what his hand would feel
like against her skin, what his mouth would taste like on the
deepest of kisses.

She'd been wrong.

Dreams were phantoms, painted on a shadow, danced to
music of the mind. They lived in the night where nothing was
real, where substance was only imagined and the sweet caress

126   ISN'T IT ROMANTIC?

of a lover was nothing more than the whisper of a sultry night breeze.

Brooke lay in the daylight, bright, strong sunshine that sharpened the world and defined reality. She rested on the earth, the wet, cool grass that tickled her back and cushioned her thighs. She was kissed by a real breeze, the same one that ruffled Pete's hair and teased the trees to whispering. She moved in Pete's arms, those solid, strong arms that had held her in grief and in joy, that had cushioned her falls and supported her first steps into adulthood. She looked into his eyes, and they weren't the eyes of a dream, half-seen, shadowy and dim so that emotion was only a wishful thing. Brooke saw the emotion, saw the heat rise like smoke from a slow fire, darkening that sensuous green, widening his pupils and lowering his lids. She heard the emotion in the sudden staccato of his heart, the rasp of his breathing, the sharp, surprised groans of pleasure he offered her.

She felt the rasp of impatient fingers as he pushed up under her shirt to find her breasts and torment her nipples into delicious pebbles that ached with a splintering impatience to have the warm slide of his tongue against them.

She knew it was real, knew she was stepping over a boundary that should never fall. She knew that after this moment she could never go back and reclaim her friend, but it didn't matter. She'd wanted it too long, and suddenly in this hot summer when everything else was changing, she couldn't deny it again.

There was no patience in their hunger, the only finesse that of trying to work around sore ribs. Need met need and fed the hunger that mated mouths and hands and bodies. There on the grass in the broad, bright sun, they danced, hands capturing tender secrets, tempting, torturing, exploring and exposing. They sang, mouths joining and then parting to seek separate feasts, always murmuring, moaning, their music like the wind and the undulation of the trees around them.

They joined, bodies slick and urgent, hunger exploding into excitement and stoking shudders of delight into whirlwinds of light and sensation, hands scrabbling for purchase, mouths greedily plundering, spending themselves in each other with surprised little cries of discovery.

And then, in spent silence, easing back to rest in each other's arms.

ISN'T IT ROMANTIC? 127

* * *

"Henry, where did you put the diapers?"

Brooke's eyes flew open. Coop was even faster. He'd no more than heard that first car door slam right over the rise before he was halfway to his feet. Then he was back on his knees.

"Damn it—"

And naked as the day he was born.

"Come on," Brooke urged, fighting the desperate urge to giggle as she threw him his jeans and grabbed hers. "They're closing in fast."

He was still rubbing at the ribs that had finally decided to protest. "Let 'em see me, I don't care."

"Mo-o-m, can I go over there?"

So much for not caring. Pete flipped over onto his backside and began to struggle into his slacks. Brooke was already hopping around on one leg, trying to do the same, an eye to that rise, praying that no towheaded witnesses would appear too quickly. For the first time in her life, she couldn't seem to get her bra to work. She finally ended up tossing it in with the picnic stuff and throwing her top over her head.

Just in time, too.

"Hi. Are you having a picnic, too?"

Brooke didn't have the nerve to look over at Pete. "Yeah, we sure are," she answered, her voice breathless with the laughter that crowded perilously close. Another little face appeared alongside the first one and waved. Brooke waved back.

"Get your shoes on," she hissed at Pete. Out of the corner of her eye she could see his shoulders heaving beneath the shirt he'd just managed to yank over his head. She wasn't sure whether he was laughing, too, or suffering from the sudden movement again. At least he was dressed.

Then the third head popped up, but this one belonged to an irritable adult female. And it took her no more than one arch look to correctly assess the situation.

"Darryl, LuAnne, you come away from there," she commanded, yanking on little arms.

That was what did Brooke in. Finally giving in to temptation, she collapsed in gales of laughter right alongside where Pete was still trying to pull on shoes with shaking hands.

"They won't be back," she informed him gleefully, holding her own sides.

128   ISN'T IT ROMANTIC?

He looked as if he were caught dead center between silly mirth and dour disgust. "I almost had a heart attack."

She looked over at him from where her head lay in the grass. "I felt like my father had just surprised me in Bill Elliott's car out on the street. You can move almost as fast as Bill could."

Pete settled for a scowl. "I've been shot. I get a handicap on that."

"You can't get your shoes on, either," she admonished, the adrenaline of discovery still jangling in chorus with the residue of passion along her nerve endings. Shaking her up, whirling her around like a ride on the tilt-o-wheel at the school picnic. Making her hands shake, too, making her unforgivably giddy and shy.

"I don't think I want to finish lunch," she admitted, grabbing Pete's other shoe and doing the honors while he finished the first one.

"I don't think Darryl and LuAnne's mother wants you to, either," he admitted. "I think I'm bleeding again."

Brooke lifted a saucy glare at him. "Serves you right," was all she said. But she met Pete's gaze and saw that it was no more certain than hers, no less disjointed and unsettled.

They'd both given in to impulse, and they'd have to deal with it. But not right now, they both knew. Not just yet, with a surprise family of vacationers within earshot and the jumble of emotions and sensations still too raw to sift through.

"Well, if I take your shirt back off to look at the bandage, LuAnne's mother will call out the police for sure," Brooke advised, dropping her gaze, pulling her hands away. "And I think I've spent enough time with those fine people for a few days. Will you be okay for a while?"

Pete ran his hands through his hair, settling it back into some semblance of order before getting to his feet. "I'll hold out a mile or two."

Brooke got to her own still-shaky legs. "Just make sure you don't get blood all over Mamie's good upholstery."

She got a glare from him, which she returned in kind. At least that broke the tension enough to provoke tentative smiles from them both.

"Hey!" A voice suddenly came from the top of the hill.

Both Pete and Brooke turned toward it, bracing themselves for the worst.

ISN'T IT ROMANTIC? 129

The woman had her hands on her hips, her head thrust forward, her eyes wide. "Aren't you Pete Cooper?"

Pete shot Brooke a dismal glance. "Why?"

The woman proceeded to hold out pen and paper. "Can I have your autograph?"

It did serve him right. Letting his hormones get out of control right in the middle of a park like a randy teen, risking having Brooke exposed, hurt by anybody who might have passed by. He was lucky he hadn't just been discovered, but struck by lightning.

More than an hour and seventy miles later, Pete still couldn't name the single impulse that had pushed him over the edge, couldn't pinpoint the moment he'd known he was going to make love to her, right there in the grass in the middle of the afternoon. At some moment, though, when he'd been caught battling her low sense of self-esteem, when he'd realized suddenly just why Mamie had so relentlessly championed Brooke's cause all these years, his rigid control had given out. Proving her worth got mixed up with salving old hurts and breaking through self-imposed loneliness. Delight and frustration and yearning had boiled over into hunger and sent his edit mode straight into shutdown.

He should have regretted it more. He knew Brooke did. He could see it in the haunted, fragile look that had appeared in her eyes once the laughter of discovery had died, that betrayal of the small wild thing that still existed within her very sophisticated exterior.

She could be so easily hurt, and he'd forgotten. He'd lost it somewhere in the feel of her satin-smooth skin in his hands, the taste of arousal on her breasts, the scent of sandalwood and sunshine in her hair. He'd forfeited caution in the slick, honey-eyed depths of her where he'd found fulfillment for the first time in his long, sorry life.

Brooke. The tagalong, the persistent, annoying little girl with braces and freckles who'd battered him with her attention and unflinchingly defended him against the rest of the town's prejudice. The kind of friend he'd been able to count on when he hadn't counted on his compatriots, his wife, his lover. Brooke, always there for him, as comfortable and easy as a face in the

130 ISN'T IT ROMANTIC?

mirror, as dependable as an accountant, as delightfully surprising as spring.

Brooke.

Damn it, she was right. He was falling in love with her, and that was going to change everything.

Somewhere between question and realization, Pete pulled the car off the side of the road. They were somewhere along the Natchez Trace, the road a slice of wilderness, restful and uncluttered and historic as it dipped and soared through the rolling landscape of Mississippi. Pete noticed none of it.

Brooke looked around as if expecting to find a trooper on their tail. "What's the matter?"

Pete noticed that she'd slipped on sunglasses, and thought of the protection they provided. He made it a point to pull his off.

"We have to talk."

Her head shot around. He could see her eyes widen, even behind the screen of colored glass. "Are you bleeding all over Mamie's upholstery after all?"

Pete made a try for her hand, but she was too fast for him. "Brooke, listen. I'm sorry...."

That worked so well she jumped right out of the car. Pete sighed, berating himself for being a half-assed clod, and followed.

She was standing along the side of the road, her eyes out to the distant blanket of green, her posture rigid, her glasses in her hand.

"That's not what I meant," Pete said, walking up to her.

Her small laugh wasn't pleasant. "What did you mean?" she countered. "My mistake?"

His patience a little thin, he reached out and turned her to him. "I meant that you were right. Everything's different now, isn't it?"

For a very long moment, Brooke looked at him, her eyes huge and dark, brimming with a pain that speared Pete through like the report of that little pistol the night before.

"I guess we forgot to think about that while we were tossing our clothes around," was all she seemed able to say. Pete expected her to sound bitter. Instead, she sounded sad. Lost. Frightened.

He tightened his hold on her, unable to banish the memories of how those arms had felt around his chest, how easily she'd

ISN'T IT ROMANTIC?

fit into his embrace, how perfectly he'd fit into her. It was enough to make a man swear.

"You want to know the worst part?" he asked, crooking his mouth a little.

She shrank even more into herself, not anticipating him at all. "What?"

Pete tried out a smile on her. "I want to do it again."

He knew her too well after all. He saw the relief skim the sky of her eyes, saw the exultation before caution took hold and dimmed the blue into denial.

"No," she demurred, pulling her gaze away. "I don't think the first time was a good idea, and I've never condoned compounding mistakes."

"Was it a mistake?" Pete demanded softly, his thumbs rubbing against the bare skin of her arm, his memories finding their way to his eyes. "Was it such a surprise?"

She battled him with every ounce of obstinacy in her, chin right out there, eyes blazing. "Both," she challenged.

"You didn't enjoy it at all?"

He knew he could catch her there. Brooke was a miserable liar.

She dropped her gaze, tucked in her chin. Avoided him as she answered. "I didn't say that."

"And there's no going back, right?"

That brought her head back up, and with it a glisten of tears that she refused to let fall. "Isn't that what I told you?"

Pete nodded, something new swelling in his chest, something he'd never had to face, even on the night he'd asked the legendary Alicia to marry him at La Tour D'Argent in Paris. Something sweet and sore and perilous.

"Then why don't we just go on ahead?"

That brought the tears to a crest, swelling the shy blue of her eyes, expanding the terror Pete had never expected to see there. "It won't ever be the same," she mourned.

But Pete refused to concede. "But can't it be better?"

Her smile was so sad. "You've always been my best friend. I don't want another one."

"Can't I be your lover, too?"

She shook her head, and Pete thought she'd break his heart. "I don't know," she whispered.

The wind up on this small ridge picked at her hair and sent the sun tumbling through it, a breathtaking gleam of pure ore,

132 ISN'T IT ROMANTIC?

the most beautiful color Pete had ever seen. A color he'd known his whole life but never recognized before. A precious commodity he'd never really known how to protect.

"Come on, Brooke," he urged with voice and eyes and hands. "You have the guts to try."

"I don't have guts at all," she retorted dismally. "Not really."

Pete refused to concede. "You were the one who convinced me to go to college. You shoved me on that plane to New York."

She nodded. "And then I stayed home, right where I belonged."

He pulled her into his arms, close enough to surround her with the strength she'd allowed him, near his heart so she could draw from his certainty.

"But things can't ever be the same again anyway," he said, his hand seeking that delicately spun gold, his eyes closed above the top of her head. "So, what would Mamie tell you to do?"

He actually got a chuckle out of her as she wrapped her arms carefully around him. "To know better than hang around a bad influence like you."

"I mean after that."

"That what's done is done. No use ruing yesterday's rain."

"And?"

She actually sighed, a sound of tentative capitulation that made Pete smile. "Go for the gusto."

Pete nodded against her, closing her even more tightly to him. "Might as well go with friends."

For a bit they remained where they were, wrapped together in silence, hearts still tattooing in a syncopated rhythm, posture newly shy and uncertain. Finally, though, Brooke looked up, and Pete saw a new determination in her eyes.

"Do you really think Mamie would mind if we missed Memphis?" she asked. "I don't think I could face the crowds just yet."

Pete drew a finger along her cheek to collect the few tears that had fallen. "I don't think she'd mind at all. We'll just stop at the next decent town we see, and maybe we won't leave there for a week or so."

Humor fighting its way back into her expression, Brooke raised an eyebrow. "And what about that nasty boss of yours?"

Pete shrugged. "I'm sure there's a cat or two in town."

ISN'T IT ROMANTIC? 133

* * *

Pete wasn't sure how they kept doing it, but they did. Not only was the next town furnished with a quaint bed-and-breakfast in probably the only New England Victorian-style house with a widow's walk in all of Mississippi, but a local Safe Travel Inn whose floor show was everything a will could ask for.

"Tap-dancing Elvis?" Brooke demanded gleefully, standing before the sign. "Oh, I'm not sure about this." She kept trying to sound serious and failed dismally each time the giggles broke through. "You might not survive it."

"One should never look a gift from the gods in the mouth."

"That's a gift horse," Brooke retorted wryly.

"No problem. He probably does Elvis, too."

"We only have one room left," the little woman demurred with a coy smile that reminded Brooke of Letitia.

"Well, now isn't that perfect?" Pete responded with his best smile as he settled a proprietary arm around Brooke's waist. "We just got married."

Brooke battled to keep a straight face as Pete grabbed hold of her left hand to prevent inspection.

The proprietor's smile was at once dubious and delighted. Too much the gracious Southern lady to ask indelicate questions, relieved at the semblance of propriety under her unique roof.

"My name is Sally Mae Merriweather," she introduced herself, a plump hand out. "And you are?"

"John Cooper," Pete allowed with suspicious ease as he bent over her knuckles. Then he turned to Brooke. "And this is Brooke Fer—well, it's Cooper now, isn't it, sugar?"

Brooke overcame the urge to groan. He was enjoying this far too much. Especially when her chest was still on fire. This wasn't going to work. It wasn't going to prevent disaster....

"Cooper," Mrs. Merriweather sang out as she stepped behind her little desk to rescue the key to their room. "You know, you look very much like..."

"Cousin Pete," he assured her. "The resemblance is always causing us trouble," he admitted with a sly smile. "I'm forever getting my picture taken, and he's bein' asked for advice on pork futures."

134   ISN'T IT ROMANTIC?

"Oh, you're in trading?"

"Pigs. Can't have a better friend in the barnyard, Mrs. Merriweather. Intelligent animals, much maligned by the chicken people. I mean, I ask you, what's a few calories among friends. Can you get a good ham from a chicken? Ever heard of chicken chops?"

Brooke didn't think Mrs. Merriweather could care less. Standing stock-still in her flowered organdy dress, the key dangling all but forgotten in her hand, the woman was much too distracted by the mad twinkle in those deadly green eyes.

"Dearest," Brooke admonished dryly, "Mrs. Merriweather doesn't want to hear about your old pigs. Besides, I'll just perish if I don't get myself a nice, long bath. Been driving all day long, don't ya know, Mrs. Merriweather. It fair wears a girl out."

Damn, this stuff could become habit-forming. Brooke beamed at the little woman and couldn't believe when she came to life to give her a conspiratorial pat on the arm.

"You're so right, my dear. Now, if ya'll want to just come along with me."

They came along to the third floor, high above the nodding trees and somnolent town, where the setting sun tinted church steeples pink and gilded the pastureland beyond. Brooke fell in love with the place, with Mrs. Merriweather. With John Cooper, whoever the heck he was.

Which was the problem. She couldn't resist him. Even when she knew what a stupid thing she was doing, she couldn't say no. Just when she should be settled into an uncomfortable chair, Pete's hands in hers, telling him that there was no future for them together, that the best thing for the both of them would be for Brooke to return posthaste to her predictable life in Rupert Springs, he pulled the rug under her feet and got her to laughing again.

This time she at least waited for little Mrs. Merriweather to flutter her way back down the stairs.

"Pork futures?" she demanded, flopping onto the chenille bedspread that topped the old brass bed.

Pete dispatched one of his most unapologetic grins. "I used that one in England once. Got a tabloid stiff off my case, and ended up with a pretty nice story in the English press about American farmers."

"Cousin John would be so pleased."

ISN'T IT ROMANTIC? 135

He joined her on the bed. "Wouldn't he, though?"

She just shook her head. "You're nuts."

"All newlyweds are nuts," he allowed brightly. "It's to be expected."

She wanted to laugh again. She wanted to reach out and hug him, delighted with their silly ruse, their escape from reality in this transplanted museum from a fishing village. But, of course, she couldn't anymore. Suddenly the idea of having her arms around Pete conjured up different images, different expectations. Sunshine and whirling delight, the sound of her name gasped like a plea. The full, hot hardness of completion, and then, inevitably, the loss.

So she kept her hands to herself and rued the moment she'd given in to impulse.

"Would it be too much, Mrs. Cooper, to ask you to check my bandages?" Pete asked, his voice still light and easy.

For the briefest of moments Brooke resented him. Resented the fact that it seemed so easy for him to move on, when she felt as if she were negotiating her way through quicksand, where one wrong move would inadvertently lead to disaster. It didn't deter her from getting up, though, or being her most gentle when dabbing out the wound with hydrogen peroxide and reapplying the dressing.

"It probably needed stitches," she said, just to let him know he wasn't getting off scot-free.

Sitting there in only his jeans, his bare chest provoking even more memories, Pete flashed her an impudent grin. "It'll make a much more impressive scar this way."

"Which you can't show anybody anyway," Brooke retorted, tearing tape, "because you can't tell them you've been shot because they should have known already."

She didn't seem to be bothering him. "Are you always this crabby?"

"Only when I'm not on the phone."

He rolled his eyes. "Now she tells me."

She shot him a suspicious look. "Now that I've spent five fun-filled days dodging bullets with you, is there any other little thing you want to fill me in on about your life away from Rupert Springs?"

Patting at the new tape along his side, Pete looked insulted. "I tell you everything," he protested.

"Except that you have an affinity for disaster."

136   ISN'T IT ROMANTIC?

He shrugged. ''Well, yeah. That. It never seemed to come up in the conversation.''

''Any lady friends meet untimely deaths in your company?''

He chuckled at that and reached over to gently wrap a hand around the back of Brooke's neck. ''Not even the lovely Alicia. And I can't think of anyone who deserved it more.''

Brooke couldn't pull away from him as he bent to kiss her. She couldn't protest or demur. It seemed that once tasted, this particular fruit was addictive. Sweet, succulent, as nourishing as a ripe peach on a hot summer day, as darkly sensual as a slow dance.

''Why?'' he asked against her mouth, sparking sudden fires. ''Are you telling me you don't like a little excitement in your life?''

Pete returned to demand even more, his lips capturing hers with sure command, his tongue seeking slow plunder. And Brooke, who had dreamed of such kisses once, had never known their power.

''Maybe a little,'' she admitted on a sigh, the curious dance of static beginning to skitter through her chest, to drift to her belly and burn. She brought her hand up to Pete, weaving her fingers through the thick silk of his hair and deepening the kiss in her own way. Demanding and conceding, dancing in age-old invitation with only her mouth touching his. Terrified, fatalistically certain that she was already lost, that she would go home truly alone from this trip. Still unable to battle the chemistry they had uncorked. Knowing truly how Pandora felt the instant she first saw the treasures peek from her forbidden box.

''You know,'' Pete offered, feathering kisses across Brooke's jaw on the way to her ear. ''I bet we wouldn't have to worry about picnickers showing up at the wrong time.''

Brooke's head fell back before his assault, the intimate dance of his tongue against her ear inciting the most delicious chills. ''What about Elvis?'' she managed, eyes closed, aching and uncertain and shuddering with need.

Pete never let his attention stray. ''Let him get his own girl.''

His hands, she thought distractedly, arching into his clever touch. His magic, hungry hands. They praised her and delighted her and tormented her, lifting her against him, opening her to him, stirring her to whisper with him. Capturing her

ISN'T IT ROMANTIC? 137

throat, her shoulders, her arms, commanding and gentle at once, hot, hurried, as if he needed to fit all of her into his hold at once.

Brooke writhed in his touch. She whimpered with the lightning that speared through her, gasped at the surprise of his cool, coarse fingers against her heated skin.

Gently, never allowing her to slip from his embrace, Pete pulled her to her feet. He slid his hands along her waist, down past her hips and her thighs, the race of his touch intriguing through denim. Never taking his mouth from hers, sipping, savoring, capturing, he bunched her blouse in his hands and lifted it. He cupped her breasts in cool hands, claiming them, and Brooke arched into his grasp. She lifted her arms to him, to those shoulders that could hold her up when her knees were failing. She dueled with him, her kisses as hungry as his, her hands as anxious to reach his skin.

"You like a little excitement, huh?" he rasped, burrowing his face into her throat, his thumbs teasing her nipples to aching stiffness.

She couldn't quite get enough breath for a sensible answer. Come to think of it, with what Pete was doing to her with his hands and mouth, she couldn't have come up with a sensible answer if she'd had the breath. So instead she answered in the same manner he provoked. She let her hands fall to the waist of his jeans and repaid the attention.

Her body was singing, glowing, a fluid core of pulsating heat that responded only to Pete's touch, his kiss. Her heart hammered against her ribs and her bones disappeared so that only Pete was holding her up.

"You're sure," Pete gasped, lifting her shirt completely away to settle his mouth against her breasts, "that you want just a little excitement?"

They tumbled to the bed, shedding clothes like inhibitions until Brooke lay naked alongside Pete in the gentle dusk, the air cooling her and the darkness allowing her mystery.

"Maybe more," she admitted, taking his hand to her lips and kissing his palm, "than a little excitement."

His smile was beautiful as he bent over her, strong and fierce with possession. His body was taut and glistening, his weight sweet against her. His promise was in his eyes, and Brooke couldn't ask for more.

138   ISN'T IT ROMANTIC?

And yet, he gave it. He lavished it, discovering her body like a long-awaited treasure, caressing and suckling and tasting, until she was frantic for communion. Kissing the inside of her elbows and the skin at the base of her neck, inciting her with the rasp of his beard, tormenting her with attentions to throat and belly, and, finally, the soft triangle at the apex of her thighs.

"Who'd figure?" he whispered against her ear, his fingers sparking lightning as they dipped into her.

She gasped, bucked, unprepared for the languid torture he was inflicting. Raking at him, she pulled him closer, urged him home where he belonged.

"Figure," she managed, filling herself with the coarse pleasure of hair-roughened skin, "what?"

He bent back to her, capturing her mouth with his, his tongue plundering, his fingers magic. "That you'd grow up to be so beautiful," he admitted on a satisfied smile.

She didn't think to object. She couldn't pull her whirling, swooping mind from the stunning effect of Pete's attention, from the stumble of exhilaration in her chest when she took him, slick and tumescent in her hand and tormented him right back. She couldn't imagine that she could provoke that kind of harsh groan of pleasure, and smiled for its power, for the hot, sweet taste of satisfaction that she could do this to Pete. That he would want her to. That he would battle his own arousal to satisfy her.

The shudders built, surprising, shattering explosions of sound and scent and sweet agony in her, throwing her back, curling her closer, giving her voice to beg.

"Coop...Coop, please..." Her hands on him, her hips lifting to meet him, her eyes open to him.

And he came home. His eyes on hers, his mouth covering her cries of astonishment, his hands nestling her to him, he slid gently into her, filling her, sating her, driving her right over the splintering edge of control. Plunging deeper, stroking, riding the crest of her climax and then following her, his own sharp cry of release her most precious gift.

And there, in the gathering dusk, they lay wrapped in each other's arms, where no one else could find them, and slept.

Ten

Entertainment World, MAY 30:

Hot tip for Pete Cooper watchers. Word out of New Orleans is that our man has been seen escorting a new lady. Lifting himself from his sickbed to arrange a slam-bang jazz funeral for his aunt, Cooper has been spotted everywhere from Antoine's to the not-so-elegant New Orleans police station with the mysterious redhead. Further observation is recommended. . . .

"**Y**ou're lying."

Brooke laughed as she resettled herself on the side of the bed. "Now, how the hell could I make up something like that? Actually, he wasn't bad at all on his feet. It was the fact that he couldn't pronounce his *R's* that was really hard to take. Have you ever heard somebody sing, 'Wuv Me Tendew'?"

At the other end of the phone line, Allie dissolved into giggles. "And I'm sure you two handled the whole thing like the adults you are."

"Sure. We got up and joined him for the encore. 'Jaiwhouse Wock.' Did you know Pete knows how to tap-dance?"

140   ISN'T IT ROMANTIC?

"He would."

"Yeah, that's what I said."

"Does he still do a mean lick on the guitar?"

Brooke grinned, that silly delight bubbling in her chest again at the memory of how happy he'd looked the night before in his jeans and T-shirt slamming into "Blue Suede Shoes" all on his own. Brooke would have given anything to have seen him gear up on country like he really wanted.

"He not only brought the house down, he ended up with four pairs of women's underwear."

"Hang around him long enough, you won't have to worry searching out those lingerie sales anymore."

"I don't think so. Leopard-skin bikinis are not my style."

That provoked another round of laughter.

"So, where do you go from here?" Allie asked.

Brooke took a second to sip her coffee. Pete was still downstairs helping Mrs. Merriweather with the dishes. Another twenty-four hours of that kind of behavior, and he'd get himself written into her will. He'd been so attentive to the quaint old lady the three days they'd been there so far, that Brooke was half convinced they were sneaking off to be alone when Brooke wasn't looking.

"I'm not sure," she admitted. "Pete doesn't really want to go right back to Atlanta just yet, and Shiloh's fairly close. You know the Fillihue men fought there in the Late Unpleasantness."

"You mean the Civil War?"

"You must be a Yankee, my dear. Letitia and Emily would never sully their tongues with those words. Anyway, we might pay a visit. I've always wanted to go."

"And how are you and Pete getting along?"

The twenty-four-thousand-dollar question. Brooke took another sip of cooling coffee to give herself more stalling time. It wasn't that she hadn't expected Allie to ask. After all, she'd seen the look in Allie's eyes when they'd pulled out of the driveway. But somehow, faced with it like this, she suddenly didn't know what to say. *He's great in bed? We can't seem to keep our hands off each other? We haven't so much as mentioned the word* future *since the first snap of a bra fastener?* Whatever she'd say, it would be half-truths, half explanations. Because the truth of the matter was, just as she'd predicted, she didn't know quite how they were doing. When they weren't in

ISN'T IT ROMANTIC? 141

bed, they acted as if nothing had changed. When they were in bed, they proved that it had. Repeatedly. Enthusiastically. Delightfully. Brooke had never felt so thoroughly cherished or so blastedly frustrated in her life.

"Broo-ooke," her friend called in a singsong reminder. "That last question was to you."

Brooke sighed. "Well, besides the fact that we've played hide-and-seek with a tornado, gone a round with a mugger and gotten caught in flagrante delicto in a public park, just fine, thanks."

Leave it to Allie to pick up on the pertinent facts. "What park?"

"I'm not sure. Someplace in Mississippi with not nearly enough ground cover."

"You mean . . . *really* flagrant?"

Brooke scowled. "I mean . . . really."

"Well, hot damn. Can I make a bid on Mamie's house since you're not coming home after all?"

"What are you talking about? Of course, I'm coming home."

"Don't be silly. So, *you're* the redhead I read about in the tabloids. I can't wait to visit you in Atlanta. Maybe he'll take me to nifty restaurants like that, too. Then I can try and take him away from you and end up splashed on the front page of *Daily World*, just like Madonna."

"Allie," Brooke protested. "Get a grip."

"What," she demanded with salacious delight, "was it like? Was it heaven? Was it fireworks? Was it everything you ever dreamed of?"

Old friends definitely held on to too much embarrassing information. Allie was the only one in the world with knowledge Brooke had never passed along to Pete. That being, of course, because it was about how she'd felt about him when still a young and impressionable girl.

"Was it?" Allie insisted.

"No," Brooke said.

There was a stricken silence on the other end. "Don't do this to me," she begged. "We small folk need our heroes."

Brooke fought a grin. "It was better."

She had to hold the phone away from her ear to prevent hearing loss when Allie whooped in delight. "Wow, better than heaven. I may have to hurt you."

142   ISN'T IT ROMANTIC?

Brooke didn't bother to tell her friend that she wouldn't have to. Brooke had the feeling that inevitability was about to do it for her anyway.

"I will not tolerate gloating," Brooke warned blackly.

"None," her friend assured her in a gloating tone of voice. "No 'I told you so's.'"

"Never."

"Not even a single snicker when Pete's back is turned."

"Not one. Can I be maid of honor?"

"Only if you wear your uniform."

"Oh, kinky. This just gets better and better."

"Allie."

Allie was perceptive enough to hear the true caution in Brooke's voice. "Yeah, hon."

"This isn't as cut-and-dried as you'd like it to sound. We, uh, we haven't seemed to make it past the...uh..."

"Mutual attraction."

"Yeah, thanks. Nothing else has been settled. Nothing else has really been discussed."

"Well, what the heck? You have a few days before you're due back."

Brooke's laugh was not amused. "Yeah, isn't life always that simple?"

Just then the door slammed open and Pete walked in. "Hello, darling, I'm home."

"Well, if it isn't heaven itself," Allie said. "Should I ask why he's in your room?"

"You mean my new husband, John Cooper, the famous pig broker?" The lovely Mr. Cooper bent over and deposited a very suggestive kiss in the vicinity of Brooke's free ear.

"Is that your boss or mine on the phone?" he demanded.

"It's Allie."

Pete didn't bother relaying messages. He just plucked the phone away and settled himself onto the bed alongside Brooke.

"Where were you when I needed you?" he demanded. "Did you know I got mugged?"

Brooke could hear Allie's protests, and left the two of them to harass each other in peace. Climbing from the bed, she walked over to the window to see that the world went quietly on in Buford, Mississippi. A school bus was discharging its small passengers down by the grocery store, and a tractor was cutting through a pasture on the far side of town. People strolled

ISN'T IT ROMANTIC? 143

the streets and stopped to chat, people born and raised here, just like Rupert Springs, simple, unpretentious people for the most part. People who knew their friends and their enemies, and who had formed a definite picture of themselves. Unchanging, unwavering in the face of uncertainty and upheaval. Blessed with a limited enough imagination that they didn't know what they missed beyond the confines of their small town, that the television was enough of an education for them and getting through each day enough of a challenge.

Then there were the changelings like her, caught dead center between two worlds, desperately unsure into which she belonged. Unhappy enough to be restless, uncertain enough to be afraid.

Caught by the truth just shy of where she'd always wanted to be.

Brooke didn't realize that Pete had finished his conversation with Allie and hung up the phone until she felt his hands on her shoulders.

"What's wrong?" he asked.

Brooke leaned back into him, soaking in the feel of his strong, supple body against hers like sunlight on her face. "It's a beautiful little town, isn't it?" she asked.

Pete took a moment to watch over her shoulder. "I guess."

"But not one you'd want to live in."

"Hard to if I expect to hold down a job in broadcasting. I don't think they have much of a market share in Buford."

Brooke nodded instinctively. Expectations, accomplishments, disappointments. More personally felt in a small town, more singularly experienced. Each person a familiar face, each family with its place in the pecking order. Brooke and Pete had grown up in the same town, different ends of the pecking order. It had made all the difference in the world.

Gently Pete turned her away from her view. "Do you want to talk about it?" he asked.

She challenged him just as carefully. "Do you?"

She surprised a smile from him, a small, wry thing that had no place on Pete Cooper. "Not really. For these few days, I want to live in the present perfect. No past, no future, no problems. Just us and the tap-dancing Elvis and lunch down at the Do-Right Diner."

She couldn't give much more than a nod. "Sounds wonderful."

144   ISN'T IT ROMANTIC?

He pulled her gently into his arms. "But it isn't, is it?"

She did her best to smile. "At times."

"I hope I'm at least in the same room at those times."

"You're usually sharing auras."

"But that's not enough."

She pulled away enough to face him. "Coop," she admonished. "I never thought I'd hear you say something that trite. Of course it's not enough. If it were, you'd still be with Alicia and I'd have let Purvis Waller a lot closer to my front door."

Pete arched a disbelieving eyebrow. "Purvis Waller?"

Brooke found she had a smile for him after all. "Never judge a book by its first name. Purvis considered it his duty to properly initiate every female fellow classmate interested in the rites of spring."

"He dressed up as half goat and played a flute."

She shook her head with satisfaction. "The softball team motto was Make Me Howl Like a Coyote, Purvis."

Pete struck a pose of outrage. "I'm shocked."

She grinned. "You're jealous."

"But you didn't—"

She shook her head. "The only howling I did was the night Allie and I snuck out after curfew and followed you to the little campsite you favored so much."

He stiffened even more. "That was *you?*"

Her smile was satisfied. "I heard that Mary Lou Ellerby swore for weeks that a wolf had nibbled at her toes. But you don't want to know about that."

Pete was busy shaking his head, his expression still caught dead center between outrage and amusement. "No wonder we were always baby-sitting you. You were trouble."

"Trouble?" she protested. "I wasn't trouble."

He scowled at her. "You were a pain in the butt. You dated everything from pig callers to parolees just to get a rise out of your daddy."

"How else was I going to get noticed?" she demanded more hotly than she'd realized. "After all, Annie was already perfect, and it's hard to top that. I decided to be wicked."

Pete lifted a hand to test her hair again, his voice soft. "You weren't wicked."

"No," she sighed in disappointment. "I didn't have the guts for it. I was just—"

"A pain."

ISN'T IT ROMANTIC? 145

End of story, end of glory. It was kind of the way things went in Rupert Springs. Life was played out on a small, intimate scale. No great cataclysm, no world news. When a child saw greatness in himself, it was usually perceived within the scale of his home. The best teacher rather than the president. A banker rather than a power broker. And usually, it was enough. Unless you were never quite sure you belonged in that town in the first place.

Still, Pete held her, his head just above hers, his hands soft and supportive.

"I love you," he offered simply, but that was different, too. They'd said it countless times over the phone, friends shortening the miles, shoring up confidence, stating the obvious.

But since that moment out in the field, it wasn't so obvious anymore. It wasn't the same at all.

"I love you, too," Brooke answered instinctively, knowing that her own meaning had changed and changed drastically. The treasures had been loosed from Pandora's box, and she couldn't love him the way she used to anymore. It hurt now. It shuddered in her, a live thing, hot and bright and fatal, with the power to overwhelm her logic, her sense, her identity. It terrified her, because by unleashing what Brooke had held in check for so long, Pete had walked them both to the very edge of a precipice, where one wrong step would send them tumbling into disaster. And if there was one thing Brooke was beginning to realize, the fall into love was something that never helped a person's balance.

"What do you think we should do when we get back?"

Brooke squeezed her eyes closed against the unfamiliar agony of dread, of terrible hope.

"I thought this was the present perfect," she countered a bit unevenly.

He dropped a gentle kiss to the top of her head. "Not when you look like Bambi after the hunters came, it isn't."

Her smile was sad. "I'm being a pain again."

Pete turned her toward him, and Brooke thought her heart would break. There in his eyes was a pain she'd never thought to have inflicted on him. A sore confusion that shouldn't have come between two friends.

"What do you want, Brooke?" he demanded. "Tell me."

She tried to shy away from him, her eyes down. But he trapped her again in his hands and forced her back to face him.

146   ISN'T IT ROMANTIC?

"What do you know that I don't?"

It made her want to cry. She should have had something big to tell him, something devastating. All she had were small truths. Disappointments.

"I want things back to the way they were."

He didn't understand. "You want to stay in Rupert Springs? You really want to spend the rest of your life caught in that little box?"

"No," she answered, meeting his gaze head on. "Yes."

His lips quirked a little. "One answer at a time is more than enough."

"But don't you see?" she asked. "There is no one answer. Maybe it's simple for you. You always hated Rupert Springs. For as long as I've known you, you've been itching to get out. Well, it's been different for me. Sure, the town's stifling at times. As far as being on the cutting edge nationally, it's about on a par with silent films. But it's where my stability is, my sense of identity. Now, suddenly, everything's different. My parents are gone, Mamie's gone, you're...we've..." She shook her head, frustrated with the inefficiency of words for what she needed to tell him. "I need my pole stars, Coop, and Rupert Springs is the only one left."

He was already shaking his head. "But you don't belong there any more than I do. Any more than . . ."

She stopped him, her hand to his mouth, knowing what he was going to say. "I'm not her," she said. "I'm me. And the truth of the matter is, I've never been blessed with those hot fires of vision. I've never been driven or committed or obsessed." She stepped away from him, needing motion for her words, for the final truths she had to admit. "Maybe I don't see the world the same way the town does. Maybe my ideas are a little bigger. But I'm not all that sure I ever had what it takes to redefine the way we see the world or see my name on a museum letterhead. And if I didn't, I've at least had a good family, better friends and a place I could call my own, so I figured that I was still ahead of the game. Now, suddenly, that's all changed, and you've..." She reached the back of the bed, running her hand along the smooth tube of the post, her chest churning with the upheavals, the shattering longing he'd unleashed. The reality that was sure to follow, when even he was gone.

"I've fallen in love with you," he challenged.

ISN'T IT ROMANTIC? 147

"Which means what?" she retorted, chin back up, eyes brittle. "Where do we go from here? How do we handle all this, especially when you go back to being who you are instead of John the Pig Man?"

"But don't you see?" he asked. "I'm giving you the chance to finally get out of there. You can create a new place for yourself. Heck, if you need stability, do it in Atlanta."

She shook her head. "That just isn't the kind of universe I orbit, old boy."

He stared at her. "Are you kidding? You knocked 'em dead in New Orleans."

Brooke scowled, sinking onto the bed, her hand still around the post, her heart leaden. "This isn't a road company of *Mame,* Pete. I'm not auditioning for anything."

"You don't have to audition for anything, damn it," he argued. "I'm telling you that you could take Atlanta by storm."

She lifted a fierce gaze his way. "And I'm telling you I don't want to. Besides, if I moved to Atlanta, what good would that do you?"

"What do you mean?"

She scowled at him. "Who calls me to say that he's tired of all the attention, that he can't get on another plane or sign another autograph or put up with the holier-than-thou image any longer? And who's the one in charge of defusing all that idiocy, of putting the famous newsman's priorities back into order when the fans are banging down the door? Well, the reason I've been able to do that so well is because I haven't been anywhere near the fray. I don't think I'd do any good from ground zero."

"That doesn't matter."

"It does," she insisted. "It does to me. I just don't think I belong there, Pete."

"But don't you want more?" he demanded. "Don't you want to get out?"

"Of course I do!" She shook her head, the frustration of impasse gnawing at her. "But I'm not you. I can't just pull up my roots and see where they take seed."

"But you're passing up your big chance!"

"At what, greatness? I don't want greatness, Pete. I want happiness. I'd like to find work I love, but it's more important for me to be somewhere I can make a difference around me.

148   ISN'T IT ROMANTIC?

Where I can have friends and home and continuity, and that just isn't a condo in Buckhead.''

"But I'd be there with you," he insisted.

And that was where the truth would come between them. She lifted her eyes back to him, unhappy and afraid. Wishing for anything but the necessity of this conversation. "Would you?" she asked.

He looked as if she'd just hit him. "Now, what the hell does that mean? Have I ever let you down?"

Her smile was sad. "You never made love to me, either, but we seem to have changed that situation pretty thoroughly."

"That doesn't change *anything*."

"It changes *everything*. In the last three days, we've completely thrown out the book on our relationship, and we haven't had time to write new rules. I don't know where we're going, Pete. I don't know what either of us wants to do—" Giving way to a blush, she managed a rueful smile. "Well, except for one thing."

An answering grin flashed across his features and died again. "What do I want to do?" he mused, doing a little pacing himself. "You're right, I hadn't gotten that far."

"You haven't had the energy," she accused gently.

He arched an eyebrow at her. "Careful," he countered. "You're toying with a well-won reputation."

"Which is another thing." She sighed miserably, shaking her head.

He stopped to look at her. "My reputation?" he demanded. "You know more about the truth than any person on earth."

She lifted her face to challenge him. "But I've never had to battle the myth. I was always safe from that kind of thing—at least I was until New Orleans."

Pete actually got down on a knee to be able to face her. Plucking that taut hand from the bed rail, he took it in his. "You mean you'd chicken out just because you couldn't stand a camera or two in your face? You'd forfeit nights out at the opera and the Ritz to stay anonymous?"

If she hadn't seen the glint of humor way at the back of that question, Brooke would have been a lot more upset. "I've managed to suffer through the first twenty-six years without needing anyone to unfold my napkin for me."

For a moment, he didn't speak, didn't answer her question or pose one of his own. Brooke watched him in silence, that

ISN'T IT ROMANTIC? 149

face she knew so well, that she suddenly didn't know at all. She wanted to have back the ease they'd had at the beginning of the trip, so that she could pull him tightly against her and let them forget everything else but having a nice few days off. She wished she could jump up and announce that it was time to search out that country bar, and Pete would slide on those roach-stomping boots and follow her right out the door.

But things just weren't that simple anymore. The piper was here with his hand out, and they couldn't get back out the door without coming up with reasonable coin. They couldn't go forward, and they certainly couldn't go backward. And if the caldron that bubbled in Brooke's chest was any indication, they couldn't stay where they were.

This falling-in-love stuff was for the birds.

When Pete finally lifted his gaze back to her, Brooke wasn't prepared for what she saw. Or, come to think of it, what she heard.

"Marry me."

She probably shouldn't have laughed. It just popped out, as unexpected as the proposal.

"What are you talking about?" she demanded.

Pete shrugged, singularly unruffled for a man who'd just had a proposal of marriage laughed at. "You wanted to know what I wanted. I want you to marry me."

Brooke tried to yank her hand back. Pete wouldn't let go. "Pete, that's not funny."

"I don't think I'm the one who laughed."

"I laughed because it was ridiculous, not because it was funny."

Still he held on, even as she lurched from the bed. "Why is it so ridiculous?" he demanded. "I'm a very eligible bachelor. I make a fair living and don't have any outstanding debts I'm aware of." Gaining his feet, he winced dramatically. "Try not to move too fast. My side still hurts." That didn't seem to keep him from following her to the window. "True, I travel a lot, but you've never sat in your rocker waiting for my calls any other time in your life. You certainly know all my bad habits, and we don't have to sweat getting to know the in-laws."

"Come on, Pete," she objected, shrinking away from him, her voice miserable. "I mean it. I don't consider this a joking matter." It seemed the only retort that worked its way through her overloaded brain.

150   ISN'T IT ROMANTIC?

He threw her off balance again, pulling her right into his
embrace so that she couldn't escape the sudden steel in his eyes.
"Did I say it was?"

She gave him her best glare. He glared right back, that soft,
seductive gray green suddenly the texture of granite. "What did
you think all this was leading up to, anyway?" he demanded.
"You know me better than anyone in the world. You know how
I think, how I act. And you usually know it before I do. Do you
think I was just killing time before going home, or doing you a
favor? Did you think I expected us to just head our separate
ways when we got home and forget this ever happened?"

"No," she answered, then, miserably, "Yes."

He rolled his eyes. "There you go again."

It took her a moment to clarify. When she did, she couldn't
quite face him. "Hoped for the one, expected the other."

That was the first thing to really make him mad. "You'd
really think I'd do that?"

Brooke lifted a hand to his face. "Don't be stupid. I was too
afraid to want more."

A great, beaming smile broke through. "Then it's settled."

She shook her head. "It is not."

He was really getting those scowls down pat. "I'm beginning to lose my patience."

Brooke continued to stroke his cheek, the rasp of his new
beard delicious against her fingers, the hard planes of his face
comforting and familiar. "If you were John Cooper and sold
pigs, we might just swing it without complications. But we're
on a Disney ride right now, Coop. Not reality. We can't make
any commitments caught in this time warp—" Suddenly her
eyes widened and her voice died. Pete's offer had finally really
sunk in. "You mean it?"

He was still caught between consternation and confusion.
"Mean what?"

But Brooke could only shake her head, tears brimming. She
couldn't ask, she couldn't say it. He couldn't mean it after all.
It was just something that sounded good two floors above reality.

But he meant it. She saw it when his eyes darkened. When he
took her hands back into his and smiled for her. "Brooke Ferguson, we've known each other too long for me to lie to you.
You were my best friend even when I was married to another
woman. You know more about me than the IRS and have never

ISN'T IT ROMANTIC?

151

once held it against me or betrayed my confidence. You bring sanity to an insane world and laughter into a dull one. And, after all these years, I found to my amazement that you're also the most beautiful, sexy, compelling woman I've ever known. I love you more now than I ever have. In ways I never imagined. Will you marry me?''

Caught in Pete's grasp, her view of him blurred through the tears he'd provoked, the sweet joy of his words squeezing the air from her, Brooke gazed up at him and said the only thing she could. "No."

Eleven

IBN Network, 10172 Peachtree Parkway, Atlanta...
Memo from the Chief:

If anyone has seen or heard from Pete Cooper in the last five days, notify the executive offices. If Mr. Cooper calls in, transfer him. If he shows up, detain him for questioning.

"**No?**"

"That answer's not any different than it was yesterday."

"It still doesn't make sense, either. Do you love me?"

Brooke set her suitcases down on by the front door and turned on him. "Yes."

Pete never bothered to let his bag go. "Do you enjoy making love with me?"

Brooke fought an inevitable smile. "Yes."

"Do I have morning breath, or dandruff or an obscene tattoo that offends you?"

Brooke lost the fight. "No."

ISN'T IT ROMANTIC? 153

Pete lost his patience. "Then why won't you marry me?" he demanded very loudly just as the front door swung open between them.

Much to her discomfort, it was Mrs. Merriweather. "Oh," she trilled uncertainly, wide eyes swinging between Pete and Brooke, hand to ample bosom. "Oh."

It seemed that the first "oh" was for interrupting a delicate conversation. The other was for the fact that she'd shown up with half the town to witness it.

"Oh," they all chorused out on the front porch. And then the cameras began to flash.

Pete swung on them with the grace of a cranky pit bull. Luckily the famed gray green eyes were hidden behind sunglasses and his hands were full, or there could have been mayhem.

Brooke blinked a couple of times, trying to clear away the little red suns that kept dancing across her vision. "Good morning," she greeted the throng.

They never even saw her. "You're Pete Cooper," Mrs. Merriweather accused gaily, waggling a finger at Pete's chest. "We finally uncovered the truth yesterday when Billy Ray Watson saw that article about your rout of that criminal in New Orleans in *People* magazine. Such a brave thing to do. Of course, Eldon Harper—that's our very own tap-dancing Elvis, don't you know—claims that you stood up on stage singing and dancing with him the other night." She tsked a couple of times. "And you with laryngitis and all, Mr. Cooper. Really."

From that moment on, Brooke felt like a carrot in a pot of boiling soup. Tossed around, poked and prodded, and then shoved aside in favor of the much more interesting chicken she'd found herself sharing the water with. She was a nice person, they were sure—had she *really* spent three days in Mrs. Merriweather's bridal suite with Pete Cooper without benefit of license?—but Pete was the real story. Which brought up the inevitable, what-was-Pete-Cooper-*really*-like questions, some of them so personal Brooke wouldn't have asked him herself. To his credit, the big chicken himself defused quickly and proceeded to handle the crowd with ease and charm.

Brooke ended up packing the car and listening to a half hour of the Saturday Morning Hillbilly Hour on the car radio before Pete managed to break away and join her.

154   ISN'T IT ROMANTIC?

"Well, aren't you just the most fascinating man on the planet?" she cooed with black humor as he waved one more time and pulled the car away from the curb.

His sigh was heartfelt. "Want to know what I had for breakfast?"

"I know what you had for breakfast. It wasn't interesting then."

"Where are we going?"

She sighed right back. "Home."

One hand on the wheel, the other settling sunglasses in place, Pete shot her a look of pure irritation. "Come on, Stump. Don't start up with that again."

Her answering smile wasn't a happy one. "I was just thinking as I sat here listening to Earl Scruggs, about how this was a good example of why I can't marry you."

"Because of Earl Scruggs?"

"Because of Mrs. Merriweather. Because of Buford, Mississippi, and New Orleans, Louisiana, and Atlanta, Georgia. Because you're Pete Cooper, world-famous hero, lover and all-round nice guy. I'm a bean counter in a small town who's only purpose when she's standing next to you is to answer questions like, 'Does he wear briefs or boxers?'"

Pete flashed her a look of alarm. "How did you answer?"

"I said you wore those cute leopard-skin things that were tossed to you on stage the other night."

At least he laughed. "Trust me, Stump. You'd never get lost in the crowd."

Brooke looked down to where she was twisting the dime-store ring Pete had gotten her to play their part. Sham, fantasy, fun. They'd always been able to share that. Would they still when she was threatened with being submerged by his fame?

"Coop," she protested gently. "I love you. I have since I've been a girl, and nothing's going to change that. But I can't be any good to you if I lose what I am. What I can give you."

"What do you mean?"

"I mean that whatever else Rupert Springs did or didn't do, it gave me the security to be the person I am. And I'm not sure someplace like Atlanta would—especially if I showed up on your arm."

"But I'd be there with you."

She smiled again, caught between that kind of promise and the ramifications of it when it came to him. "I know."

ISN'T IT ROMANTIC? 155

He looked over. "You don't sound especially happy."

She shrugged. "Maybe this was all previews for *Mame* after all," she acknowledged. "And after playing Philadelphia this morning, I'm just not sure I'm ready for Broadway."

"Would you stop speaking in allegories?"

"I know who I am at home. I wouldn't get the chance in Atlanta," she objected. "Even with you there beside me. And I'd have to deal with a lot more than just marriage and house hunting if I decided to do it."

"Then what do you want to do?"

She shrugged, impatient, uncertain. Wishing with all her heart she could just throw her objections to the wind, aching for a simple solution that would make as much sense to Pete as it would to her.

"I guess I want to figure out what I can find in Atlanta— besides you—that would compel me to leave Rupert Springs."

His expression was more hurt than outraged. "I'm not enough?"

Brooke reached over and patted his leg, wondering still if he understood. "If you were," she said, "I wouldn't be the woman you need."

Pete was really trying his best. Patience had never been his long suit, although persistence had been mentioned in a review or two. He simply couldn't understand why Brooke didn't see herself the way he did. Brash, bright, with the common sense of a judge and the whimsy of a child. He loved her, damn it. And not just as a friend, although there would always be that. He'd let her stay in Rupert Springs all those years without raising serious protest. Now, soaking in the astonishing magic of her, he wanted to go back and drag her out with him. He wanted to give her everything she'd been denied. Everything she'd denied herself.

Once he'd made the decision that suddenly seemed so inevitable, he wanted Brooke with him. Now. Always. Lighting up when he walked in the door, slapping him down when he got out of hand. Helpmate and companion, counselor and confessor, conspirator and inspiration; he wanted all those things in his wife, and he hadn't realized it until it had dawned on him that his friend had been those things all along.

156   ISN'T IT ROMANTIC?

And lover. But that was the icing, the subtle, special flavoring to her. Stump, that ferocious child and pragmatic woman, had matured into a generous, demanding lover. She danced in his hands, sang and laughed and whimpered in his arms, and provoked him to the same, again and again, each time better, each time sweeter as they discovered the only secrets they'd kept from each other.

"So, what is it you want to do?" he asked as they strolled through the soft woods of Shiloh.

Brooke never looked away from the soft, sad hills, the trees that dripped with rain. "Can you feel it?" she asked in a voice as hushed as the breeze.

Pete looked over to see the pain in her gaze. The empathy. He took his own look around, reacquainting himself with the site Mamie had taken him to as a child where he'd run his hands over the piled canon balls and imagined the nameless dead buried beneath.

But he'd never told anyone about the feeling the place had given him.

"The sorrow?" he asked. "Yeah. It kind of rises up out of the ground."

"I think," Brooke allowed, bending to run her fingers over old, pitted iron, "that there was so much blood shed here, that it permeated the place. All those boys, all that noise and smoke and terror. It's still trapped here."

Pete couldn't help but smile. Of all people, of course it would be Brooke who would understand. He didn't even need to tell her. He just reached across and took her other hand, sharing the silence with her in a place where it seemed even the birds couldn't speak.

They walked that way for a long time, honoring the Fillihue men who'd died there, the other thousands who must have walked these same paths on their way to battle.

"Have you been to other sites?" Brooke asked.

Pete nodded. "Most of them. Evan wanted a retrospective when they were trying to sell off part of Bull Run that time."

Brooke nodded absently. "Oh yeah, I forgot."

Pete answered the question she didn't ask. "They all feel the same. Maybe Shiloh hurts worst because it's such a beautiful place. Nothing like that should have happened here."

ISN'T IT ROMANTIC?

* * *

"History," she allowed hours later when they'd returned to the road, the time they'd spent in that lush, silent valley weighing on them. Still picking at her ring, that silly cheap toy she wouldn't take off, she looked over at him with introspective eyes. "If I had the chance to do something new with my life, I'd want to work preserving something with a sense of history. And beauty."

Pete offered a small smile. "Well, that narrows it down."

She managed one in return. "And I like working with people. It's what's so fun about working at the trucking company."

"Anything else?"

She shook her head slowly. "Don't you think that's enough for now?"

They spent the day wandering through southern Tennessee, and the night in the foothills of the Appalachians, anonymous and comfortable, isolated from the notoriety that was brewing out in the real world, from work and responsibility and consequence. When they made love, it was with a heightened hunger, as if the happiness they shared these few days would have to last them, and when they laughed, it echoed with a more brittle, unstable sound.

"I'll call my friends on the art museum board," he offered as they strolled hand in hand through the Hunter Art Gallery in Chattanooga. "You have a degree. I can find you a job there. Maybe teaching or being a docent or something."

They wandered through the back roads of the Unaka Mountains right at the border to North Carolina and skimmed the edges of the Great Smoky Mountains National Park.

"Evan's always talking about doing more programs devoted to the arts," Pete offered. "You know, something probably right up your alley. I'll call him when we get back tomorrow."

So caught up was he with his feverish plans and possibilities that Pete didn't even notice how quiet Brooke was becoming.

It was as they drew closer to Atlanta that Pete finally began to understand what Brooke had been trying to tell him. When they stopped for breakfast, other tourists began to gather like flies after bad meat, at first spotting them, then approaching, then making demands.

158 ISN'T IT ROMANTIC?

"Oh, you're Pete Cooper," they'd say, which was no longer any surprise to him. "May I have your autograph/advice/inspiration? What did you think of that war/trial/Elvis sighting?"

Brooke would be referred to as "that redhead in the *Entertainment World*" report and nodded to in passing. If any interest was shown at all, it was in the "What do you do, dear?" form, which was never satisfactorily answered. They wanted her to tell them she was a model/rock singer/notorious bimbo to the stars. And although Brooke handled it all with admirable equanimity, Pete finally saw what he was asking of her. He saw that one of the most special aspects of their friendship had always been her distant objectivity on the whirlwind of his life. She'd never signed on for this bus ride, and suddenly he was asking her for the fare.

Lunch was worse, even though they did their best to use the drive-through. The Thunderbird, it seemed, had made the news. Pete's health was asked after, his career, his relationship with any given movie star. Until this moment, such interest had never really affected him. Rude questions and obsequious flattery had always rolled right off his back with equal ease. He'd always known that no matter what, he could make that call to the one sane voice in the world.

And now he was asking that sane voice to jump into his fishbowl. Without water wings.

"Where are we going to have the dress-up dinner?" Brooke asked quietly as they cruised south through Georgia.

"Do you want to do it at an antebellum home?" Pete asked, the new stress eating at him. "Or in the privacy of the Cooper manse?"

"I thought you decorated it in Southwestern."

"I did."

She shook her head. "Hard to get that old plantation feeling with a cow skull hanging on the wall."

"You still need to get your costume."

"I have it."

He actually turned around, as if looking. "You managed to pack a hoopskirt in that stuff?"

"No hoopskirt," she allowed. "Scarlett was not my favorite character."

He looked at her, surprised. "Melanie?"

Brooke just grimaced.

ISN'T IT ROMANTIC? 159

"No, I didn't think so. Well, then, who?"

"You'll find that out at dinner." She sighed. "Of course, the way things are going, so will all of the free world. Did you bring a costume?"

"I got it in Buford."

He managed to get a grin out of her on that one. "Don't tell me. The tap-dancing Elvis also does readings from *Showboat* on the weekends."

"I plead journalistic confidentiality."

She snorted. "What you should plead is insanity. I never realized that your life was quite so..."

"Bizarre?"

She shook her head, still groping for the right words. "Smothering. And you've been on vacation. I can't imagine what it's like on a day-to-day basis. It's a good thing I got you some time off."

Pete allowed a soft smile for the turbulent pleasures of the last days. "Now you know why I want you to stick around?" he asked.

She never took her eyes from the road, the trees reflecting from her glasses. "Now you know why I'm having so much trouble saying yes?"

Pete turned his attention back to his driving, her words caught in his chest with the inevitability of returning to that pallid, empty apartment, to the rat race that had been getting just a little too crazy lately without respite. He'd lived with it before. He'd just always counted on Brooke to defuse some of the tension. Now the precarious balance he'd maintained was threatening to tumble around him.

Suddenly he didn't want to be alone. He wasn't sure he had the patience to wade back into all that insanity without a change in his life. And the one real stabilizing force, the one constant he could always count on, wasn't constant at all anymore. All because he'd done the unimaginable and fallen resoundingly in love with his best friend.

"Yeah," he finally admitted. "I do."

"It's not that I don't love you," she protested, turning on him now, her forehead creased, her posture intense. "It's that I don't want to become inseparable from you. It wouldn't do either of us any good. Do you understand?"

He could only nod. "When we get into Atlanta, I can set you up with those people I mentioned. Maybe contact an antique

160   ISN'T IT ROMANTIC?

dealer or two who might be interested in help. If you can take
a couple more days off before heading back to Rupert Springs,
we can get you all set up in something. That would help.''

''Pull over,'' she commanded.

He stared at her. ''What?''

''I said pull over, or I'll step out of this car while it's doing
fifty-five.''

It seemed that the decision was taken out of Pete's hands.
Before he could even get the chance to turn back around to the
road, a tire blew. Suddenly the car was veering back and forth
across the blacktop, the wheel bucking like a live thing in Pete's
hands. They barely missed two oncoming cars and sideswiping
a truck as they careened a short distance down a hill.

''Here we go again,'' Brooke moaned, eyes closed, hands
gripping anything she could find.

All that time spent riding jeeps through deserts and jungles
hadn't gone to waste. Neatly skirting two street signs and a
telephone pole, Pete managed to get the car onto the shoulder
without turning them on their heads. And then, for a few minutes, they just sat there.

''You wanted to stop?'' Pete asked, his voice suspiciously
quiet.

''That's another thing,'' she said, eyes still closed, hands
clenched around dashboard and door handle. ''I'm not sure
how many more lives I have to offer. Or how many more times
I feel like changing my underwear on short notice.''

Pete couldn't help chuckling, which brought Brooke's eyes
snapping open. He could see her trying very hard to hang on to
her anger. In the end, though, she broke down, too.

''Well, you can't say life isn't interesting around me,'' he
offered with a grin.

She snorted. ''I think 'interesting' might be too pale a word.''

He gave her his best grin. ''You want to get out now?''

''Once my legs start working again.''

She wasn't as wobbly as she claimed. In fact, she was the one
who dug into the back for the spare tire while Pete rolled up
shirtsleeves and tackled the jack.

''What was it you were in such a hurry to tell me?'' he asked,
bent over the wheel.

Occasionally a car whirred past, and tucked into the dense
trees a little farther beyond, the first residential rooftops peeked
through. They had just about reached the edges of suburbia.

ISN'T IT ROMANTIC? 161

Home. Reality. Pete wasn't so sure he was all that anxious to get there.

"The tire's no good."

He straightened to see only her hair above the lifted trunk. "That's what you were going to tell me?"

She leaned to the side and flashed him a rueful grin. "No, but it is."

Pete gave the half-elevated jack a considering look. "Well, then I guess this is wasted effort. Looks like we should be in our hiking shoes."

She gave the car a look of her own. "Are you sure we should leave it here?"

"I don't see how we can bring it along."

She had a really cute grimace on her. "I mean one of us should stay."

"If one of us stays—" he informed her, stepping up to join her by the back of the car "—both of us do. I want to find out what was so all-fired important back there."

She wrinkled her nose at him. "I think you just want to find out what my costume is."

He flashed her an impudent grin. "Can't be better than mine. Now, what's it to be? Walk or stay?"

Brooke answered by slamming closed the trunk and holding out her hand. "A lovely day for a stroll, Mr. Cooper, don't you think?"

Damn her, why couldn't she see how good this was? he thought. Why didn't she want to spend all her days just like this, teasing each other, lightening the load of the rest of the world, shoring each other up over the rough spots. Just like before, only better. Much better. Damn near as perfect as a man could expect.

"Do you realize that you're getting as bad as they are?" she asked without preamble, her attention down on the uneven terrain they were trying to negotiate along the side of the road. It wasn't a big road, one of those lost little thoroughfares Brooke was so adept at finding, so that the shoulders were kudzu and rocks, and the turns all blind.

"Getting as bad as who?" Pete demanded.

She waved her hand in an all-encompassing motion. "All those people who see me as part of your chicken soup."

162 ISN'T IT ROMANTIC?

Pete almost tripped over a vine trying to figure that one out. "I don't think I want to be many more chicken soups," he warned.

"You know what I mean," she objected. "The Pete Cooper Time and Space Continuum. All the Buffys and Muffys and Gidgets who've orbited your planet since Alicia's departure. Reflecting the Cooper light into the night sky without possessing any of their own."

"I don't see you the same way I see Buffy," he protested.

"Probably because my braces are already off."

"Cheap shot."

She grinned with great satisfaction. "I know. But I didn't mean that you saw me as Buffy, but that you've been treating me a little like all the fans have. Haven't you seen it?"

"No," he answered honestly. "I haven't."

She nodded contemplatively, her forehead pursed again, her chin out. Pete wondered whether that was a good sign or not. "What did I think about that museum idea of yours?"

He wasn't following her at all. "What do you mean?"

She went right on walking, her eyes down, her steps careful, her hand in his as if they were strolling through the park. "What about the antique store, or the job at IBN, or the art gallery job you were going to get for me?"

This time she stopped, because Pete did. He looked down at her, unsure what to expect, suddenly understanding what she was trying to say. "I don't know," he admitted. "I didn't stop to ask."

Frustration flashed across those brash features, hesitation, unhappiness. "You assumed," she said, shaking her head a little. "Coop, don't you see? I feel like I'm being sucked into your force field so that I'm going to look up in a few months and find that I'm not even there anymore. And buddy, if there's one thing I've learned on this pilgrimage, it's that you definitely need me to be me."

Pete took her in his hands, facing down the truth there on the side of the road. "I'm trying to find a way we can work this out."

She shook her head. "You're trying to find a way we can be together. It's not the same. It never would have occurred to you to try and make my decisions for me two weeks ago. No matter how anybody else in the world saw me or treated me, you

ISN'T IT ROMANTIC?

believed that I could call my own shots. Since we've made love, that's changed.''

"That's because I'm in love with you, damn it!''

Her smile was sad. "That's the worst reason to take over somebody else's life, and you know it.''

"And if I leave you alone, you're going to crawl right back into that town and shrivel up and die.''

She looked down, her shoulders slumping a little, and Pete thought his heart would break. He thought he'd pushed her away from him by using the argument that mattered most to him.

"You've been my friend a lot longer than you've been my lover,'' he insisted. "And in that time I've seen you put your life on hold for other people. I've seen you stuck in that town like a...like a lily in a field of dandelions. And I know what that can do to a person, Brooke.'' He shook her, shook her hard. "Do you hear me? I know, and I won't let it happen to you.''

She lifted her gaze back to him, and everything she felt for him filled those beautiful eyes, both the love and the pain and the frustration. "But you can't save me by making me you. Give me a chance to do this myself, Coop. Let me find my own way to carve out a special, separate niche from the Pete Cooper legend. It's the only way we'll ever manage it.''

"Away from Rupert Springs,'' he insisted. "With me.''

She took a breath, teetering on the edge of decision, her expression betraying the price he asked her to pay.

"I'll do anything you ask,'' he told her. "I'll wait, I'll step back, I'll pay your way through a grand trip to Europe if that's what it's going to take, but I want you to get away from there and see what your potential is.''

"I don't...''

"I mean it. Live a completely separate life than mine if you want until you're sure you're ready, but at least take the chance.''

She was trembling in his hands, torn between the comfort of the past and the upheaval of the future. Balanced between dread and possibility. And she only had Pete to hold her up.

"It's out there,'' he persisted, his eyes locked onto hers, his grip fierce, his belief in her all she'd allow him to give her right now. "Whatever it is you want, you can have it. But not if you don't go for it.''

164 ISN'T IT ROMANTIC?

"How do I know that?" she asked, her voice small.

And Pete smiled for her, his best smile, the one he'd only discovered since falling in love. "Because I tell you it is. And if there's anybody I know who can help you find it, it's me."

She lifted a hand in exception. "Help."

Pete fought the urge to crow. "Advice and support only. Deal?"

Briefly, that young Brooke peeked through, the one so earnestly seeking comfort and approval, the shy, gawky girl with no one to ask to the prom, and suddenly Pete was giving her a second chance.

"I'll try," she finally allowed.

Pete took a second to pull her to him, filling his senses with the feel and smell and sounds of her, closing her to him like a part of himself he'd almost lost—the best part.

And then he turned them back along their way. "Now that that's settled, let's make the most of this nice, quiet summer day before I have to go back to work."

They'd taken ten steps when the nice, quiet day opened up on them, in buckets. Caught a good half mile from the car, Pete elected to pull Brooke back into a stand of pines along the side of the road for temporary shelter.

"Maybe it's you," he complained, his hair already dripping in his face as he squinted out into the downfall. "I usually don't get this much action in a week, even in a war zone."

"Pete," Brooke gasped, her attention caught by something over his shoulder. "Look!"

He turned, fully expecting to find at least Bigfoot bearing down on them, if not the real Elvis. All he found was a battered, faded little sign that hung by one frayed wire from a low-hanging tree limb.

"Bed-and-breakfast?" he demanded, bending a little to peer past the overhanging limbs of the first three or four oaks to see the sign. All he came up with was a very overgrown driveway. "When did they put that sign up, after Appomattox?"

But Brooke was already dragging him back through the dripping trees. "Come on, let's find out."

And that's how they came to discover Eleven Oaks.

Twelve

Georgia Travel Guide, 1939:

Continuing in our tour of stately antebellum homes, we chanced upon the aptly named Eleven Oaks, lovely home of Mr. and Mrs. Beauregard Hansard. A classic Greek Revival building with colonnaded balconies and sculpted gardens, it is reputed to be haunted. The young couple is quite handsome and charming...

"**I** *do* believe in spooks, I *do* believe in spooks...."

Brooke punched Pete in the ribs. "Shut up, Coop. This place is great."

"Yeah, if you're a trick-or-treater," he allowed, taking a step or two to the left to avoid the steady drip from the porch roof. "What do you bet Bette Davis answers the door?"

Brooke gave the bell another push and then took some more time looking around the untended grounds and decaying building. Once a great beauty with simple, elegant lines that invoked images of garden parties and high-stepping horses, in the flat gray light of a rainy afternoon the old antebellum

166 ISN'T IT ROMANTIC?

mansion looked about seventy years past its prime. Past its decline as well, come to think of it.

On the other hand, so did the old man who pulled open the great front door.

"Afternoon," he drawled, his posture picture perfect, his papery skin wrinkled and yellow beneath a neatly trimmed white mustache and goatee, his threadbare attire carefully proper. Shirt, tie, sweater and suit, all on a hot, muggy, rainy afternoon. The best part, though, was the ivory-headed cane he used to support himself. "Can I be of some help?"

Brooke spoke up before Pete had a chance to. She knew he was just going to ask for a phone. Suddenly she saw a way to not only avoid Atlanta tonight with all the choices that waited there, but neatly close their service for Mamie. "Your sign out front," she answered with her most demure smile, hoping the little man would overlook her bedraggled hair and damp clothes. "Would there be a room available this evening?"

Pete swung accusing eyes on her. She dispatched a swift, silencing elbow to the ribs. The gentleman of the house didn't seem to hear Coop's rather inelegant "oomph."

"Why, yes, my dear, there is," the old man answered with a formal nod. "Won't y'all come in?"

They were stepping through into the dim foyer when a voice floated down the long staircase that swept up before them.

"Beauregard?"

Coop turned incredulous eyes on Brooke again, but she ignored him. The last thing she needed was to burst out laughing right in the old gent's entry foyer. Even as they gingerly stepped onto the front rug to prevent getting water on the battered hardwood floor, they were joined by a will-o'-the-wisp in pastel flowers and Demur Blonde #2 hair coloring.

"We have guests, Evaline," Beauregard announced, stepping back to show them off.

Brooke turned to follow his line of sight to find Evaline floating down those stairs in her organdy dress and pearls as if on the way to a cotillion. Considering she couldn't have been a day under eighty, Brooke figured that was no mean feat.

"Why, bless my stars if we don't, my dear," she gushed, one hand to birdlike breast, the other hand extended.

ISN'T IT ROMANTIC? 167

Pete took his cue well and bent over her hand. That practice back in Buford must have paid off. The sparrowlike woman tittered with girlish glee.

"How lovely to see you," she greeted them. "Y'all must have seen the piece in *Old Southern Living* on Eleven Oaks."

"Eleven—" Pete didn't get any further, obviously wishing he would have counted on the way up to the porch.

"It's a lovely place," Brooke agreed easily, her peripheral gaze taking in yards of heavy, patched damask drapery and original early Victorian furniture, back when it was still light and delicate. All lovingly polished, all threadbare as its owners. The rooms were dim and dark from age and penury rather than taste.

"My name is Beauregard Hansard, sir," the old man introduced himself, shaking hands with a suspiciously straight-faced Pete. "You have met my lovely bride Evaline."

Pete bowed again like a British waiter. It seemed the thing to do. "My pleasure, ma'am. I'd like to introduce you to my wife, Brooke—"

She shot him a warning glare, which he handily ignored, and had her own hand kissed by her new host.

"You're most welcome here, my dear."

"Thank you," she said with a genuine smile, enchanted in a way she hadn't been since she'd said goodbye to Mamie. They were originals, and there weren't many of those left.

"And my name is Pete Cooper," Pete finished.

"Of the Lickskillet Coopers?" Evaline trilled in delight.

Brooke could see Pete choking back his instinctive response. "No ma'am, I'm afraid not. My kin are from Alabama."

"How lovely for you. They fought in the late war, did they?"

Brooke fought her own grin this time as she watched Pete try and decide just which war she meant. If he'd paid more attention to his aunts, he would have realized that there was only one worth mentioning in this kind of household.

"Oh, yes," she answered for him. "As a matter of fact, on our way here, we visited Shiloh. Several Fillihues—Peter's mama's people—are buried there." This kind of stuff got easier the longer one did it. Brooke had the feeling that if she

168   ISN'T IT ROMANTIC?

wasn't careful, she was going to slip right into hog futures any minute.

Evaline invoked a sigh. "How lovely."

Brooke decided it would be safer to figure she meant the visit rather than the deaths.

"Fillihues, you say?" the old man piped up.

Pete nodded. "Yes, sir."

The man nodded, still watching Pete. "A fine name, sir. A fine name."

"We have the Jackson room prepared, if that would be all right with you," Mrs. Hansard offered grandly.

"Do you have luggage?" her husband asked.

Brooke turned on Pete, unable to conceal the alarm at the idea that this frail old man would consider carrying their bags anywhere—much less a half mile down the road. She even less wanted them to know that the only reason they'd stopped was because of a flat tire. It would have seemed cruel.

"If we could see our room and freshen up," Pete suggested smoothly, "I'll get our things in a bit."

Both of their hosts smiled with ill-concealed relief.

They were guided up the great staircase—down which Robert E. Lee's boyhood backside had slid—and along a gloomy, barely lit hallway to the east wing of the house. Brooke never stopped looking around, cataloging the original touches rehabbers would have spent fortunes uncovering from remodeled homes, aching for the missing light bulbs and tattered carpeting that betrayed the Hansard's financial state. This house, and these people, deserved better than that.

But whatever they had had obviously been lavished on Stonewall Jackson.

He glared down from an old hand-colored photo over the fireplace. A canopied mahogany four-poster bed shared space with a rocker, dressers, nightstands with working ewers, and even a red velvet fainting couch that looked like one good attack of vapors would send it crashing to the floor.

"Would this be...to your liking?" little Evaline asked, the love of the place evident in her eyes, her hands clasped nervously before her.

"It's perfect," Pete assured her.

ISN'T IT ROMANTIC? 169

Brooke turned to find that he was as taken with the place as she, as beguiled by its owners.

Both of them nodded in chorus and turned for the door. "By the way," Beauregard announced. "We'd be most happy if y'all'd join us in the parlor at seven for cordials. Dinner is at seven-thirty."

Brooke could barely wait for the door to close behind them.

"Isn't this incredible?" she demanded on a whisper, circling the room to test furniture.

"Quick," Pete suggested, doing his own testing. "Check the hallway and make sure Rod Serling isn't standing out there."

"Oh, come on," she protested, plopping down on yet another chenille bedspread. "Where's your sense of adventure? This place is a hell of a find. Aren't they the dearest things you've ever seen?"

His grin was telling. "I feel like I just stepped into an H. G. Wells story about time travel. How old do you think they are?"

Brooke reached over to the bedside table and picked up a picture. "Eighty-five. Look at this."

It was a framed clipping from a society column describing their marriage in 1932, and behind it an old, grainy photo of Evaline standing at the top of the staircase in her bridal gown.

"She was gorgeous. And look at what the house looked like then. It gleamed like a penny."

Pete took the frame from her hand and considered it for a minute. "They're cousins."

"Of course they are. Are you surprised?"

Pete turned his gaze on her, amazed and amused, shaking his head. "How do you do it?" he demanded.

"What?"

He waved the frame at her. "Find things like this."

She arched an eyebrow at him. "I don't think that's absolutely true. After all, I'm not the one who ran the car off the road."

"You wanted to stop anyway."

"Well, that had nothing to do with this."

He waved the frame again, as if indicting her with its presence. "I'm telling you, there's something not quite right about all this. We're going to wake up in the morning back in 1862

170   ISN'T IT ROMANTIC?

and the reb enlistment party's going to be knocking on the door."

Brooke faced him with hands on her hips. "Excuse me, what was all that stuff about taking chances with your life? What's this but a little chance?"

"It's a bigger chance than moving in with me," he protested. "At least you know I won't sneak in during the middle of the night and chop your head off."

"Beauregard is not going to chop your head off."

"Yeah, but did you see that glint in Evaline's eye?"

Brooke just smacked him. "When you get the luggage, don't peek in my big suitcase. My outfit's in there."

Pete arched a disbelieving eyebrow. "You're planning on doing that here?"

She shrugged with a delighted grin. "What better place? We're havin' cordials in the parlor at seven. Now, my dear. Ya don't wanna be late."

Pete left the room shaking his head.

It wasn't just a find, it was an adventure. While Pete labored to get the bags upstairs, Brooke cornered little Evaline and talked her into a grand tour. And a grand tour was what she got, from cellar to attic, every room complete with a long, rambling, sometimes incoherent story, every corner revealing another surprise. The moose head hanging over the dining room table. The claw-footed bathtub in the old master's bedroom right before the fire. The personal family ghost, an irascible old secessionist who'd had the bad taste to meet his maker while dallying with a married guest. The slave cabins that still stood at the back of the property, and the faded copy of *Old Southern Living* spotlighting the house—in 1948.

Brooke had so many questions, about the house, about the fact that it had survived the war intact—a dark blot on the family history, according to Evaline. Brooke figured that meant they'd lent it to Union troops as a headquarters. How come no one had snatched it from its aging owners, and how had those owners still managed to take the care of it they did? She asked, but Evaline was so lost in her mama's time, and her grandmama's time, often mixing the two of them up, that Brooke knew better than to expect a straight answer. All she could do

ISN'T IT ROMANTIC? 171

was enjoy the visit and consider herself lucky at the find. She and Pete had come much too close to passing it by altogether, and there just weren't any places left like this one anymore.

"That's what I'd want," she admitted, her eye to her reflection in the mirror as she retied the black material around her throat. "A place just like this."

"A crumbling white elephant?" Pete asked from the other side of the bathroom door.

Brooke chuckled, the excitement of discovery still bright in her chest to war with regret that she'd never find anything like this to own, to restore, to show off.

"A house with a real history," she informed him, placing the hat so that it raked just so over one eye. "With real beauty. A one-in-a-million treasure that can't be found anymore. I still can't believe some hotel chain hasn't bought this place up."

For a moment there wasn't a sound from the other side of the door. Brooke was dying to know who Pete was dressing up as in there. He'd whisked his bag by her so fast that she hadn't had a chance to peek, and it was already past six-thirty.

"You mean it?" he asked.

She turned at the subdued tone of his voice. "Mean what?"

"That you'd like something like this?"

That provoked the only response she considered appropriate. She laughed. "Sure. You know one that's up for sale?"

Only Pete didn't respond as she'd expected him to, with more cracks about ghosts and time travel. "What would you do with it?" he asked instead.

"Coop," she demurred, eyes closing against the sudden, sharp regret. "I'm not serious. It's a stupid, romantic idea that just isn't feasible."

"What would you do with it if it were?"

"Same thing Beauregard and Evaline are doing. Run a B-and-B. Except I'd have a bigger sign out front . . . and fresh flowers on the foyer table, and a cook to do real meals, maybe an art gallery in the music room. . . ." Her voice faded off with the plans that had formed without her realizing it while she'd walked through the old house. Dreams. Wishes she hadn't even known she'd made.

172   ISN'T IT ROMANTIC?

Well, leave it to her. She finally discovered what it was she'd like to do with her life, and she couldn't afford it. She couldn't even afford to visit it. For just a few fleeting minutes, as she'd run her hands over that old flocked wallpaper, though, she'd thought of how nice a place would be where she could live and work for herself and accept Pete home from the wild ride of fame and he could be safe and quiet. A testament to history, to permanence, to beauty.

She'd learned a long time ago not to dream. Now she knew why. Suddenly it seemed as if a life with Pete were even further away than ever.

"Are you ready?" she asked, flattening her finger over her upper lip one more time.

Still she got a pause, as if Coop's mind were on other things. "Yeah. You?"

She gave her hat another pat for luck and turned to the door. "You'd better not be dressed as Rhett Butler," she warned blackly.

"Why?" he demanded from behind the still-closed door. "Don't you like him either?"

"Of course I like him. He's only one of the two characters I do like. But if you dress up like him, we'll look silly."

"Because you did, right?" he retorted, swinging the door open. "I knew it!"

He stood before her, arms out, showing off his own costume. Brooke couldn't say anything. She couldn't so much as close her mouth to begin a word or, for that matter, a thought.

"You do look pretty dashing, Captain Butler," he said with a cocky grin that looked absolutely out of place. "Although I personally think the breasts are a nice addition."

The giggles built from beneath her breastbone. Tight, silly, wild giggles that would ricochet around these old walls like bullets. Brooke slapped her hand across her mouth, but that didn't stop them.

"You can't—" She couldn't get that out, either, her voice rising precariously.

Pete stood proudly before her, smiling like a pirate, hands on his skirt.

"You can't go…"

ISN'T IT ROMANTIC? 173

His teeth flashed a brilliant white. "As my favorite character?" he asked. "You dressed as yours."

"But mine wasn't Prissy!"

That did it. There was no controlling either of them. Holding on to each other in their ridiculous getups, tears running down their faces, they dissolved into laughter, friends once again.

"We can't...go down like...this," Brooke gasped, and then took another look at the kerchief Pete had tied around his head and went off on another paroxysm.

"Why not?" he asked, picking her hat back up from where it had fallen to the floor and replacing it. "They probably won't even notice."

But Brooke nodded vigorously. "They'd notice you," she assured him.

He looked down at the front of his homespun dress with a certain dignity. "I think I look quite nice."

"For a baritone with a five-o'clock shadow."

He looked back up at her. "What do you suggest we do?"

"Change outfits?" she asked. "At least the breasts would be on the right person."

He scowled. "But Rhett wasn't my favorite character, and that was Mamie's stipulation."

"She also figured we'd be doing this for Rupert Springs, and it'd serve them right to see you in a dress. I don't think we want to be responsible for the Hansards' health."

"What about the old dress in the closet?" he asked.

Brooke took a moment from wiping her eyes to face him. "What dress?"

He lifted an eyebrow at her. "You didn't see it? The one with the hoops?"

Brooke spun on her heel and threw open the closet door. There, on several padded hangers, was a beautiful green watered silk dress that looked as if it would have been worn sometime during the Civil War, its neck low and its skirts full. Brooke took in a breath.

"Do you think they'd mind?"

"Want me to ask?"

She shot him a distasteful glare. "Not in that, I don't."

174 ISN'T IT ROMANTIC?

He motioned to her attire. "Let me see if I fit into your costume."

"But I didn't like any of the women in that book," she protested.

"Tough. We're not in Rupert Springs anymore, Toto. We'll have to do it right."

And so it was that when Brooke entered the salon on Pete's arm at seven, she was clad in the most sumptuous, flowing, feminine—and tight—dress she'd ever worn. Her breasts swelled over the line of flowers at the neckline, and her modern heels were hidden by the rustling sweep of the skirts. In an attempt to maintain the image, she'd pulled her thick hair up on the top of her head so that it hung in loose ringlets down the sides and back of her neck, around which Pete had supplied a simple black choker fashioned from the tie from Prissy's apron.

Pete, at her side, made a most dashing Captain Butler, right down to the mustache he'd painted on with her eyeliner. He looked properly rakish and handsome in the fawn breeches and cutaway coat, the black tie and hat, even if they were a mite small. She could easily see him riding up on a stallion to the lawn party and sending the women into a swoon. Now if she could only stop him from calling her "Scor-let" way in the back of his throat all the time.

"Isn't it lovely to have company for dinner, Beauregard?" Evaline asked as the two of them swept into the little room.

They were in more formal attire, just as threadbare, just as eccentric. If they noticed that Brooke and Pete were clad in clothing about a hundred and thirty years out-of-date, they failed to make mention of it.

"They said, of course," Pete had announced upon returning to the room earlier, "that they always tried to keep spare clothing in case the guests might need it."

"For a costume party?" Brooke had demanded. "Attended by a five-foot-ten-inch woman? You're right. This *is* weird."

But Pete's attention had already been snagged by the fit of the dress. "I don't care how weird it is," he retorted with a salacious grin. "It's now my favorite fantasy."

Brooke couldn't overcome the feeling of dislocation as they first sat in the little salon sipping at sherry, and then proceeded in to join the moose for dinner. It only took a little work

ISN'T IT ROMANTIC? 175

to figure out how not to embarrass herself with those hoops, but it demanded constant attention. Brooke was sure she never would have made a good Southern belle. Just as well anyway, she figured. Her family had probably been the shop clerks in town anyway.

The Hansards, obviously trained in the Old South school of hospitality, and even more obviously glad for the company, kept up a continuous stream of conversation throughout what turned out to be the most formal stew Brooke had ever shared. They talked of weather and family and the importance of loyalty. They asked about Brooke and Pete and were only slightly intrigued by Pete's job.

Not for them, the outside world, it seemed. Brooke could well imagine. It was as if stepping down that driveway she and Pete had crossed a kind of time warp, where the real world didn't exist. She knew that tomorrow they'd reach Atlanta. After all, it was only about half an hour away. She knew she'd have to go back home and come to grips with the idea of starting a new life at twenty-six if she ever hoped to keep the kind of promise she'd made to Pete.

But for now, she could lose herself in the timelessness of good food, good manners and good company. She could listen to the whispers of an old house as it told its tale and cherish the fleeting moments she spent with its fragile, proud owners. And she could share that with Pete, because no one else she knew would have understood how special this evening was.

"Would you like to retire to the drawin' room?" Beauregard asked, patting his lips with his napkin.

Dessert had been Jell-O and coffee, served on fine old Sèvres china.

Chairs scraped as the men got to their feet.

"Would you like me to help you clear?" Brooke asked, wondering how she was going to get through that kitchen door in this skirt.

"Oh, no, my dear," Evaline protested with a flutter of her hand. "Tilly will take care of it later."

Brooke didn't know whether there really was a Tilly, or whether Evaline was just protecting her pride. It didn't matter. She conceded with a nod and got to her feet as well.

176   ISN'T IT ROMANTIC?

"Well, my dear," Beauregard announced from the door. "Would you care to join us, as well? I think we have something to discuss with these young people."

Brooke exchanged puzzled looks with Pete as she followed the little woman into the drawing room where a fire had been laid out in the fireplace. Thankfully, it wasn't lighted. Brooke did her best to fit on the same couch with Pete and not poke him in the eye with one of her hoops as she settled in, still waiting for either Beauregard or Evaline to make some comment—any comment—about their attire.

Beauregard poured brandy and a little more sherry for the ladies. Brooke thought of how she preferred her sherry on Chinese food, and sipped quietly.

Leaning heavily on his cane, Beauregard approached the little group and raised his glass. "To Eleven Oaks," he announced in that fine, cultured voice of his.

They raised their glasses and sipped.

Then Beauregard turned to Pete. "You said your mother's people were Fillihues, sir. Did you not?"

His forehead pursed in bemusement, Pete nodded. "Yes, sir, that's right."

Beauregard nodded contentedly and then consulted silently with his wife, who nodded him on. Stepping carefully over to the fireplace, he rested his drinking arm on the mantel. "In that case, sir, I'd like to make a proposal, if I may."

Brooke fought the urge to run check her calendar for the year. Maybe Pete was right. Maybe they were about to discover the rebel forces outside the front door, or maybe the first shots had yet to be fired on Fort Sumter.

"The Fillihues are a fine family," Beauregard began, eyes up to the collection of paintings on one wall. "My father's cousins were Fillihues." He nodded to himself, as if passing judgment. "I always found them to be honorable men."

Not much to say to that, Brooke thought. Pete was hardly in a position to argue. He did have that reality-check-time look in his eyes again, and she didn't blame him. Of course, she was the one sitting in hoopskirts, not the Hansards.

Clearing his throat, the old man brought his gaze back to his guests and smiled. "I apologize. Old men often find the past a much more vivid place." Especially here, Brooke thought. "My

ISN'T IT ROMANTIC?

wife and I have for some time been approached by people wishing to buy Eleven Oaks to turn it into an amusement park or some such thing. That is, of course, out of the question. It is our home. It was my daddy's home, and his before him, with the exception of the time he rode off with General Jackson himself. But, to be perfectly truthful, it has become more difficult lately to maintain it in the style we wish.'' He waved his hand a little. ''Times bein' what they are.''

Pete was very quiet. Evaline's eyes glittered suspiciously as she watched her husband, her head up, her hands calm in her lap.

''How can I help you, sir?'' Pete asked, as if he'd known the old man his whole life, instead of just that afternoon.

Beauregard turned his attention full on Pete and gave him a rare old smile. ''Buy Eleven Oaks from me, boy.''

Thirteen

Hamlet, Act I, Scene 5:

There are more things in heaven and earth, Horatio,
Than are dreamt of in your philosophy.

Brooke's first reaction was to suspect Pete of collusion. Surely
he'd worked something out with the old couple earlier when
he'd walked down to ask about the dress. But even Pete wasn't
that good an actor. He was openmouthed with astonishment.

"Excuse me?" he finally asked.

Brooke couldn't even manage that much. Beauregard's
words had lodged somewhere in her throat, getting in the way
of her vocal cords. Tied up with silly hope and futile wishes and
unmanageable futures.

Beauregard turned to bestow a delighted smile on his wife.
"What did I tell you, darlin'? Speechless. I knew they were the
couple."

"But we've only been here since noon!" Pete protested.
"You haven't even had the time to get to know us."

ISN'T IT ROMANTIC? 179

The man bestowed that same smile on Pete. "I'm eight-seven, boy. If I don't make my decisions quick, I don't have time to make 'em at all. Now, Evaline says that your little lady here was quite taken with the old place. Asked her all the right questions, showed the proper respect. And we find that we like you both very much."

Pete actually made it to his feet. In a really bizarre way, he looked perfectly at home having this discussion in this house in that getup. Brooke kept blinking, waiting for one of the old people to furnish the punch line.

"And that's enough for you to want to sell us your home?" Pete asked carefully.

"You're a Fillihue," Beauregard assured him, clapping a hand on his shoulder before he had a chance to mount further protest. "That's enough for me."

Pete shook his head. "Have you made this offer to anyone else?"

Both of them demurely shook their heads. "I told you," the old man said. "We've been waiting for the right couple. Why, even old Ezekial likes you."

Pete turned pleading eyes on Brooke. "The ghost," she allowed with a small shrug, wondering how Ezekial had made his point.

"It would ease the old man's mind to know the house is still in the family," Beauregard said. "I'm the only Hansard left in the world now. And even though the Fillihues weren't Hansards..."

Pete nodded his concession. "They were honorable."

"They were Southern gentlemen."

Brooke found herself battling the first giddiness of impossibility. If he thought the Fillihues were gentlemen, she was going to have to introduce him to Letitia and Emily. It still hadn't occurred to her to wonder how in the heck out of all of the South, they'd tripped over an available antebellum mansion complete with long-lost family.

Pete shook his head, still trying to make the old people see some sense. "I simply can't take your home from you," he protested.

"I'll buy it," Brooke said.

180   ISN'T IT ROMANTIC?

All three people looked her way. She hurried on before the urge to retreat overcame the swooping rush of possibility.

"I may not have a very interesting job," she told Pete, "but my credit is great. I can take out a business loan, use the money I get from selling my house as a down payment..." Turning again, she faced the couple who reminded her so much of Mamie in their own way. "What would you ask for the house?"

The old man took the change in tactics completely in his stride. "What would you like to pay?" he asked.

That stopped her cold. She clenched her hands in her lap and lifted a silent plea for help to Pete. It took him a minute to answer. First he had to believe that it wasn't all a joke. Then he had to assimilate Brooke's offer. By the time he smiled, Brooke knew that he really understood what was happening.

"Whatever the cost is," he said to her, "I'd like to be the one to make you that loan." Then, smiling, he continued, "I'd like to be a silent partner, if it's okay with you."

Brooke battled tears. It was just what she wanted. Just what both of them needed.

"Would we be able to work that out, Mr. Hansard?" she finally asked.

His smile was courtly and sweet. "You must call me Beauregard, my dear. I insist."

Brooke dipped her head in acknowledgment, wondering what the hell she was doing. Figuring that it wasn't any crazier than anything else she'd done on this trip. Knowing as suddenly as the Hansards had that she and Pete could have the house, that this was her chance. It was what she'd waited her whole life for, a little world of her own, for her to rebuild and cherish and share. An island of tranquility in the real world where Pete could escape. A solid, secure base from which she could attack the rest of the world.

Then, without warning, the inspiration became complete. "You would never mean to leave Eleven Oaks, would you?" Brooke asked the couple.

They exchanged quick, furtive glances, caught between their own need and the best interests of their beloved house.

Brooke turned to Pete for his support to find that he was following right with her and in perfect agreement.

ISN'T IT ROMANTIC? 181

"It's your house," he told her. "You are planning on continuing its tradition as a fine bed-and-breakfast, aren't you?"

There was so much she wanted to say to him, to share with him. To give him. At that moment, the best she could manage was a bright, happy smile.

"Of course you'll stay," Pete insisted to the couple. "I don't think my wife would accept your offer under any other conditions."

"If you really mean for us to have it," Brooke said to the couple.

Both Beauregard and Evaline nodded their heads decisively. "Oh, we do, my dear."

Brooke smiled at them both, content with her new family. "Then we will work to maintain Eleven Oaks together. I would so like your help in ensuring that this home remains the gracious, hospitable place you have kept it."

Beaming, bright tears swelling her eyes, Evaline reached over to pat Brooke's hand. "You are an answer to a prayer, dear. An answer to a prayer."

Brooke beamed right back. "So are you, Mrs. Hansard. So are you."

It was deep into the night when the house spoke the most, little creakings and moanings from age, the rustle of an overgrown oak against the back eaves, the whisper of the breeze through the sheer curtains at the window. Nestled in the big, soft bed, Pete and Brooke watched the shadows shift and collect, listened to the lazy chorus of insects outside, and talked about the future.

"You really don't want a big wedding?" he asked, fingering the auburn curls that tumbled over his chest.

Curled into his arms, her ear to his heart, Brooke shook her head just a little. "Families," she said. "Everybody else can read about it in the *Daily World.*"

"I could move in a little early...."

"No. You'll stay right where you are till we get married." She laid her hand against his chest, flat against his skin, as if she could better impart her feelings, as if she could somehow make them closer than they were. "Not until I've renovated the house

182   ISN'T IT ROMANTIC?

and gotten all of Mamie's things in. I still need to accomplish this all by myself before we share it.''

She felt his hand begin to stray, and it sent chills chasing before it.

"I don't know," he hedged, his fingers teasing the soft skin along the base of her throat. "I've suddenly become awfully impatient.''

Brooke smiled to herself, hearing the rhythm of his heartbeat change, feeling her own match it. She let her hand do its own straying. "I think insatiable is the word you're looking for," she retorted, distracted by the play of her pale fingers against the darker, rougher texture of his chest, mesmerized by the torture a simple set of fingers could inflict with no more than a caress to her breast.

He chuckled, so that it rumbled against her. "Just making up for lost time.''

"You're trying to . . . ah, get your way. . . .''

Her body, finally cooling from the last session of lovemaking, began to hum again, instinctively arching to Pete's touch. Pete responded by feathering kisses along her upturned face.

"It's called the fine art of compromise," he assured her.

She didn't care what it was called. She just didn't want him to stop.

"You don't mind . . . aah, commuting from here?''

He didn't mind. He whispered as much, just before he nibbled on her ear.

"And children?" she asked on a sigh, as much from her own explorations as his.

That brought him to a temporary halt. Brooke held her breath. "Well, that's one conversation we've never had," he admitted.

"How do you feel about it?''

He lifted himself up on an elbow, his eyes a little more serious than they had been. "Amazed," he admitted.

Brooke did her best to keep her eyes from straying to where the waning moonlight poured over his shoulders and chest. She did her best to keep her mind from wandering to the thought that she wanted to lap that moonlight up like milk.

"Why?''

ISN'T IT ROMANTIC? 183

"Think about it," he admitted, settling into position enough to run a finger along her breastbone and produce new shivers. "Do you realize it's only been ten days since we've buried Mamie? Suddenly we're engaged, you're quitting your job and moving from Rupert Springs to renovate and run an original antebellum mansion and Allie's going to live in Mamie's house."

"And Bud's dedicating his poolroom to Mamie," Brooke added, suddenly distracted again. "Ten days..." she murmured, her hand stilling against Pete's chest.

"What about it?"

"I don't know... are you sure you didn't arrange that little scene with the Hansards?" she asked yet again, still not quite believing their luck.

"If I had," he assured her, "I probably would have been more coherent when they made the offer. After all, what kind of coincidence would land us in a house with Fillihues in it?"

Fillihues... suddenly the bit of information she'd been trying to remember hit home like a baseball bat. "Omigod," Brooke gasped, jumping out of Pete's grasp as if he'd slapped her with a fish. "The letter!"

Pete ended up flat on his back as Brooke hopped out of bed.

"What letter?"

She was already digging desperately through her belongings. "Oh, God, I hope I didn't lose it in the tornado. I completely forgot about it."

Clothing flew into the air like shadowy birds, and purse contents rattled against the dresser. With everything that had happened in the past few days, Brooke had completely forgotten the letter Mamie had wanted her to have. The one to be opened exactly ten days after the funeral. Hip deep in her search, she didn't notice that Pete flipped on the bedside light and sat there in bed, watching like a spectator at a dwarf-tossing contest.

"What letter?" he asked.

"Aha!" She straightened from where the contents of her purse lay in an untidy pile, the crumpled, water-stained envelope in her hand.

"I think I saw this in an Agatha Christie movie once," was all Pete would say.

184 ISN'T IT ROMANTIC?

Still as naked as the day she was born, Brooke hopped back up on the bed and ripped into the envelope. "It's from Mamie," she explained. "Allie couriered it over from Harlan the day of the funeral. I was to read it exactly ten days after the funeral."

Coop's eyebrow quirked. "*You* were?" he demanded, making a grab for the missive. "Why didn't she want *me* to have it?"

Brooke shot him an arch look. "Probably didn't trust you not to lose it."

He let one lingering look over at her belongings answer for him.

"'Dear kids,'" Brooke began, just the sight of that handwriting transporting her right back again.

"Kids?" Pete countered.

She shrugged and read on. "'I hope I've given you enough time. By now, I imagine you've finally found each other.'" Brooke looked up, a funny chill of prescience crowding her chest. She could see that Pete was no less affected. He motioned her to read on.

"'I knew you would have eventually, but why waste time? You're good for each other, and I figured the funeral request would do the job. I imagine you went out on the road. It's why I did it. I didn't figure anybody else in that town would have the guts to fulfill those requirements. Nobody left there with any life but you two. So, now that you've sung my songs and visited different places and made love, I imagine you've discovered what I've known all along. All I ask is that you take care of each other, and have some fun along the way. It's the only way to go.'" This time when Brooke looked up, there were tears in her eyes. "'All my love, Mamie.'"

Pete was shaking his head. "Crafty old thing, wasn't she?"

Brooke shrugged. "She loved you. She wanted you to be happy...oh, wait, there's something on the back...oh, my God..."

Pete leaned over. Brooke handed over the letter, her hand suddenly trembling, her chest closing off. "How did she know?"

He read the P.S. and lifted a stunned gaze on Brooke. "She couldn't have. Not possibly."

ISN'T IT ROMANTIC?

"But the tire . . ."

"An accident."

"The family tie . . ."

"A coincidence."

Brooke shook her head. " 'There are more things in heaven and earth, Horatio.' 'Oh, by the way,' " she read aloud over his shoulder. " 'I knew you'd take care of Beauregard and Evaline. Enjoy the old place.' You call that coincidence?"

Pete sailed the letter off into the shadows. "I'm not calling it anything," he insisted. "I'm not about to jinx the best thing that's ever happened to me."

And before Brooke could so much as protest, he swept her into his arms and rolled them back beneath the covers.

"I don't care if Mamie and Ezekial conspired somewhere on a ghostly plane," he insisted, settling back down to taste Brooke's throat. "You and I are getting married, and settling down here and raising our children to love country music and the Three Stooges, and we'll live happily ever after."

Her hands already tangled in Pete's hair, her body remembering just where they'd left off, Brooke smiled up at him in the soft light. "Is that a promise?" she asked.

And he stopped long enough to seal his words with the expression in his eyes. "Oh, yes," he assured her. "It's a promise."

"But can we still be friends?" she asked, sating herself on the sight of him, the feel of him, the promise of him.

The smile he gave her was like a gift. "Till the end," he promised. "Till the very end."

A woman couldn't ask for much more than that.

Entertainment World, October 15:

It was a dark day for Pete Cooper fans yesterday when the famed newsman traded vows with childhood friend Brooke Ferguson on the lawn of their newly renovated home, Eleven Oaks, just outside Atlanta. The ceremony was an intimate one, with just immediate family and friends. A very romantic story all around, although we might question the influence the new Mrs. Cooper wields after receiving reports of attendance by the Hell's Angels and an Elvis impersonator who assisted a country-western band in entertaining guests....

* * * * *

The spirit of motherhood is the spirit of love—and how better to capture that special feeling than in our short story collection...

Curtiss Ann Matlock
Carole Halston
Linda Shaw

Three glorious new stories that embody the very essence of family and romance are contained in this heartfelt tribute to Mother. Share in the joy by joining us and three of your favorite Silhouette authors for this celebration of motherhood and romance.

Available at your favorite retail outlet in May.

SMD92

YOU'VE ASKED FOR IT, YOU'VE GOT IT!
MAN OF THE MONTH: 1992

ONLY FROM
◐ SILHOUETTE® *Desire*™

You just couldn't get enough of them, those sexy men from Silhouette Desire—twelve sinfully sexy, delightfully devilish heroes. Some will make you sweat, some will make you sigh... but every long, lean one of them will have you swooning. So here they are, men we couldn't resist bringing to you for one more year....

A KNIGHT IN TARNISHED ARMOR
by Ann Major in January

THE BLACK SHEEP
by Laura Leone in February

THE CASE OF THE MESMERIZING BOSS
by Diana Palmer in March

DREAM MENDER
by Sherryl Woods in April

WHERE THERE IS LOVE
by Annette Broadrick in May

BEST MAN FOR THE JOB
by Dixie Browning in June

Don't let these men get away! *Man of the Month*, only in Silhouette Desire.

MOM92JJ-1R

NORA ROBERTS

Love has a language all its own, and for centuries, flowers have symbolized love's finest expression. Discover the language of flowers—and love—in this romantic collection of 48 favorite books by bestselling author Nora Roberts.

Two titles are available each month at your favorite retail outlet.

In April, look for:

First Impressions, Volume #5
Reflections, Volume #6

In May, look for:

Night Moves, Volume #7
Dance of Dreams, Volume #8

Collect all 48 titles and become fluent in

THE LANGUAGE of LOVE

Silhouette®

LOL492

WHERE THERE IS LOVE

Annette Broadrick

Secret agent Max Moran knew all too well the rules of a road where life-threatening danger lurked around every corner. He stalked his prey like a panther—silent, stealthy and ready to spring at any moment.

But teaming up again with delicate, determined Marisa Stevens meant tackling a far more tortuous terrain—one that Max had spent a lifetime avoiding. This precariously unpredictable path was enough to break the stoic panther's stride... as it wove its way to where there was love.

Last sighted in CANDLELIGHT FOR TWO (Silhouette Desire #577), the mysterious Max is back as Silhouette's *Man of the Month!* Don't miss Max's story, WHERE THERE IS LOVE by Annette Broadrick, available in May... only from Silhouette Desire.

SDAB

"GET AWAY FROM IT ALL" SWEEPSTAKES

HERE'S HOW THE SWEEPSTAKES WORKS

NO PURCHASE NECESSARY

To enter each drawing, complete the appropriate Official Entry Form or a 3" by 5" index card by hand-printing your name, address and phone number and the trip destination that the entry is being submitted for (i.e., Caneel Bay, Canyon Ranch or London and the English Countryside) and mailing it to: Get Away From It All Sweepstakes, P.O. Box 1397, Buffalo, New York 14269-1397.

No responsibility is assumed for lost, late or misdirected mail. Entries must be sent separately with first class postage affixed, and be received by: 4/15/92 for the Caneel Bay Vacation Drawing, 5/15/92 for the Canyon Ranch Vacation Drawing and 6/15/92 for the London and the English Countryside Vacation Drawing. Sweepstakes is open to residents of the U.S. (except Puerto Rico) and Canada, 21 years of age or older as of 5/31/92.

For complete rules send a self-addressed, stamped (WA residents need not affix return postage) envelope to: Get Away From It All Sweepstakes, P.O. Box 4892, Blair, NE 68009.

© 1992 HARLEQUIN ENTERPRISES LTD.   SWP-RLS

"GET AWAY FROM IT ALL" SWEEPSTAKES

HERE'S HOW THE SWEEPSTAKES WORKS

NO PURCHASE NECESSARY

To enter each drawing, complete the appropriate Official Entry Form or a 3" by 5" index card by hand-printing your name, address and phone number and the trip destination that the entry is being submitted for (i.e., Caneel Bay, Canyon Ranch or London and the English Countryside) and mailing it to: Get Away From It All Sweepstakes, P.O. Box 1397, Buffalo, New York 14269-1397.

No responsibility is assumed for lost, late or misdirected mail. Entries must be sent separately with first class postage affixed, and be received by: 4/15/92 for the Caneel Bay Vacation Drawing, 5/15/92 for the Canyon Ranch Vacation Drawing and 6/15/92 for the London and the English Countryside Vacation Drawing. Sweepstakes is open to residents of the U.S. (except Puerto Rico) and Canada, 21 years of age or older as of 5/31/92.

For complete rules send a self-addressed, stamped (WA residents need not affix return postage) envelope to: Get Away From It All Sweepstakes, P.O. Box 4892, Blair, NE 68009.

© 1992 HARLEQUIN ENTERPRISES LTD.   SWP-RLS

"GET AWAY FROM IT ALL"

Brand-new Subscribers-Only Sweepstakes

OFFICIAL ENTRY FORM

This entry must be received by: April 15, 1992
This month's winner will be notified by: April 30, 1992
Trip must be taken between: May 31, 1992—May 31, 1993

YE$, I want to win the Caneel Bay Plantation vacation for two. I understand the prize includes round-trip airfare and the two additional prizes revealed in the BONUS PRIZES insert.

Name _____

Address _____

City _____

State/Prov._____ Zip/Postal Code_____

Daytime phone number_____
(Area Code)

Return entries with invoice in envelope provided. Each book in this shipment has two entry coupons — and the more coupons you enter, the better your chances of winning!
© 1992 HARLEQUIN ENTERPRISES LTD.   1M-CPN

"GET AWAY FROM IT ALL"

Brand-new Subscribers-Only Sweepstakes

OFFICIAL ENTRY FORM

This entry must be received by: April 15, 1992
This month's winner will be notified by: April 30, 1992
Trip must be taken between: May 31, 1992—May 31, 1993

YE$, I want to win the Caneel Bay Plantation vacation for two. I understand the prize includes round-trip airfare and the two additional prizes revealed in the BONUS PRIZES insert.

Name _____

Address _____

City _____

State/Prov._____ Zip/Postal Code_____

Daytime phone number _____
(Area Code)

Return entries with invoice in envelope provided. Each book in this shipment has two entry coupons — and the more coupons you enter, the better your chances of winning!
© 1992 HARLEQUIN ENTERPRISES LTD.   1M-CPN